The Swansea Arena Murder

by

Peter Black

The final part of the Morgan Sheckler trilogy

First published in Great Britain in 2024

Copyright © Peter Black 2024
The moral right of the author has been asserted.

No part of this book may be used or reproduced in any manner without permission from the author in writing. The book is sold subject to the condition that it shall not be lent, resold, hired out or otherwise circulated without permission from the author in writing.

This novel is a work of fiction. Names, characters, businesses, places, events, locales, and incidents are either the products of the author's imagination or used in a fictitious manner. Any resemblance to actual persons, living or dead, or actual events is purely coincidental.

ISBN: 9798337638003
Imprint: Independently published

Chapter One

As much as she had enjoyed watching 'Hamilton' at the new Swansea Arena, police Inspector Jenny Thorne was still put out at having to travel forty plus miles for the spectacle when there was a perfectly good theatre in Cardiff Bay.

She wasn't normally into musicals, but being newly married to a woman who was far more political and with a greater interest in history and social justice than she herself could ever muster, Jenny decided it wasn't worth complaining about.

She was only there for the entertainment; she'd leave the political stuff to her mother-in-law, who'd accompanied them, the infamous Aileen Jenkins, the South Wales Police Commissioner, and Labour stalwart of many decades. And besides, Aileen had paid for the tickets.

Jenny was dressed in jeans and a T-shirt that showed off her slim body and firm breasts. Her natural blonde hair and piercing blue eyes were turning heads among the crowd as the three of them made their way out of the auditorium. She smiled at Dawn, whose hazel-coloured eyes sparkled with happiness. Wearing a flowery summer dress, she was still tanned and refreshed after their two-week honeymoon in the Mediterranean.

Dawn held hew wife's hand tightly, while discussing the finer points of the show with her mother, who was dressed in a Hillary Clinton-style mauve pantsuit, with her hair dyed to match. Jenny thought that the police commissioner had been attending too many official dinners recently, as the weight that had been lost for the wedding had returned with a vengeance, and then some.

It wasn't an accusation that could ever be levelled at Jenny, who, toned body aside, was used to standing out. Her west country accent was still strong and distinctive, despite the many years she had spent in South Wales, while she exuded a natural authority developed through her years as a police officer… one that some took for arrogance, but which was just decisiveness.

She was also not afraid to take unorthodox action when she needed to, as was evidenced in how she'd dealt with the former mayor of the Cardiff region, Morgan Sheckler when he threatened Dawn's future.

Shooting him down in cold blood may have cost Jenny her soul, but it had won her a wife. It was a secret they shared between them and nobody else, despite the continual angst, regret, and nightmares they both still suffered as a result.

Jenny looked around again at their impressive surroundings. They'd emerged from the auditorium into a large ante chamber bedecked in what looked like gold tiles on one wall, contrasting with the black pillars and a black painted wall elsewhere. The area had been accessed by descending a large winding staircase.

She recalled that outside, the external walls were covered in LCD lights capable of flashing up messages and pictures, while access across the busy Oystermouth Road dual carriageway was facilitated by an ornate golden footbridge that looked like the inside of a Crunchie bar.

She was looking for the toilets, thinking that she should avail herself of the facilities before the drive back to Cardiff, when she became aware of a disturbance in that direction and a man dressed in jeans and T-shirt, running towards them shouting for somebody to call the police.

He looked flustered and was struggling to speak and run at the same time. It was clear that if somebody didn't stop him then a first-aid responder would soon be needed to revive him.

As the man approached, Jenny managed to grab him, pull her badge from her bag, and flash it in his face. He was babbling something about having found a man in the toilets with a stab wound.

'There's blood everywhere!'

Jenny took charge, instructing Aileen and Dawn to ring 999, find the manager and his head of security and direct them towards her. She then escorted the man back to the toilets.

As they neared the Gents, a woman in jeans and a dark blue hoodie, pulled down to obscure her face, pushed past them. For a split-second Jenny thought about stopping her, but the man was pulling her forward, anxious to put his ordeal behind him and go home once he'd shown her the scene of the crime.

A large crowd had gathered at the toilet entrance, beyond which she could just make out a male figure leaning over the body. Jenny pushed her way through the crowd, holding onto her informant as she did so.

As she got through, she paused, turned back towards the crowd, flashed her badge, and ordered them to stand further back. She placed her informant to one side and told him not to move, and then turned her attention to the man trying to revive the victim.

She asked him to stand back so that she could take a closer look at the crime scene. The victim was male, in his late forties, of average build, with closely cropped blond hair. He was wearing a dark two-piece suit with an open neck white shirt and black leather shoes.

Jenny pulled on a latex glove, which she found in her bag - she always had a couple of pairs tucked in there for work - and felt for a pulse but couldn't find one. The carotid artery had been slashed causing a huge pool of blood to form beneath. There was no sign of the murder weapon She turned towards the Good Samaritan a couple of feet away and asked him to identify himself.

His name was Chris Davies, a local businessman. He was clean-shaven, with silver-grey hair, parted at the side. She guessed he must be in his late fifties, and looked like he kept himself in good shape; his clothes were casual, but looked expensive – *were* being the key word because now they were smeared in blood,

He told her that he'd seen a woman in a hoodie slash the victim's throat as he'd come out of one of the cubicles. She'd then walked calmly away as if nothing had happened. Unfortunately, he didn't see her face as she had her back to him throughout the incident.

'I rushed over to see what I could do to help. I know a bit of first aid having done a course recently and tried to put that to good use. It was too late, and I couldn't save him.'

Jenny thanked Davies and asked for his contact details, He handed her a business card – something about personal finance - which she pocketed before asking him to stand to one side until somebody could come and take his statement.

She told him that he would also need to provide fingerprints and a DNA sample as he'd handled the body, and they would need to exclude him from any other forensic evidence they may find. Davies seemed quite happy to cooperate.

She looked around, there was blood everywhere, on the walls, the sinks, and the floor. She started to tick off the various procedural steps in her head that she needed to follow in this situation when she saw that Dawn and Aileen had appeared with the manager and the head of security, who she instructed to secure the building to prevent anybody from entering or leaving.

It was most probably a bit late for that, she thought. Many of the audience would have left already, but it was better to hold onto those they had and get statements now to cut down on the work of chasing them up later. Jenny knew that most of those attending the show would have booked online, so it would be possible to contact them through the Arena's database.

She was about to turn her attention to the manager when Aileen cried out:

'Gareth!'

'Did you know him?' Jenny asked. She could see that her mother-in-law was struggling to speak. Eventually, she managed to spit it out.

'Yes, his name is Gareth Tresham, he's a councillor in Cardiff and the cabinet member responsible for community safety. Oh, my God, what am I going to tell his wife and daughter. Do you think they're here? Shall I go and look?'

Jenny decided that locating the next of kin would be a useful thing for Aileen to do. It would also keep her busy and away from the crime scene.

'Please do,' she said.

Just then two uniformed officers appeared. Jenny showed them her warrant card and instructed them to summon the duty detective Inspector and a forensic team. She then tasked them with taking statements from those members of the public still in the building, starting with Chris Davies and the man who had alerted her to the murder in the first place, who had subsequently identified himself as John Pinnell, a forty-year-old council worker.

She looked around for Dawn and then realised she'd gone with her mother to find the Treshams. She needed somebody to rope off access to the toilets to prevent anybody stumbling onto the crime scene. Fortunately, the head of security reappeared so she sent him way to get a couple of rope barriers from the reception area.

A few minutes later she was joined by two Swansea-based detectives. Detective Inspector Simon Waddingham was mid-thirties but looked older largely due being a heavy smoker. Twenty-a-day was not conducive to good health or to a good bank balance. Aside from his laboured breathing, the nicotine stains on his fingers were a giveaway. Unlike many other heavy smokers, he'd refused to switch to e-cigarettes instead.

Balding and sporting designer stubble, his growing beer belly was testament to his drinking habits, mostly while watching rugby with his mates.

His colleague, Detective Sergeant Rhodri Quinn, was a complete contrast to his boss. He was in his late twenties, with curly brown hair and a narrow, pointed face dominated by a long thin nose. Jenny knew him as a regular marathon runner, who often approached colleagues to sponsor him for one of his favoured charities.

She took Waddingham to one side to brief him. She explained that she'd been on the scene when it happened and that she'd secured the area and done her best to keep as many potential witnesses in the building as she could.

'Mr Davies, who is currently giving a statement to one of your officers, witnessed the murder,' she said. 'He believes that it was committed by a woman, who was wearing a dark hoodie. Somebody fitting that description pushed past me as I was making my way here.

'I suggest that once we've got things under control we go and look at the buildings' CCTV and see if we can identify her. I'm sure she's long gone, but any clues will help.'

Waddingham agreed. By now, several police officers were taking statements. A forensic team had also arrived and were photographing and scouring the area around the body and taking DNA samples from selective witnesses.

A pathologist was examining Councillor Tresham's body prior to having it removed, while the Arena manager looked on from behind the extended roped off area,

Jenny glanced across towards the auditorium doors and saw Dawn and Aileen comforting two women, one in a designer blue midi dress, the other in a crop-top, tartan skirt and doc martens. By the way Aileen was restraining them from rushing over to the murder scene to inspect the victim she assumed these were Mrs Tresham and her daughter. Jenny took Waddingham over there and introduced him to the police commissioner.

Aileen was still in shock but had managed to compose herself enough to tell the Treshams what had happened and to now give the detectives some background on the family.

Julia Tresham was Gareth's second wife and was ten years younger than him. Tall, attractive with expensively layered, shoulder-length maroon-coloured hair, she looked as if she exercised regularly. Jenny was convinced she'd seen her before, at the gym, a memory that Dawn later confirmed for her.

Her daughter, Emily was studying law at Swansea University. Like her father she was politically active and had recently taken up the position of women's officer in the students' union.

She had closely cropped hair and a piercing beneath her lower lip; there was a tattoo on her right shoulder, but Jenny couldn't make out what it portrayed.

'My name is Inspector Jennifer Thorne,' she said 'and this is Inspector Simon Waddingham. I'm sorry for your loss.'

Julia Tresham seemed relieved to have somebody in authority to talk to. She grasped Jenny's hand tightly, while Emily continued to cling to her mother.

'Do you know what happened?' she sobbed. 'Who would do something like this? Gareth wouldn't harm a fly.'

'We don't know anything at the moment, Mrs Tresham,' Waddingham said, cutting in. 'I'll be the Inspector in charge of this investigation. We're doing everything we can to find the person who attacked your husband.'

'Do you know anybody who might have a grudge against Gareth?' Jenny asked. 'Has he received any threats recently, for example?'

Julia Tresham shook her head.

'Not that I know of.'.

Jenny put a reassuring hand on the woman's shoulder.

'Look, there isn't much you can do here for now. We'll come and talk to you again in more detail after the shock has worn off a bit, but in the meantime, it's best if you make your way home. Do you have family or friends there who can support you?'

At this point Aileen cut in.

'Don't worry, Jenny, Dawn and I will look after them and see that they get home safely.'

Jenny indicated her appreciation and suggested to Waddingham that they should move on. The Arena manager was surveying the chaos that had engulfed his facility. They went over to him and asked to see the CCTV footage taken during the attack.

A few minutes later they were sitting in front of a monitor. There were, of course, no cameras in the toilets, which they presumed was one of the reasons why the murderer chose that spot, but Jenny could clearly see the woman in the hoodie leaving the vicinity straight after the murder.

She zoomed in and could see some blood spatters on the woman's sleeve, which she'd obviously tried to conceal as she walked calmly, but at pace, across the concourse and towards the stairs. The woman was holding her hand in an unnatural position as if she was carrying something and trying to keep it out-of-sight, maybe the knife itself. It wasn't that clear.

The murderer's demeanour convinced Jenny that they were dealing with somebody who'd done this before. Could it have been a professional hit? Who would pay somebody to kill an obscure Cardiff councillor?

She looked across at Waddingham, who looked unfocussed as if he needed a cigarette, however, it was clear that he had the same idea as Jenny.

'This is a professional hit,' he said. 'She knows where all the cameras are and is deliberately hiding her face from them. She's so calm and collected, you'd think this is just another day's work to her.'

Jenny tapped away at the keyboard and switched from camera to camera as they followed the murderer's progress out of the arena. The woman exited the front door and turned to her left through the park area at the rear of the building and into the Paxton Street carpark.

They knew they would need to contact the council CCTV centre for subsequent footage, but they could just see at the far reach of the Arena's camera's scope that she had put on a helmet, mounted a motorbike, and sped off onto Oystermouth Road in the direction of the M4.

They arranged for a copy of all the CCTV coverage to be sent to Waddingham. He thought it was possible that the woman might be recorded earlier on without her hood up, though Jenny was sceptical.

The attack looked like it had been meticulously planned. Somehow the attacker knew that Tresham would be attending this show, had mapped out the building and then waited for her opportunity. She wasn't going to be so careless as to reveal her face to a camera before the murder.

Could she be on camera checking out the Arena, maybe the day before? It was a possibility. Jenny suggested this to Waddingham, who changed his request to include CCTV for the whole week.

As they got back to the crime scene, the forensics and pathology team were finishing up. There would be a full post-mortem the next day, while any DNA and fingerprints found would be run through the system. Neither detective was optimistic.

They watched as the body was wheeled away on a stretcher towards a waiting ambulance. Tresham may have been unknown elsewhere, but he was a major public figure in his own community and every effort would be made to expedite matters.

Jenny shook Waddingham's hand.

'Well, it's over to you now, Simon. I'll write up my statement as soon as possible and send it your way. If you need anything else, you know where to find me.'

'I'll walk you out,' he responded. 'I'm dying for a cigarette.'

Jenny looked around for Dawn and Aileen, and then realised that they'd gone back to Cardiff with the Treshams. They'd come in Aileen's car, which she presumed they'd taken back to Cardiff. She was stranded.

'You'd better show me the way to the railway station,' she said.

Chapter Two

The next morning Jenny arrived at the police station feeling a little worse for wear. She'd got home quite late following a long and tedious train journey that seemed to involve stops at every minor station before taking a detour through the Vale of Glamorgan, and then she'd slept badly.

The sight of another dead body had triggered more bad dreams. She didn't used to be like this, but ever since discovering that the gun she'd used to kill Morgan Sheckler had been used in another murder, she'd started to exhibit the classic symptoms of PTSD.

Dawn had tried to help her through this, drawing on her own therapy sessions for inspiration, but it was a long road back to good mental health, and Jenny had been unable to draw on any of the counselling resources normally made available to police officers suffering in this way without giving away her guilty secret.

This was her first day back after the honeymoon, and no doubt her colleagues would be expecting her to be relaxed and happy, instead she felt like death warmed up and was having difficulty focusing.

As she walked into the detectives' office, she saw that Pyke and Stoneman were waiting for her.

As a burly, six-foot-two rugby player, Detective Sergeant Darren Pyke stood out in any environment. He was in his early thirties, with short blond hair and a penchant for ill fitting brown suits.

A popular figure in the office, when he wasn't playing rugby, he was one of the many baritones in a local male voice choir and was always in demand at police socials for the karaoke and his capacity to hold large quantities of beer.

Married with two sons, he could often be observed on a Saturday afternoon cheering one of them on at the side of a muddy football pitch.

By contrast, Detective Constable Jane Stoneman was a slim, five-foot-four, twenty-something with mousey brown hair, expensively organised into a bob, who always turned out smartly dressed in a skirt, blouse, and jacket combo.

Recently married herself, she was fiercely intelligent, methodical, and perceptive and could always be relied upon to ferret out difficult-to-find information, or to produce a decisive question in an interview. Jenny had her marked out as a high-flyer and knew that her bosses felt the same way.

The two detectives stood to greet her.

'I hear that your honeymoon ended rather abruptly last night,' Pyke said.

'Yes, it wasn't very pleasant. I'm hoping for a quieter day, today.'

'Alas, your hopes may be in vain, the Super wants to see you.'

Jenny sighed. A summons to see Superintendent Craig Brook was the last thing she needed on her first day back, and she hadn't even had her first cup of coffee, yet. She asked Jane if she could fetch her a strong coffee, while she deposited her stuff and then, grasping the mug, headed towards Brook's office.

She had had many run-ins with Brook in the past, not least over her tendency to ignore his instructions when it came to seeing Dawn. But she knew too, that Brook was also wary of the fact that the police commissioner was her mother-in-law, and that made it even between them.

Brook was another marathon runner, with a thick beard and swept-back brown hair. Those officers who reported to him tended to fear being summoned to his office. Many found his penetrating eyes, quick intelligence and brusque, no-nonsense approach intimidating. Jenny was no exception.

She knocked the door of his office and entered. Brook was staring intently at a computer screen, typing as fast as he could with two fingers. As she entered, he looked up and invited her to sit down.

'Well, Jenny, I hope you are suitably refreshed after your little sojourn in the Mediterranean.'

'I was, sir, until last night.'

'Yes, I heard. You did well, my counterpart in Swansea was well impressed.'

'Thank you,' she responded warily. Jenny was not used to praise from Brook.

'I know that you're going to be writing your statement up today, but unfortunately it isn't going to be so easy to just walk away from this one.

'Councillor Gareth Tresham was a good friend of this police force, and we're going to pull out all the stops to find his killer. The Assistant Chief Constable thinks this murder is a potential timebomb PR-wise with a clear Cardiff dimension, and I agree.

'Whatever the motive, the chances are that it originated here, and we need to get to the bottom of it before things get out of hand. We're setting up a multi-city taskforce, and you and your team are going to be the Cardiff-side of that.'

Jenny was unsure how to react. On the one hand, this was a high-profile case that was good for her career, on the other she'd only just got back from holiday and needed to ease herself back into the job.

'Am I being chosen because I was first on the scene,' she asked.

'That, and the fact that you have experience dealing with politically sensitive cases. I suggest you get to work.'

Jenny acknowledged the assignment and headed back to give Pyke and Stoneman the good news. They'd already been alerted and were clearing the decks so they could focus entirely on this new case.

She spent the next hour writing her statement about the events of the night before and entering it onto the police's HOLMES 2 system. Meanwhile, Jane set up a video conference with Waddingham and Quinn, while Pyke put together some background information on the Treshams focusing on social media and news items regarding the councillor's work.

This was also entered onto the computer system so that it would be available to the Swansea team members and form part of the case records.

By the time the conference call got underway they had the preliminary forensics and pathology reports in front of them. As expected, death had been almost instant after a single knife stroke had cut Tresham's throat.

The pathologist speculated that the angle of the cut indicated it had been administered from behind and that the assailant was a good foot shorter than the victim. Marks on Tresham's mouth suggested that a gloved hand had covered it and pulled his head back to facilitate the action that delivered the fatal wound.

Unfortunately, the killer's DNA or fingerprints were not on the knife or the body, while the fact that the murder took place in a lavatory meant that there were a lot of samples that could not be matched to anybody at this time.

Quinn reported that he'd trawled through the CCTV for the whole week, right up to the murder, but where the killer did appear on camera, she was careful to hide her face.

He added that the witness statements they had were vague and uninformative, though they were still in the process of contacting all those who'd bought tickets that night. Jane said she'd also gone through the statements and agreed that there was very little there to assist them.

Pyke added that there was nothing unusual in Tresham's social media to suggest that he might be in danger. There were no obvious threats, while recent news reports featuring the councillor were run-of-the-mill and unlikely to arouse any hostility in anybody, though people were unpredictable and there was no telling what might prompt somebody to pay for a professional hit.

Waddingham grimaced at this. He agreed that it looked like the act was carried out by a hired killer. He didn't want to jump to any conclusions however, and was worried that if this was a professional hit then it would make establishing a motive more difficult.

'We need to know more about what Tresham was up to,' he said. 'Jenny why don't you head over to the family home and see what you can find out. Get his laptop and we'll get the tech boys to have a look at them. You never know what they might find. We'll focus on gathering the remaining statements.'

* * *

By the time Jane and Jenny had edged their way through traffic and pulled up outside Tresham's home in one of the more prosperous Cardiff suburbs, a blanket of cloud had rolled in, banishing the morning sun.

It was a large, semi-detached house with a generous driveway and a huge bay window, the curtains of which were closed.

'I thought drawing the curtains as a sign of mourning had gone out of fashion,' Jane said.

'Either that or they're not up and dressed yet,' Jenny responded. She pointed out the CCTV cameras at the front and side of the property alongside a movement-activated floodlight and burglar alarm. 'Plenty of security, wonder what they were afraid of.'

The Tresham's car was sitting in the driveway, having been driven back from Swansea by Dawn, while Aileen chauffeured Julia and Emily. A brand-new Mini Cooper sat next to it, its red paintwork glistening in the shaft of light that had broken through the clouds.

Both Julia and Emily Tresham were wearing dressing gowns, their faces drawn and stressed. Neither seemed in any hurry to make themselves presentable for the day ahead. Jenny didn't blame them.

She and Jane were ushered into a large kitchen dominated by a central island unit surrounded by stools. Emily hauled herself onto one, while her mother poured coffee from a large cafetiere for the two detectives and started a fresh cup for herself.

Once they were all settled, Jenny introduced Jane and explained what they needed from the family if they were to find the murderer.

'I'm so sorry for your loss,' she began. 'I want you to know that we are doing everything we can to find the person who did this, but we do need your help.

'Can I start by asking if you're aware of any threats against Gareth in recent weeks? Was he behaving out-of-character in any way, or did he appear to be worried about anything?'

Julia Tresham sat in silent contemplation for a few minutes.

'I'm not aware of anything in particular,' she said. 'Everything has been routine. Gareth had his work of course, and he was always rushing off to meetings, or taking phone calls at all times of the day and night, and of course he was always on that bloody laptop of his.'

She pulled a tissue from a nearby box, dabbed at her eyes and blew her nose. Emily was sitting quietly, her eyes red from crying. She also took a tissue and held it in her hands, ready to use. Her mother composed herself and then continued.

'I suppose the only break from the usual routine was his trip to Swansea a few days ago. He was very secretive about it, but I just assumed it was council business and didn't inquire further.'

'Did he give any indication of where he went or why he was going there?' Jane asked.

'No, not at all. I did ask but he said it was business.'

Jenny turned to Emily.

'You're a student at Swansea University, aren't you? Did he call on you when he was there?'

Emily looked perturbed.

'No, I didn't even know he was in the city. Maybe he thought I was busy, or that I wouldn't want him walking in on me without notice. I've been very protective of my independence in the past. I'm surprised that he didn't phone me, though. We could have gone for a coffee.'

Now, she was dabbing at her eyes as tears started to flow. Jenny let her recover her composure before pressing further.

'Perhaps he felt there was no need because all three of you would be together last night,' she said. 'He may have been genuinely busy and not had the opportunity.'

Emily wiped her face with a fresh tissue while acknowledging the explanation as a plausible one. Her mother placed a hand on hers to try and comfort her.

'We've been inundated with messages of condolence and support,' Julia said. 'We even had Mike Jones, the council leader call around half an hour ago. It's been non-stop.'

'Of course,' Jenny said. 'We'll try not to intrude on you anymore than we need to.'

'Oh no,' Julia seemed shocked. 'I wasn't trying to get rid of you. I know that you have a job to do, and we'll do anything we can to help.'

Jane, as if sensing that there was more to hear, turned to look at Emily.

'I know that you've been living away from home, but in your conversations with your father, had you noticed anything unusual in his manner? Did he tell you of any worries, or talk to you about his work at all? Apart from last night, when did you last speak to him?'

Emily paused to gather her thoughts.

'We've been speaking recently. I'm the women's officer at the students' union. One of the students came to me for help but the problem was so big that I needed to involve my dad.'

Jenny and Jane sat up straight at this information. Julia was listening intently. She seemed unaware of this development.

'What was the name of this student,' Jenny asked.

'Allison Hill. She's active in the local asylum seekers support group in the city centre, and she'd heard reports of women being trafficked to a house in Swansea.

'She didn't want to go to the police as the person who told her about it was afraid of authority and wouldn't talk to them, and she had no proof, just an address.'

'Do you have this address,' Jenny asked.

'No, I'm sorry. Allison knew that my father was a councillor in Cardiff who'd done a lot of work with asylum seekers and people who were trafficked, and of course he had a national role with the Welsh Local Government Association on modern slavery, so I put her in touch with him.

'That was the last I heard of the matter; neither of them mentioned it or discussed it with me again.'

'Do you suppose that your father's trip to Swansea was something to do with what Allison had told him?' Jane asked.

'I don't know. It could have been. As I said we never talked about it.'

'What about Allison? Do you have her address?'

'No, I'm sorry. The university will have that information, I do have a telephone number for her though.'

Emily pulled out her phone, scrolled through it and showed the screen to Jane, who wrote down the number displayed.

Jenny was beginning to feel that they were getting somewhere at last. Was the murder related to this report of human trafficking? Had Tresham started to investigate himself and stumbled onto something he wasn't meant to see? Had he got himself in too deep? She needed to find out more.

Jane could see that the women were struggling and signalled to Jenny that it was time to go. Jenny raised a hand to indicate that she understood.

'I'm really sorry to have kept you so long,' she said. 'I'm sure you have a lot of things to do, and no doubt family and friends will be wanting to speak to you as well. We'll leave you alone, but if you think of anything else, please contact me.'

Jenny handed Julia Tresham a card and they shook hands. She hesitated as if there was something else that she had forgotten.

'Oh, I'm sorry, but could we have your husband's phone and any computer or laptop he may have used? We need to examine them to see if there are any clues as to what Gareth was doing in Swansea. There may even be threats in there he hadn't told you about. Anything he has would help.'

'Of course, I'll get them for you, but most of them belong to the council. They'll want them back.'

'Don't worry about the council, we'll clear it with them. Do you mind if I come with you? It might help if I could see where your husband works.'

Julia agreed and led the two detectives into a small room off the main hall. A large desk with a laptop on it dominated the limited space. There was a pile of paper stacked neatly alongside it. A filing cabinet was sitting in a corner with a sound system on top.

'Gareth liked to listen to music as he worked,' Julia said. 'She ejected a CD from the machine and placed it into an empty case. He loved the Arctic Monkeys,' she said. 'We saw them in Swansea not so long ago. He had all their CDs.'

Jenny placed her hand on Julia's shoulder to comfort her.

'If it's okay, we'll take the laptop and the phone. Jane will be touch later to have a more thorough inspection of the office if that is okay with you.'

'Yes, that's no problem at all.'

'Would you have any idea what passwords he might have used?'

'I'm sorry, I don't.

Jenny handed her a notepad.

'Perhaps you could jot down some likely ones, maybe birthdates for the three of you, the date of your wedding anniversary, when Gareth was elected, the names of pets and anything else you can think of. We'll get our techs onto it.'

As Mrs Tresham wrote down the requested details, Jane bagged the two machines, and then they headed back towards the front door. As they approached, Jenny paused.

'Does Gareth's car have a satnav?' she asked.

'Yes, why do you ask?'

'Would you mind if I had a look at it? We may be able to determine where he went in Swansea.'

Julia Tresham fetched the keys and watched as Jenny opened the door and started the engine. She activated the satnav and scrolled through the past destinations. One stood out; it was an SA5 postcode. She made a note and turned the engine off.

'Thank you,' she said to Julia as she handed the keys back. Can you ensure that the journey log isn't erased. One of our technicians will come and download it in due course. Jane will be in touch to carry out a more thorough examination of Gareth's office. Once again, we're sorry for your loss.'

As they left another car pulled up and a man got out. It was Byron Harris, the regional mayor. He greeted Jenny like an old friend.

'Jenny, how nice to see you. How was the honeymoon?'

'Lovely thank you, Byron. I take it you've come to see Julia and Emily Tresham.'

'Yes, what a tragedy,' he said, shaking his head. 'Such a shock. Gareth was such a lovely bloke, wouldn't harm a fly. Who would do this to him?'

'We're hoping to find out. I'm sorry but we need to get on. Mrs Tresham is waiting at the front door for you. I'm sure she will be comforted to see you.'

Harris pulled himself together, put on his best sympathetic face and headed down the drive. Jenny and Jane placed the evidence bags in the boot of the car and set off for the police station.

Chapter Three

As they left the Tresham's, Jenny phoned ahead to ask Pyke to get what information he could on Allison Hill and the asylum seeker support group she worked with in Swansea.

She was worried that if Hill had passed on information to Tresham that got him killed then the student might be in danger as well. The least they should do is get her into protective custody.

It was not yet noon, so she believed that there was time to follow up another of the leads from the Tresham house. On getting back to the station, she tasked Stoneham with getting Tresham's phone and laptop analysed and writing up their visit, while she set up another video call with Waddingham, who reported that the full post-mortem was now available and loaded up on the system. There was nothing new that might assist the investigation, however. Interviews were ongoing with those in attendance at the Arena, but these were also looking like a dead end.

Quinn said that they'd located the suspect's bike on traffic cameras and had traced it as far as Sarn motorway service station, after which it had disappeared. The number plates were fake and unregistered. Local police had searched the area for the motorbike without finding anything.

He suggested that it might have been loaded into the back of a van so that the killer could continue her journey undetected. CCTV in that area was being checked to see if there were any likely vehicles, but he was not optimistic.

If the killer had made the switch on one of the local roads behind the service station and continued her journey through some of the nearby villages, then there was no way of tracking her.

Jenny reported on the visit to the Treshams and suggested that they retrace the councillor's steps from a few days ago. She was determined to go in person, rather than leave the visit to Waddingham and suggested that she meet them at the location in a few hours' time.

He agreed, so Pyke and Jenny set their satnav for the SA5 address and headed for the motorway.

The directions took them to a cul-de-sac in the Blaenymaes district of Swansea, containing twenty council houses, all with the same postcode. Waddingham was already there, standing next to his car, smoking a cigarette, while Quinn was scrolling through his phone.

A strong breeze blowing up from the direction of the sea was shaking the branches of nearby trees, while the whine of a scrambler motorbike on the nearby common cut through the silence like a hacksaw, setting Jenny's teeth on edge.

The houses looked to be post-war and in need of renovation. Some had old furniture and black bags full of rubbish stored in their front garden, while one frontage contained a half-dismantled car and various parts that had either been stripped from the vehicle or were scheduled to be put on it.

Jenny looked around, apart from the four police officers there was nobody in sight. A quiet cul-de-sac like this was an ideal place to conduct an illicit operation.

As she and Pyke approached the Swansea detectives, she noticed an empty, boarded up house at the end of the cul-de-sac. The garden was heavily overgrown with brambles and the property had clearly seen better days.

She decided that this was as good a place as any to start their investigation. Perhaps this was the address Tresham had been directed to.

The four detectives agreed to divide their efforts. Pyke and Quinn would conduct door-to-door inquiries, while Jenny and Waddingham would investigate the empty house.

As they got closer, Jenny noticed that there were brackets and some wiring on the wall of the property as if cameras had been placed there but had been hastily removed.

Waddingham agreed with her analysis and confirmed that it wasn't the local council's policy to install CCTV on their empty properties.

'It's too expensive,' he said, 'and besides, who has the time to monitor them? We certainly don't. If that's the house we're looking for then whoever or whatever was in there had them installed but had to clear out in a hurry when Councillor Tresham appeared.'

'It's also possible, that if there were cameras there, then that is how they identified him,' Jenny added. 'Of course, we have no idea what actually happened, we're just speculating.'

'Yes, but if they did identify him from their camera footage, then they must have had access to some sophisticated facial recognition software and a database. That seems unlikely to me.'

'Or they knew him already,' Jenny said. 'Or maybe he introduced himself, we really don't know.'

Waddingham shrugged, he clearly didn't have a clue either.

They pushed aside a ramshackle iron gate and walked up the path, taking care not to get their clothes snagged in the brambles that were growing everywhere.

'Should have brought some secateurs,' Waddingham said. 'I hope we don't find Sleeping Beauty in here.'

Jenny looked at him. 'You're not exactly the prince who fought his way into the castle.'

Waddingham was about to retort but then thought better of it. 'No. Well... you have a point.

The front door was bolted shut and covered in a metal panel. They walked around the building noting that the back door and all the windows were similarly covered.

Waddingham looked again at the panel on the back door, something wasn't right. He pulled at the metal sheet, and it came away.

'Well, whoever was here didn't put the bolts back in properly,' he said. 'They really must have left in a hurry.'

Jenny surveyed the back garden. It was piled high with black bags, mixed with used disposable nappies and piles of rubble and what looked like asbestos. She'd seen tidier landfill sites.

At that moment Pyke and Quinn joined them.

'Most of the residents were out, or not answering,' Pyke said. 'One even came to the door clutching a claw hammer - he said it was for self-defence, but soon put it down when I showed him my warrant card.

'However, his neighbour saw Tresham's Mercedes a few days ago. Let's face it that vehicle would stand out like a sore thumb up here. He said he was curious, so watched from his bedroom window.

'And what did he see?' Jenny asked

'He said the driver spent some time looking around this property and trying to see inside. He dropped out of sight for a bit while he explored here, in the rear garden, but in the end appeared to give up and left in a hurry.'

'Did he know how long the man was out-of-sight?' Waddingham asked.

'Quite a while, apparently. Certainly, long enough to have gained access.'

'That's not all,' Quinn added. 'The resident I spoke to didn't see the Mercedes, but he did say that a black van has been seen at this end of the cul-de-sac on several occasions, and that he'd observed a group of people being ushered into this house around about the time that Councillor Tresham would have been up here. He hasn't seen the van since.'

'People trafficking?' Jenny asked, more for speculative effect than seeking an answer.

'Very possible,' Pyke said. 'You did say that was the issue raised with Councillor Tresham by Allison Hill, didn't you?'

'Yes, I did, and it's beginning to look like it was a valid concern. Was this resident able to give any more detail, Rhodri?'

'Only that there was roughly ten of them, a mix of men, women and children, who he described, and I quote, as looking a bit foreign.'

'Anything else?' Jenny asked.

'The only other person we found at home lives at the far end of the close,' Pyke responded. 'She hadn't seen or heard anything but said it's well known that squatters use this property. According to her they don't cause any trouble, so the residents leave them alone, and they don't report it to the police or the council because that's not the done thing around here.

'None of the people we spoke to were able to give a description of anybody coming or going into the house.'

'Right,' Waddingham said, 'we need to get into this house, but we need a forensics team to lead the way.'

He made a quick phone call and told his companions that there would be a team on site within an hour.

'I suggest we wait in the cars,' he said, lighting another cigarette. 'Do we all have forensic over-garments with us?'

Jenny nodded; she'd decided at the last minute to shove a couple in her car boot. She was glad that she'd done so.

Not long afterwards the forensic team arrived. The four detectives pulled on their over suits and paper shoes and followed them into the house. There was clear evidence of a hurried evacuation and a strong, cloying musty smell that Jenny couldn't identify.

Rubbish was scattered everywhere along with blankets, pillows, and personal belongings such as toothbrushes. There were dirty dishes all over the floor and stacked in the kitchen along with unopened tinned food.

Black bags full of used food cans, more dirty nappies and other rubbish were lying around, all contributing to the unpleasant odour that hung about the place. Upstairs there was more bedding and some clothing that had been left behind in the hurried evacuation.

They were able to track the wiring from the outside brackets to a central place where a monitor may have been installed, and according to one of the team they had with them, possibly a transmitter as well.

The tech told Waddingham that whoever had occupied the house had hacked into the electricity supply and a nearby phone line as well, so it was likely that they'd established a wi-fi link to monitor the site remotely.

'This was a very sophisticated operation,' Waddingham said. 'My guess is that it's part of a network of safe houses for people trafficking. What I don't understand is why somebody stumbling on just one part of the operation would lead to a professional hit person being hired to bump him off. It just doesn't make sense.'

Jenny agreed.

'There must be another motive,' she said. 'There's no obvious reason why they'd draw attention to themselves in that way. They evacuated the house, didn't leave anything behind that could lead us to them, and for all intents and purposes have safeguarded the integrity of their operation.

'If Councillor Tresham was killed because he saw what was going on here, then we're dealing with some very ruthless, and sick individuals. He must have had more, but what?'

She opened a cupboard and pulled out yet more bedding. Just then there was a shout from one of the bedrooms. Jenny and Waddingham rushed upstairs to find one of the technicians standing over the body of a child.

The boy must have been no older than ten. If Jenny had to guess, she would have placed him as of eastern European origin. He had dark hair and was dressed in jeans and a T-shirt. There was a large bruise on his head.

'He was underneath a blanket,' the technician said.

Waddingham pulled out his phone.

'We need the pathologist up here,' he said.

This investigation was getting out of hand. They stood back while photographs were taken of the scene, the body, and the surrounding area examined for fingerprints and DNA.

The blanket was bagged along with other items, and the area searched for a possible murder weapon. Jenny shook her head in despair, what a waste, she thought.

She walked with Pyke back onto the street. Waddingham and Quinn were waiting for them. The forensic pathologist had just arrived and was being directed into the house. A small crowd had gathered behind the police incident tape that was securing the scene.

'They were home after all,' Pyke said. He asked a nearby police officer to talk to the residents that hadn't opened their doors earlier to see what they knew about the safe house.

'You two might as well head back to Cardiff,' Waddingham said. 'There isn't much you can do here. We'll touch base tomorrow and let you know what we have from this crime scene.'

Jenny wasn't ready to leave Swansea yet. Pyke had discovered that the asylum seeker support group would be meeting that evening in the city centre. She decided that they would take a detour and see if Allison Hill was there. Maybe they would find the person who'd passed the information to Hill in the first place.

'Shouldn't we let Waddingham know what we're doing,' Pyke asked.

'We will,' Jenny responded, 'if we find anything. I think he's got his hands full for now, don't you?'

Jenny had learned that the asylum seeker support group held their meetings in an old chapel just outside the main shopping area. When she and Pyke got there it looked deserted, the front door locked, but a light at the side of the building suggested otherwise.

They followed three men, who appeared to be of north African origin, down a narrow passage at the side of the building towards a faint light emanating from behind a half-closed door. As they got closer, they could hear music and numerous voices all talking at once.

They were greeted at the entrance to what turned out to be the chapel's crypt by a man in his late sixties with long, straggly light brown hair and an unkempt beard. When he spoke, it was with a distinctive Swansea Valley accent.

'Good evening, can I help you?'

The two detectives pulled out their warrant cards and held them up for inspection.

'Are you in charge here?' Jenny asked.

'It's more of a collective effort really,' the man replied, looking at them suspiciously. 'I'm Graeme Reynard, I chair this support group. I hope we haven't done anything wrong.'

'No, not at all,' Jenny responded. 'We're actually looking for Allison Hill, I understand that she volunteers here.'

'Ah, I'm sorry, but she isn't here, we haven't seen her for a few weeks. I assumed she'd been busy with her degree. Is she in any trouble?'

'No, nothing like that. Do you mind if we come in, we're interested in tracking down a people trafficking ring and was wondering if any of your clients might have some information that could assist us.'

Reynard laughed.

'By all means, but I doubt if anybody here knows anything about such a thing, and if they do, they won't want to tell the police. I'm afraid everybody here has had bruising encounters with the authorities in one form or another and they are wary of anyone who represents the State, even such a liberal and caring one as we have in the UK.'

Jenny could sense the deep irony in his voice as he made this statement. She sympathised.

Reynard stood to one side to let them in. There were about twenty people in a large room, a mix of men, women, and children of all nationalities. Two teenagers were playing pool at the far end, while a group of women wearing hijabs were sitting in a corner chatting over knitting needles and wool.

'As you can see, we're all very law-abiding people,' Reynaud said. 'We get together twice a week to chew the fat, put on English lessons, offer legal advice, and assist with issues like housing.

'All of our members are seeking asylum after fleeing some terrible circumstances, war, terror, torture, starvation. We do our best to make them feel welcome and to settle them in our community.'

'And are all these people here legally,' Pyke asked.

Reynard smiled and tapped the side of his nose with a finger.

'Of course, Sergeant. They're all housed in Home Office-approved accommodation and have current claims registered for refugee status. One or two, like my friend Dani over there, have already been successful and continue to come here to mix with their friends and help when they can.'

He pointed to a young woman in her mid-thirties with dark hair, wearing a knee-length multi-coloured dress decorated with small mirrors. Jenny decided that she needed to do something to get this man on side.

'Look, Mr Reynard, we're looking for Allison Hill because we believe she may be in danger. We understand that she heard about a safe house for trafficked people while helping here and passed that information on to the father of one of her friends, who is a Cardiff councillor. We believe that information led to that man being stabbed to death last night.

'I'm trying to prevent Allison suffering the same fate, Mr Reynard. Do you think you can help us.'

Reynard's eyes widened with surprise at this information but repeated that he didn't know Hill's whereabouts.

'I really would like to help you Inspector, but unfortunately Allison didn't confide in me, so I can't tell you who gave her that information, nor do I know any more than you do as to where she might be now.

'You're welcome to question our members, but I'd be surprised if they know any more than I do.'

Jenny could see that nobody in the room was going to confide in a police officer, especially when there was so much at stake for their own future.

She handed over her card to Reynard, asked him to contact her should Allison Hill make another appearance at the group and led Pyke back to the car.

It was getting late, and Dawn would be wondering where she was. She vaguely recalled that she'd agreed to have supper with her wife and mother-in-law that evening. She looked at her watch, she was going to be late.

As Pyke started the car, she texted Dawn to give her a potential arrival time.

'You'd better put your foot down, Darren, I'm going to be in trouble with the wife.'

Pyke shrugged.

'I did tell you that getting married would change your life, didn't I?'

'Yes, yes, alright, just drive would you. Thank you.'

Chapter Four

Pyke pulled up outside the restaurant in Cardiff city centre where Jenny was due to meet Aileen and Dawn. She was half an hour late, but thanks to Pyke's driving they'd made up twenty minutes on her estimated time of arrival.

She stood on the pavement composing herself before entering, immediately spotting her two companions seated at a table in the far corner of the room. A bottle of wine sat three-quarters empty in front of them alongside three menus.

Alieen stood to greet her and kissed her on the cheek, Dawn sat grinning, still looking radiant following their honeymoon. She took her seat between them and scanned the menu. This was not a cheap restaurant.

'We held off ordering until you got here,' Aileen said. 'You must be rushed off your feet with this investigation. Poor Gareth, he didn't deserve to go out like that. He was one of the good guys.'

Dawn indicated her agreement. Jenny knew from a conversation that morning over breakfast that her wife had known the Treshams for a long time and had joined Julia on several occasions on nights out with mutual friends. Aileen continued.

'I called to see them this afternoon, I understand that you'd already been there. Jenny.'

'Yes, we went first thing this morning,' she replied still trying to make sense of the menu. 'I didn't know the Treshams, but they were clearly devastated at what happened.'

A waiter came to take their order and Aileen ordered more wine. Jenny wondered who had drunk more, Dawn or her mother. She decided it was best not to know. She had to be in work early the next day and so was taking it easy.

With the waiter heading off to the kitchen to arrange their food, Aileen finally got to the point she was trying to make.

'So, have you made any breakthroughs in your investigation, Jenny.'

'Now, you know I can't discuss it, Aileen, even with the police commissioner. You'll get me in trouble.'

Dawn laughed.

'It doesn't usually take somebody else to put you on the wrong side of your superintendent, love.'

'No, you're right, but you're both too close to this and I don't want to compromise you, or me. How were the Treshams when you went to see them, Aileen? I gather that there's been a long procession of visitors there all through the day. We even bumped into the mayor on our way out.'

'Well, naturally, they're still inconsolable. Their only comfort is the support they're getting from the local community. There was one thing though…

'Julia said that Gareth had been quite tense over the last few days, as if he was harbouring a secret. She just had no idea how dangerous that secret was.'

'Oh, does she think that's what got him killed?'

Jenny was genuinely curious. Julia Tresham had not told her about this tension, and even though it fitted with what the police knew of the murder, she wondered whether the councillor had confided in his wife, and if so, what he'd told her.

Aileen looked puzzled.

'I don't think she knows any more than that. I did wonder though what the secret might be, so I approached the council officer Gareth worked with the most often to see if he knew anything, but he was in the dark as well. Did she mention it to you?'

'Not really. It looks like Councillor Tresham was playing at amateur detective and that was what got him killed. But we're still not clear about motive, as none of what we do know makes any sense, well as far as any rational criminal is concerned anyway.'

Aileen looked even more confused, while Dawn had zoned out, as if she were anxious to change the subject. Their starters arrived and they began to eat, but Aileen wanted more information.

'What do you mean, rational criminal?' she demanded.

Jenny put her cutlery down.

'I can't really give you any more details, but for the sake of argument, if you were embarked on a criminal endeavour and somebody discovered what you were doing, but not your identity, would you bring down all the forces of law and order upon yourself and your operation by bumping them off, or would you quietly close up shop for a bit and relocate elsewhere?'

'Well obviously, as the police commissioner I would never put myself into that position, but I see what you're saying. The police have found a motive of sorts but logically it would be self-defeating; therefore, there must be something else.'

'Beautifully put, mother, now can you let Jenny eat her food, please?' Dawn interjected.

'Of course, dear. Please carry on eating, Jenny.'

Aileen turned sheepishly to her own food and started consuming it at a rate of knots. Dawn looked on disapprovingly.

As the waiter cleared away the dishes in preparation for their main course, Jenny decided to press Aileen further to find out what else she'd discovered on her visit.

'What else did Julia Tresham say about her husband?'

'Only that he made a mysterious trip to Swansea a few days before he died. Emily had put him in touch with a friend who'd needed his help. She didn't give any details as to what he was being asked to do.'

Jenny relaxed, there was nothing in what Aileen said that she didn't know already. Their main course arrived, and Dawn took the opportunity to steer the conversation into a different direction.

'We've had our offer on the house accepted,' she said. 'It's just the legal work now, and then we can move in.'

Jenny couldn't quite muster the same enthusiasm as her wife. She was looking forward to having a house of their own, with a garden and somewhere they could host barbecues, she was even liking the idea of living in a proper community with nearby shops, a park, and local pubs, but she knew that it would be a lot of work and stress before they got to that point, and that was not to be welcomed.

She remembered the amount of effort they'd put into closing down and selling Dawn's previous home, at a time when her other half was struggling with her mental health and hoped that vacating and selling her own flat and moving into this new home would be a little easier.

Aileen seemed to be in another world altogether.

'Oh, really dear, that's nice, where are you moving to?'

Now Dawn looked exasperated, not unusual when dealing with her mother.

'Pontcanna. You knew that already, you even came and inspected it with me,' she barked.

'Oh, of course, how absent minded of me.'

Jenny thought that Aileen was still dwelling on the fate of the Treshams and wasn't equipped for small talk at that moment, even about family. Nevertheless, it would be good to distract her.

'I'm looking forward to the garden,' she said, 'but I don't know much about growing things. I hear you've got green fingers, Aileen. Perhaps you can teach me.'

Her mother-in-law brightened up at this suggestion.

'I'd be delighted to Jenny; a productive garden is a healthy garden. I'll have you growing your own food in no time.'

Dawn sighed.

'We've got a long way to go before we're able to start gardening. Somehow, we've got to sort out what we're taking from each property. Don't forget that all my stuff is still in storage. And then there is the decorating, sorting out the carpets, maybe even buying new furniture.'

Jenny felt exhausted just listening to the list of tasks. She'd just come back from a two-week holiday; would she have to take more time off to sort out this new home? She and Dawn had busy jobs that could keep them away from home until late into the evening and occupy them at weekends as well. When would they have time for all this work?

Aileen rushed to the rescue.

'That sounds a lot dear. Obviously, I'll do what I can to help, but why don't you ask your father to do the decorating for you? That sort of thing is right up his street and he's a dab hand at laying carpets too.'

Jenny felt a huge weight lift from her shoulders, and she could see that her other half felt the same way. Although Dawn and her father had been estranged for some time, they had reconciled during the recent mayoral election, and he'd given her away at their wedding. She was sure that Stephen Highcliffe would jump at the chance to spend yet more time with his daughter.

'Did the solicitor give you any idea how long it will take to get all the legal stuff sorted?' she asked.

She'd left all this side of things to Dawn, who loved organising things, and already had lists for the house move. In fact, Jenny was convinced that she had lists about lists. Everything was being planned right down to the last second.

'As it happens, I had a discussion with him this afternoon,' she said. 'We don't have to wait for you to sell your flat, even though it's under offer, so we're not tied down by a chain. Our sellers are in a similar position as they're acting under probate and the house is already registered at the Land Registry.

'The mortgage is in place, so once we've got the searches and the survey out of the way, it'll just be a few days before we can complete. We'll be in there before you know it.'

'That's great news,' Aileen said. 'You'd better ring your father quickly and get him to book some time off work. I take it that you've got a colour scheme in mind?'

She looked at Jenny who, as Dawn knew, wasn't really into home improvement and would live anywhere with a bed, a television, wi-fi and a nearby takeaway pizza place.

'Oh yes,' Dawn said, 'We've already started to map out the rooms.'

Jenny knew that Dawn meant that she'd done this work on her own and would get agreement on her plans later. She was fine with this. Her strengths lay elsewhere; she was determined that sorting out the garden would be one of them.

'Aren't you due to go back to your new job soon?' Aileen asked. 'I guess that's going to take up a lot of your time.'

Dawn had previously worked for the regional mayor's office as the director of development for the Cardiff region, before Morgan Sheckler suspended her after discovering she had altered tender documents.

Her agreement with Byron Harris, Sheckler's successor, involved resigning from that role in return for any charges being dropped. She was subsequently snapped up by the company building the power plant she'd championed in her previous role. Her job was to get it built, something she was looking forward to.

It had taken some time to get all the paperwork together, and to transfer the legal options to a new company after the original tenderer, Maga Power Holdings Limited had been discredited following Sheckler's assassination, but everything was now in order, and she was raring to get it built.

'I'm starting back tomorrow,' Dawn said. 'I reviewed the planning documentation earlier today and I think we're all set to go. I'm confident that the Welsh Government will be giving us the heads-up very soon.

'I've spoken to Byron, and he says that the mayor's office is drawing up the relevant documentation to transfer the land to the new company as soon as planning approval is given.'

'That's very good news,' Aileen said. 'I'm not sure that the action group who opposed this development will think so, but it will certainly help to bring new jobs to the area.

'I'm told that Ministers are talking to Whitehall about setting up a special development area around the plant, which will offer incentives to new businesses to move there.'

'Are you expecting trouble?' Jenny asked, her police officer's instinct kicking in.

'I'm expecting protests, yes, but Gerald Rebane's action group is opposing the plant and whatever else he is, he's not a lawbreaker. He'll keep it peaceful, and once work gets underway, I expect things to settle down.'

'Well let's hope so,' Aileen said. 'That lot have been trouble from the outset, and if I need to deploy police officers to protect workers on this development then I'll do so.'

'I'm sure it won't come to that, Mum, and besides it's in another police area. I discussed this with Jack before I took the job; we're planning very strict security on site. We can't afford delays.'

Aileen grimaced. Jenny knew that she didn't particularly like Jack Chaffont, who was heading up the development on behalf of the new investors. He'd rescued the power plant project when the Americans walked away following Morgan Sheckler's death, but his loyalty had always been to his own best interests, often at the expense of those who'd considered him to be an ally.

He'd initially bankrolled Sheckler's successful bid to oust Harris as regional mayor and the campaign against the power plant, before reversing his position completely when it became clear that it was damaging his own business investments in the United States. Aileen had a long memory.

Their deserts arrived and the table descended into silence as they ate. It was getting late, and Jenny was still very tired. She felt as if she had compressed forty-eight hours into twenty-four, while her sleeplessness from the previous night was catching up on her.

Aileen got the bill and offered them a lift back to Jenny's flat on Lloyd George Avenue. She had a car and driver at her disposal, which had allowed her to indulge in a few too many glasses of wine without worrying about how she would get back to her home in the Ely Valley, near Llantrisant and Talbot Green.

The two women gratefully accepted her offer. The weather had deteriorated during their time in the restaurant, and it was raining heavily. Neither of them had dressed for this likelihood.

Jenny's first instinct on getting home was to jump into the shower to wash away the taint left behind by the traffickers' safe house from that afternoon. As she closed her eyes and let the water wash over her, a picture of the dead child, and the carnage that lay around his body flashed into her head.

No amount of hot water and soap was going to wash away that image. And then she was overwhelmed by images of Tresham, lying in a pool of blood, and Morgan Sheckler, his face half-blown away by the shot she'd fired.

She staggered out of the shower, sobbing, dripping all over the floor, not daring to reach for a towel or to move in case her legs gave way beneath her. How had it come to this?

She'd always considered herself to be as tough as nails and yet recently every little thing, every incident, every death she attended had started to get to her and haunt her dreams, and now her waking moments as well.

Dawn came into the bathroom, drawn by the sound of Jenny's sobs. She grabbed a bath sheet and wrapped her in it, pulling her into an all-embracing hug.

They hadn't talked about Jenny's Day yet, but Dawn knew what she was going through, having helped her with a previous episode of PTSD and, of course, having had her own experience due to being attacked in her own home and subsequently killing her attacker in self-defence.

These flashbacks were not regular but happened every time there was a trigger event such as Jenny attending a sudden death or some other atrocity, and because they'd started with her committing a crime, it was not possible to seek counselling for the condition. She was beginning to wonder whether she would be able to continue as a police officer.

Jenny told her wife about finding the boy in the safe house and how it had once more set off her condition.

'He was so young,' she said. 'What a tragedy. I just can't get him out of my head.'

'I know, try not to dwell on it too much. You need to switch off, try to think of something else. Use the deep breathing exercises we practised.'

Dawn dried Jenny off and led her to bed where they fell asleep in each other's arms. For Jenny, however, it was another disturbed night in which she had nightmares where Morgan Sheckler's head exploded in front of her, and of the little boy, who she dreamt died in her arms.

On several occasions, Jenny woke screaming and Dawn had to calm her down, until finally the detective settled into a troubled sleep, still struggling with her demons.

Chapter Five

Bleary eyed, Jenny made it into the office early the following morning. She was learning how to compartmentalise her emotions, a skill which had helped her to cope with the flashbacks and bad dreams and, with Dawn's help, she was starting to come to terms with these episodes by talking about and recording each episode in a diary.

Despite her good timekeeping Jenny found Jane already at her desk studying Tresham's laptop. She'd obviously managed to get into it with the information supplied by his wife.

'What have you found?' Jenny asked.

Jane jumped, startled, she'd been so engrossed in the machine that she hadn't heard her boss come into the room.

'Oh, good morning, Ma'am, actually there's quite a lot that's interesting on here, but I'm not sure yet whether there's anything useful from our perspective in solving this murder.'

'Well, at least you got into the bloody thing.'

'Yes, the password was his wife's maiden name. At least it wasn't *'password'*, but I doubt if the council ICT department will be very happy at him using such an obvious and unsophisticated means of securing his data.

'I got into his phone as well. You'd think that a six-digit code would be hard to crack, until that is you put in the actual phone number. This man didn't manage his digital security very well.

'But before we go into all the stuff Councillor Tresham was storing on these devices, I need to tell you about Allison Hill.'

Jenny sat down opposite her and took out a notebook.

'Have you managed to find her, then?'

'I'm afraid not. I've made numerous attempts on the phone number that Emily Tresham gave me, but it keeps going to voice mail. I've left several messages, but she hasn't phoned back. I've also tried ringing her on WhatsApp and sent a message there too.'

'Do you think she's avoiding us?'

'Or just not taking calls, full stop. Youngsters nowadays prefer not to speak to somebody on a phone, they'd rather send messages or voice notes. Darren got me her address in Swansea, so I've arranged for an officer to call around. Anyway, this brings me back to Councillor Tresham's phone.'

Jenny held her hand up to request Jane to pause for a minute while she wrote down what she was being told, and then indicated that the detective should proceed.

'There are a series of WhatsApp messages on there between him and Allison, mostly confirming what we already know. The address of the safehouse in Swansea is on there, referenced in a message sent to the councillor just three days before he visited it.

'She also told him to speak to her father who, she says has more information about the trafficking operation. There are no details in the WhatsApp message, but I believe that there might be an email. I was just looking for it when you arrived.'

'Great, well done. I'm going to touch base with Simon later this morning so, I'll bring him up to date. What about social media?'

'I've checked all of Allison's social media and there's been radio silence for the last three days. No clues as to where she may be.'

'Okay, thanks. Let me know if you find anything else.'

Jenny went over to her own desk and logged onto her computer. Waddingham had forwarded the autopsy report on the boy to her. Cause of death was a blow to the head following a fall.

In his email he suggested that the boy had been involved in an accident in the rush to vacate the building. Jenny wondered whether there were any relatives with him in the house, or had the boy been smuggled in unaccompanied.

She guessed that it was the latter, no mother would leave her child behind like that, not without significant coercion. Perhaps his parents could only afford to send him and were going to follow later. She desperately wanted to catch the people who would abandon a dead child in this way, without taking a second glance backwards.

They may not have deliberately killed the boy, but they might as well have done. And what about the parents, would the smugglers notify them? She hoped that somehow, he could be identified so that at least his relatives would get some closure.

Just then Pyke joined her.

'The boy?' he asked.

'Yes.'

'Terrible. I understand that Rhodri Quinn believes the boy is from Albania and has sent his DNA and fingerprints to the authorities there in the hope that they'll get a match with a relative or something. I'm afraid it's a long shot.'

'He's just collateral damage to the bastards who run this operation,' Jenny said. 'How did the Swansea lot pin down his country of origin?'

'He had a tag in his pocket with a first name, Aron, and the name of a town, Ballsh. There are only about 9,000 people living in that town, so Quinn is hopeful.'

Jenny was relieved, there was some hope of closure.

'What do you think?' she asked. 'Is there a chance of identifying him?'

'I don't know,' Pyke responded. 'If they're trying to get out of Albania the parents may be long gone, but there might be a grandmother or something. We'll see.'

Jane appeared, looking troubled.

'I spoke to the university,' she said, 'Allison Hill hasn't been at any of her lectures or tutorials all week. The officer we asked to call on her has just got back to me. Her housemates don't know where she is either, or rather they're not saying. The officer had the distinct impression they were holding out on her.

'All she could get out of them was that Allison left in a hurry yesterday, which would be around the time the news of Councillor Tresham's death was released. It looks like she got scared and ran.'

'Maybe they've been sworn to secrecy. Do we have any idea where she might have gone?'

'Well, there's her father.'

'Do you know where he lives?'

'Somewhere in London, but that's all we know for now. I'll get a photo of Allison off the university registry and check through CCTV at the bus and train station. If she's left Swansea by one of those routes, we may get a hit.'

'Good. See if you can get an address for her father. The university should have it on file, perhaps a phone number.'

'I think there are some emails on Councillor Tresham's computer that might help, and the recent calls on his phone. One of the numbers might be Mr Hill's.'

'Thinking about it,' Jenny said, 'we need to put out an alert for Allison. I don't like the idea of her being out there without protection. The sooner we find her the better. Once you get the photo circulate it around South Wales and the transport police.'

'Will do, Ma'am. Do you think we could get a warrant to look around her accommodation in Swansea? It might give us some clues.'

'I doubt it, we have no probable cause, but I'll talk to Simon Waddingham and see what he thinks.'

Jenny turned back to her computer, leaving Jane to get on with trying to find Allison Hill. She made a video call to Waddingham.

He answered on his phone, standing in the open air, smoking a cigarette.

'Good God, Simon those things are going to kill you. At the very least switch to e-cigarettes before you have a heart attack, or worse.'

He grinned.

'Got out of bed on the wrong side did you, Jenny? Don't worry about me, I'll be fine.'

'It's your funeral. Just touching base. Thanks for the autopsy report. What's the situation with forensics in the safe house?'

'The place is full of DNA and fingerprints but there's nothing that's on the system. We've sent it all over to Interpol to see if they have any matches. There may be a chance that one of the smuggling gang is known to them. We could get lucky, you never know.

'We've been reinterviewing residents up there this morning and managed to get a more accurate time when the illegal immigrants were put in the van and taken away from there.

'It's a long shot, as the van was unmarked and we don't have an index number, but I've got officers scouring CCTV all around that area to see how many black vans show up.

'If they kept to the side roads, we've got no chance, but once they're on the motorway or one of the A or B roads, it's just possible we'll get a hit.'

'What about door cameras and private CCTV?'

'Not a great deal around there, but we're identifying what's available and asking for footage around the relevant time. Do you have anything for me?'

'A few things. We've got into Councillor Tresham's laptop and phone and found a WhatsApp conversation with a Swansea student called Allison Hill, the one who gave him the address of the safe house.

'We think it was that information that led him there in the first place and, of course caused his death.

'We first got her name off Emily Tresham. Allison Hill is a volunteer with a local asylum seeker group. Darren and I called in there last night to see if she was there but drew a blank. Details are on the computer system.

'Jane Stoneman in my team has got her phone number and address and has been trying to contact her. An officer called around to her lodgings earlier, but it looks like she's done a runner. She may be scared for her own safety.

'Her father lives in London, we don't have his contact details yet, so I've got Jane checking CCTV in your bus and railway station, and she'll be putting out an alert as soon as she gets a photo off the university.'

'Good,' Waddingham said. 'Let me know if there's anything I can do to assist in that search.'

'Well, there is one thing, another longshot I'm afraid. If we could get a warrant to search Allison Hill's lodgings, there might be information there that'd give a clue as to her whereabouts, and even how she came across the smuggling gang in the first place.'

'I'll talk to my Super,' Waddingham said, 'I'm sure he knows a friendly magistrate who could accommodate us. We'll argue that we need the warrant to avoid a potential witness being harmed. I'll get back to you on that.'

'Thanks, was there anything else in the house?'

'Well, I can confirm that our first instincts were correct. Whoever was running the operation had hacked into the electricity supply and phone lines. The brackets outside were almost certainly for cameras and there is evidence that they were monitoring inside too.

'One camera was left behind in the rush to clear the place. Unfortunately, it wasn't stand alone, but was hooked into a server, which was taken, so we can't get any images off it.'

'So, the property was being monitored remotely?'

Waddingham lit another cigarette and inhaled with the relieved look of an addict getting his fix.

'Yes, it certainly looks that way. I'd love to get my hands on an IP address.'

'You and me, both. Is there anything else?'

Waddingham thought for a moment, taking a few puffs on his cigarette. Jenny sat back and moved the mouse cursor towards the end call button. She was about to click it when Waddingham spoke up.

'Oh, yes, just for information, we're letting the media know about the safe house and the dead boy we found this afternoon. My Super is doing a press conference.

'We're appealing for witnesses and asking people to let us know if they saw the black van in the area at the time the property was evacuated. It's another long shot but it must be done.'

Jenny was sceptical and said so.

'Well, I hope you've got a well-staffed action line. You're going to be swamped with calls, most of them irrelevant or hoaxes.'

Waddingham was resigned.

'I know, but if only one of them is genuine then it might help.'

Jenny accepted the point.

'Well let me know if anything pops up.'

They ended the call, and Jenny was about to walk back to Jane's desk for a further update when Superintendent Brook appeared. He looked around for a few minutes and then strolled over to Jenny's desk.

'I've just got off the phone to my counterpart in Swansea,' he said. 'It seems you and Waddingham have uncovered a real can of worms. Just to let you know that they're holding the press conference in about an hour's time.

'There's no plan to publicise the link between the safe house and Councillor Tresham's murder at this stage, as far as the public are concerned these are two separate investigations.

'That's not to say you should treat them as such. You do what you need to do to solve this. It looks like the poor bugger paid the price for sticking his nose in without going to the proper authorities.'

'That's the assumption we're working with.'

Jenny was reluctant to give Brook any more information than she needed to, at least not until she was fully confident of her facts. He had a reputation for interfering in investigations, a habit that didn't sit well with the senior officers in charge of the cases.

The theory doing the rounds was that the Super got bored easily and felt he needed to interfere with the work of his officers to keep himself amused. Brook himself called it 'management by walking around.'

Jenny felt like asking him if he had a meeting to go to or something so she could get on with her job but was saved from such a blunt intervention by Jane's arrival.

They both stared at Brook for a minute until he took the hint and went to speak to Pyke instead.

'Sorry, I hope I wasn't interrupting something, Ma'am,' Jane said half seriously. She knew Brook's reputation as well as every other detective.

'God, no, you came in the nick of time. What've you got, Jane?'

She put Tresham's laptop down on Jenny's desk and opened one of the emails. It was from Allison Hill and contained contact details for her father, Casey Hill. In the message she suggested that Tresham speak to Casey as soon as possible.

The message went onto say that Hill works for a medium-sized firm of accountants based in London, who've had dealings with the traffickers. Jenny thought that this might involve money-laundering.

'Great, let's get in touch with him,' she said.

'Hold on a minute,' Jane said. 'There's a later email. In it, Allison says that when she told her father that Councillor Tresham might contact him, he absolutely forbade it.

'She says that her father instructed her to back off, warned her that she might be in danger and told her that she should get out of Swansea for a few days. That email was sent the day after Councillor Tresham visited the safe house.'

'Wow, is there anything more?'

'Yes, there was a follow-up email in which Allison tells the councillor that her father warned her that he had knowledge of some of the people involved in this trafficking operation and that they were dangerous.

'She suggested Councillor Tresham needed to protect himself and says that as a result she's no longer getting involved. She tells him not to contact her again.

'That email was sent on the day Councillor Tresham was murdered. It's not clear if he read it or not.'

'Well, we can't say that he wasn't warned,' Jenny said. 'He should have listened. Councillor Tresham was obviously a very stubborn man.'

'Or a very stupid one,' Pyke said, joining them. 'Thanks for sending the Super over to me. It's not as if I had any work to do,'

The two women laughed.

'Don't blame us,' Jenny said. 'He found his way over there all by his self. Besides I thought you too were pals.'

Pyke snorted,

'Outside of work maybe.' He picked up a remote control and used it to switch on a nearby television. 'I thought you'd want to watch the press conference.'

The screen filled with a picture of Waddingham, his Superintendent and one of the Assistant Chief Constables.

The event went much as expected with Waddingham explaining that they had raided a property suspected of being used for housing trafficked people, only to find it abandoned and the body of a young boy concealed in one of the rooms.

He asked people watching to contact the police if they'd seen anything suspicious in the area and if they'd seen a black van entering or leaving the area, especially at the time the house was evacuated.

They opened it up to questions. Most of the journalists present focused on how they'd found the house in the first place. Waddingham told them he couldn't comment on that for operational reasons.

One journalist wanted to know if they had any more leads. Waddingham deflected that question as well. Questions about the identity of the boy were answered as fully as possible, with the Superintendent explaining that they'd passed DNA onto the Albanian authorities.

And then came the question they were all dreading; was this find related to the murder of Councillor Tresham? Jenny looked more closely at the screen. She thought she recognised the questioner.

It was Simon Jones, a freelance journalist who'd moved to Cardiff during the controversy that erupted following the murder of Morgan Sheckler. He'd started out on a provincial newspaper before rising to become a senior member of staff on the News of the World. When that paper folded, he went to work freelance.

Jenny had heard that Jones had joined a gym and put himself on a strict diet. He looked all the better for it. Even the double chin had disappeared. She knew that his sources were good and wondered what he'd heard.

Was there a leak in the department? Had somebody been talking in the local pub? There was no point worrying about that now. She knew that Superintendent Brook would be furious if there'd been loose talk, that though, was his concern.

She picked up the remote control and switched the television off.

'Okay.' She said, 'let's get back to work.'

* * *

A few hours later, Jenny gathered the team together to take stock. It had been a long, hard, and frustrating day.

Waddingham hadn't been able to secure a warrant to search Allison Hill's house, but he'd sent Rhodri Quinn around there to question her housemates more closely. They either didn't know or were staying silent about her whereabouts.

One of them had mentioned a boyfriend but didn't know his name or where he lived, or at least that was what he told the detective, Jenny thought. She wasn't buying this wall of ignorance. Were they protecting Allision, trying to hide her for some reason? It was very likely.

Jane said that she'd spoken to Hill's tutor who also denied seeing her for the last few days. She'd trawled the CCTV footage at the train and bus stations in Swansea but had not been able to positively identify the girl.

'The problem is that all these youngsters are wearing hoodies, and none of them look up,' she told the group. 'There are half a dozen youngsters in both places that could be Allison, all London-bound, but I can't categorically identify any of them.'

'What about her father?' Jenny asked. 'It sounds like he has information we desperately need to take this investigation forward.'

'Just as frustrating,' Pyke responded. 'I took that task off Jane so she could concentrate on the CCTV. The number we have for him is going straight to voicemail. I've sent him an email but no reply yet.

'I've also managed to get an address for him from the university and have contacted the local nick down there to see if they could find him. An officer called around but there was no answer.

'If we knew the name of his accountancy company, we could try them but that isn't available to us either. What about Waddingham's appeal for the van?'

'I spoke to him again a few minutes ago,' Jenny replied. 'You won't believe how many people claim to have seen a black van in the Swansea area.'

'I think I could guess,' Pyke said.

'Exactly. Waddingham says that they're following up all the sightings on road cameras. He thinks he has one promising lead, a van heading down the M4 at the right sort of time. It came off on Junction 37 apparently, and headed towards Porthcawl, but that's all he's got.

'They picked it up on camera again turning off towards the fairground. He's got an index number and has the local beat copper and the community support officers keeping an eye out. It's not going to solve our murder. however.

'Jane, do we have anything on Allison's credit or debit cards?'

'Not really,' Jane replied. 'I haven't been able to get her bank to co-operate without a warrant, and we're having the same problem as Inspector Waddingham. She's doing nothing wrong and the powers that be don't believe we have strong enough grounds to allow us access to her accounts.'

'So, another dead end then.'

'I'm afraid so, Ma'am.'

Just then Jane's phone rang. She walked over to her desk to answer it. Jenny watched as her detective constable engaged in a protracted conversation. Eventually, she ended the call and returned to the group looking grim.

'It's not good news,' she said. 'You're to expect a call from Inspector Keaton, Ma'am. She's going to bring you up to speed.'

Chapter Six

Detective Inspector Fiona Keaton was feeling pleased with herself. She'd finally secured the transfer to the Met's Major Crime Unit that she'd been after and had left the financial crimes section behind her.

There was though, one loose end that she needed to clear up before she could fully immerse herself in the new role, though she was pleased that it'd been possible to take the case with her so that it hadn't delayed the move.

A slim, statuesque blonde in her early thirties, Fiona chose to play down her looks by dying her hair bright red and having it cropped short. Her choice of clothing reflected this choice, often turning up for work in a trouser suit and, when called for, jeans and a plain top.

Nevertheless, she attracted attention wherever she went. She was tougher than she looked, had a sharp mind, an aptitude for figures and a good understanding of the financial markets all of which had served her well in her previous role.

Now, she was looking forward to escaping the largely office-based environment of investigating blue collar crime and getting back onto the streets, dealing with criminals face-to-face.

She was going to spend her first day bringing her new team up to speed. The case revolved around a firm of accountants who were involved in laundering the proceeds of drug smuggling and people trafficking. Fiona had an informer who, if he delivered what he'd promised, would enable them to break up several illegal operations.

Her number two in this operation was Detective Sergeant Alaya Chopra, a graduate in criminology and an up-and-coming officer in her mid-twenties, who always presented for work in black trousers, matching jacket and white blouse, and whose round, full face was dominated by a large pair of black-rimmed glasses, her black hair tied back in a ponytail.

They were supported by Detective Constable Pat Harmon, whose distinctive Irish accent betrayed his roots. He was also in his twenties, tall and thin, with curly red hair and dressed casually in blue chinos and an unbuttoned white cotton shirt.

Fiona knew Alaya from a previous assignment and had full confidence in her ability. She'd also heard good things about Pat. Her new Superintendent, however, was an unknown quantity but one with a fierce reputation.

Fred Appleton was a brusque, no-nonsense Yorkshireman in his early fifties with decades of experience in the Met behind him. At six-foot four, with a shock of white hair and a large beer belly he tended to dominate any room he was in.

His loud raucous laugh and sarcastic sense of humour was notorious in the department, as was his large golden retriever called Bear, who had a habit of climbing all over visitors to his home and slobbering in their face.

The whole team was gathered in the office to discuss the next steps in the case. Appleton was observing. It stood to reason, though unspoken, that this was because Fiona was an unknown quantity, and he was assessing how she did and how she interacted with her colleagues.

'No pressure, then,' Fiona thought as she surveyed her new team. She'd put in place a power point presentation to help her, a medium that she knew Appleton was not comfortable with.

He was an old-fashioned cop who was yet to come to terms with the way that many of the scams used by criminals had migrated to the internet. Fortunately, he had officers under his command who did that sort of thing for him.

Her first slide was a simplified explanation of how this particular money-laundering worked. As she took them through it, she was pleased to see that both Alaya and Pat were taking copious notes.

'Cutter Associates,' she said, 'is a medium-sized accountancy firm based in west London. Their managing partner and founder is John Cutter. The firm has about half-a-dozen junior partners and several associate partners, some of whom appear to be outside investors who aren't involved in the day-to-day business of the company but have a financial stake in it, as well as the right to attend board meetings and examine financial records when they need to.

'Our informant is an accountant called Casey Hill. He's worked for the firm for the best part of ten years. Mr Hill contacted the financial crimes unit after stumbling across some files he wasn't meant to see and subsequently carried out a bit of digging to put them into context.

'I don't have any photos of him, and he appears to avoid social media, but I do have background. He's an Oxford graduate, before that Westminster public school. His parents were both senior civil servants at the Ministry of Defence. When he left university, he trained as a chartered accountant with one of the big companies but left under a bit of a cloud and ended up in his current employment.

'He was married and has one daughter, Allison, who's at Swansea University. He lost his wife to cancer a few years ago, went through a bit of a rough patch, but got his life back on track with the help of some university friends.

'So far, he's only been willing to speak to me through WhatsApp, and on condition that I keep the messages top secret and don't share them with anybody else. He says that he's activated the automatic message deletion mode on his own phone. I have of course recorded all these messages on HOLMES 2 and formally registered him as an informant.'

She looked towards Appleton as she said this, who indicated his approval. She continued.

'I've been encouraging Mr Hill to get me copies of these documents and he has finally agreed to do so. There is some risk involved to him naturally.'

She put up a map of an area of London with a building on an industrial estate circled in red.

'He's agreed to meet us at 11am today in this empty warehouse on the south bank of the Thames, where he will hand over a USB stick containing the documents. He's chosen this venue, which I'm a bit uneasy about, but he insisted on it; he says it's out of the way, not overlooked and there's no CCTV.'

'If anything, that makes it riskier,' Appleton said. 'I take it we're going in mob-handed?'

Fiona paused to reflect on the question before answering.

'Hill is insistent that there be only two officers present. I was going to suggest myself and Alaya. However, we could station officers around the immediate area so that they're only a minute or so away if needed.'

Appleton seemed happy with this response.

'There is one more thing,' Fiona said. 'Hill wants protection for himself and for his daughter, who is, he tells me, on the way to London to meet up with him. I've told him that we'll review the material first and if we decide to bring charges then we can deal with that request at that time.

'If nobody knows he's taken the files, and he's confident that's the case, then there's no imminent danger to him.'

At this point Appleton stepped to the front so he could address the whole team face-to-face.

'I'm beginning to think that this operation has the potential to go tits-up quite quickly if your informant is caught in flagrante, so to speak. You're both firearms trained aren't you, so I want you and Alaya to attend this meeting armed and wearing body armour, Inspector. Is that clear?'

'Absolutely, sir.'

'Good, keep me informed as to progress,' he added, leaving them to their preparations.

Fiona watched Appleton leave and then turned back to address her team.

'Right, we've only got a few hours to get this show on the road. Alaya, could you please arrange some armed back-up and ask them to hang back a few streets away.'

She put up a map and pointed to a location where she wanted the van to wait.

'Could you also arrange for us to draw weapons and body armour on the way out. Pat, I've uploaded the full profile of Casey Hill onto HOLMES 2, could you review that, please and see if there's any new information we can add to it. See if his family are on social media.

'Oh, and have another look at this accountancy firm as well. See if any of the partners have form. Thanks.'

* * *

A few hours later, Fiona and Alaya parked their unmarked car alongside the derelict warehouse. There was no sign of any other vehicle. They checked their weapons were holstered properly and secured their bullet proof vests.

The building was huge - a three-storey brick wall with expansive multi-paned windows, many of them broken... the victims of bored kids who liked to throw stones.

A chill breeze buffeted the surrounding scrub and the vegetation sprouting through the cracked mortar of the building. The place was derelict and desolate, but Fiona had no doubt that some developer already had plans to turn it all into luxury, riverside flats.

Picking their way through broken glass, discarded bricks and other debris, Fiona and Akbar went in search of the entrance.

Most of the site had been secured behind portable metal fencing units, but as they turned a corner Fiona saw that one of these had been removed and pushed aside. They walked through it and headed to a large green door which had some sort of pulley mechanism above it.

As they approached it, they could see that it had been left open, wide enough to get a vehicle through. Fiona edged close to the doorway, darting her head inside for a quick survey before stepping into the gloom. Alaya followed, keeping her back to the wall.

Looking up they could see that most of the roof was missing, iron girders were silhouetted against the pale sky above. The floor was covered in moss and wind-blown branches, mixed with smashed tiles, bricks and busted wooden pallets. An eerie silence, broken only by the occasional cry of a gull, hung heavily around them.

The building consisted of one large, cavernous space with very few hiding places. Fiona wondered where Hill could be lurking, if he'd turned up for the meeting at all. There were several doors to her left, which she presumed led to offices. She signalled Alaya to accompany her in that direction.

They were now entering an area where the roof was intact, and there was a lot less light. Fiona pulled out a flashlight and used it to illuminate their approach.

She started at a movement to her right and knocked over a couple of cardboard boxes but relaxed again when a huge rat emerged and scurried away. It was then that she noticed daylight coming through a half-obscured opening in the far corner of the building. She gestured for Alaya to check it out, following closely behind her.

A gust of wind that disturbed the dust around their feet confirmed Fiona's suspicion that the light was coming from another opened exit to the outside world. There was still no sign of Hill.

She pushed at the door of one of the offices, brushing away cobwebs as she did so. The room was empty other than a wooden desk and a wheeled chair.

She approached the second office with a similar result, albeit with the addition of a disconnected old rotary dial phone sitting on the floor. Like the rest of the room, it was covered in dust.

'Bloody Hell,' Fiona said, 'that thing belongs in a museum.'

She was feeling uneasy about this whole venture. It was beginning to look like Hill had decided not to honour his side of the deal, either that or something had gone very wrong.

There was just the one office left to check. As she reached for the door handle, a noise coming from the direction of the open exit distracted her. Both officers spun round, their hands hovering over their weapons, ready to draw them if needed.

A shadowy figure sprinted from the building. Fiona called out for them to stop. The next minute they heard the noise of a motorbike engine being started.

They ran towards the exit just in time to see a leather clad figure wearing a black helmet and tinted visor speed past them. Fiona's eyes automatically went to the number plate, but it had been obscured by dirt and it was impossible to make out.

The two officers looked at each other, wondering what had just happened. There was no point calling in the back-up team, the bike would be long gone, but now Fiona's feeling of foreboding was stronger than ever.

She strode back into the building and straight towards the final office. As she tentatively pushed the door open, she saw a shape lying there in a pool of blood. It was a man. She strode over to check, but her initial suspicions were correct, he was dead.

She had never met Casey Hill and without his photograph couldn't be sure if this were him, that would have to wait for dental records and a formal identification.

The dead man in front of her was in his late fifties, about five feet eight inches tall with thick white hair, a white beard, and dark-rimmed glasses, his throat had been cut, but there was no sign of the knife.

Fiona telephoned for forensics to attend along with a pathologist. She pulled on latex gloves and conducted a cursory search of the body. She was looking for the memory stick which they'd been hoping to acquire and anything else that might assist them.

The stick wasn't there. Instead, she pulled out his wallet but all it contained was cash and credit cards which at least confirmed that they were looking at the corpse of Casey Hill.

There was also a set of keys and a very basic phone, which looked very much like a burner. It was locked and inaccessible at this time. It didn't, however, appear capable of hosting messaging software such as WhatsApp so Fiona concluded that it was not his main device. She'd hoped that it would be a more sophisticated smart phone packed with incriminating data about Hill's employers. She turned to Alaya.

'Get this place secured as a crime scene. I don't want to miss anything in trying to find the killer or give him a way out by compromising the area. Oh, and get some uniforms over to Casey Hill's home. I want it secured so we can search it later. Hopefully, the stick or its contents will be on his laptop. Thanks.'

The scene-of-crime team didn't take long to arrive. Ominously, they were joined not long after by Superintendent Appleton. He stood silently next to Fiona as she watched the pathologist work.

A technician was filming the location of the body and the surrounding area, while others were looking for clues and bagging anything that might be useful.

A fingertip search of the room was underway. It would have to be extended to take in the rest of the building and wherever it was that the killer had left their motorbike.

Either Casey Hill had not brought his phone with him, or the killer had removed it from his body. She was optimistic that it would turn up in a search of Hill's home along with the incriminating evidence he'd intended to give them. She reasoned that he must have left it there so that he could not be tracked.

The question that was burning most fiercely in her mind now though, was how did the killer know about their meeting? Had somebody discovered that the files had been downloaded and had him followed?

Perhaps Hill had let it slip to one of his colleagues, but no, that couldn't have been it, he'd been ultra-cautious in his communications with her, to the point where he was deleting messages from his phone as soon as he'd sent them.

Maybe somebody thought he was acting suspiciously and had him put under surveillance. There was no other way that the killer could have known what was going down, surely. But somebody did, and whoever that was had had the time to hire a hitman and send him to this location. It didn't make any sense.

She watched as Hill's body was taken away. Alaya had bagged all the items that had been found on him and passed them to forensics. Fiona was praying that the killer had left some DNA behind, perhaps when he'd removed the USB stick, but she wasn't counting on that either.

Her instincts were telling her that as this murder was zo well-planned then whoever had committed it would be forensically aware. She looked across at Appleton, who was standing near the exit, quietly seething as he sucked on a pipe, exhaling the occasional puff of smoke.

He'd hardly muttered a word to her since arriving on site. Maybe he suspected a leak in the department, or that she'd screwed up in some way. She'd been told that he didn't suffer fools gladly. Perhaps he'd marked her down as one of those fools. It was only her first day and already a major operation had fallen over. It was not an auspicious start.

She called Alaya back over and asked her to head off to the office and get Pat to pull down footage from all the traffic cameras in the area. Any information that could be gleaned, even a partial index mark or just direction of travel would be useful. At that moment Appleton appeared at her shoulder, pipe in his hand.

'I think you've done all you can here, Inspector, shall we reconvene back at base in half an hour for a debrief?'

'Yes, of course, no problem, Sir,' she stuttered, but Appleton was already halfway to his car.

'How rude,' she thought, and then she realised that Alaya had taken their ride. Fortunately, there were still some officers on the scene, so she hitched a lift off the first one she could find.

Chapter Seven

As Fiona walked into the squad room, Alaya glanced in her direction and raised her eyebrows in a signal of silent solidarity. Appleton was at the far end of the squad room looking discombobulated. This is going to be fun, she thought.

Fiona put on her most serious face and strode purposefully to join the team. She was determined not to be intimidated on her first day in the new job. Further she was not going to accept responsibility for this disaster.

Everything had been planned meticulously, if Hill had died because he was planning to pass on information about a criminal enterprise, it hadn't been her fault nor that of any of the officers working under her.

He'd clearly compromised himself or had been found out. Nothing the police had done had led to the sad outcome they now had to deal with, she believed.

As she reached Alaya and Pat, Appleton drew himself up to his full height and demanded an explanation in his broad Yorkshire accent.

'Report, Inspector! How did this fuck up happen?'

Fiona refused to be rushed into responding.

'I think, sir, that we were unlucky. As you saw at this morning's briefing, the entire operation was planned to the last detail, nothing was left to chance. If Mr Hill was compromised, then it wasn't because of anything we did.'

Appleton seemed happy with this answer. Fiona knew that he had a reputation as a ball-breaker, but she was also aware that he took his management responsibilities seriously, was fiercely loyal to his officers and was scrupulously fair when it came to operational culpability. Her answer calmed him down almost immediately.

'Yes, you're right, of course. I reviewed the operation in detail myself. It's just so bloody frustrating to have a major coup like this whisked away when we were so close to sealing the deal.

'But you understand that I need to conduct a post-mortem, right?'

'Absolutely, sir.'

'Right then, are we sure that there is nothing we did that could have got Hill killed? Could the arrangements have leaked?'

'I don't see how that is possible,' Fiona responded. 'None of our communications were put in writing. All the arrangements were conducted through WhatsApp and, as I said at the briefing, Hill was deleting those messages straight away.

'Even if his phone had been tapped or accessed in some other way, he would have had to have been bloody unlucky for those messages to have been seen before they disappeared.

'WhatsApp is an encrypted service. It shouldn't be possible to get into somebody else's conversation without access to the phone the messages were sent on.

'The only other record is what was entered onto HOLMES 2. You can go through that in detail if you wish, everything was recorded contemporaneously, nothing has been added or altered.'

Appleton seemed satisfied.

'I know,' he said, 'I've already reviewed the file on HOLMES 2. Good, so our priority now is to find the killer and to try and retrieve those records.'

At this point Pat piped up.

'I may have something,' he said sharing his computer screen to a larger wall-mounted one nearby. 'I've been pulling up footage from all the traffic cams around the warehouse at about the time Mr Hill's body was found. I believe that this is the motorbike that left the crime scene.'

A picture was highlighted on the screen of a black leather-clad motorcyclist speeding down the A200.

'I've managed to follow the bike for a few miles on the cameras we have access to but then it disappeared.'

'What about the number plate?' Appleton asked.

'They're false. I'm afraid. No doubt at the bottom of the river by now.'

Appleton grunted. Fiona however went to look more closely at the picture.

'Can you sharpen this up a bit?'

Pat made adjustments to improve the picture's resolution. Fiona continued to stare at it for a few more seconds and then turned to the others.

'Is it me,' she said, 'but could that be a woman?'

'Either that or a slightly built man,' Appleton said.

'Right, then let's not jump to any conclusions on who this murderer could be,' Fiona said. 'Where are we on the forensics?'

'Too early,' Alaya said. 'Preliminary conclusion on the scene was death was caused by the slicing of his carotid artery, clinical and instantly fatal. We need to wait for the pathology report to get anything more, including any supposition on the type of knife used, if that is even possible.'

'Okay, what about the daughter? Mr Hill told us she was on her way to London. Do we have any contact details for her? I'm worried about her safety, and I'd hate for her to find out about her father from somebody else.'

'No, we've got nothing,' Pat said. 'I'll get onto her university and see if they have a mobile number for her.'

'Thank you,' Fiona said. 'That just leaves us with Casey Hill's home. Have you heard anything from the officers we sent to guard it, Alaya?'

'No, everything seems to be secure there.'

Fiona rattled the set of keys she'd taken from Hill's body.

'Right, let's go see what we can find there. Alaya, you're with me. Pat, can you keep digging into Hill's past, please, and the company he works for? The more background information we have the better.'

As they grabbed their jackets and prepared to leave, Appleton turned and moved towards an internal door, stopping briefly to address them one more time.

'I'll leave you to it,' he said. 'You seem to have everything under control. Well done, everybody.'

* * *

Casey Hill's home was a first floor flat in a converted two-storey house in Queen's Park. A low wall topped by a substantial privet hedge hid a small garden containing a few shrubs and two plastic bins. A tiled path let to a big wooden door flanked by two pillars holding up a brick porch. To its right was a large bay window with the view through it into the building barred by thick curtains drawn across its full width.

As Fiona had requested, a uniformed Police Community Support Officer was standing guard. He confirmed that there had been no movement into or out of the property since he'd arrived.

She put on latex gloves, pulled out the keys and let herself in, Alaya followed suit. A pile of unopened post, most of it junk mail, littered the entrance hall. Fiona made a note to check it later. She was now faced by two white doors, one of which she thought must be the entrance to Hill's flat.

She chose the door on the right and went to insert the key in the lock, only to notice that it was already ajar. She pushed at it tentatively and stood back. It swung open to reveal a carpeted stairway.

They climbed the stairs slowly, alert for any movement in the flat above. At the top was a long passageway leading to various rooms.

She noted two doors on the righthand side and a further door facing them at the bottom of the hall, all three were ajar. Slowly, she and Alaya walked to the first door. It opened onto a cavernous living room, complete with three-piece suite, a television, and a vintage four drawer bureau desk. Prints of Renaissance art were hanging on the wall.

The room was a mess. Cushions had been flung from the chairs onto the floor and the linings beneath slashed open. The desk drawers were open, and their contents flung anywhere in what appeared to have been a frantic search for something.

Fiona picked up a discarded picture frame. The glass had been broken, but the photograph was still there. It was of Casey Hill and two women. One was slightly older and could have been his deceased wife, the other looked to be a teenager, presumably his daughter, Allison. She removed the picture from the frame and bagged it.

They moved into the next room, which turned out to be a small kitchen. Again, all the contents of the drawers and cupboards had been turned out onto the vinyl flooring.

There was a door at the far end of the kitchen, which opened onto a glass-walled conservatory overlooking the rear garden. This area had been set up as an office, with a desk, a fan heater, and an ergonomic swivel chair, however the laptop that fitted into the docking station sitting on top of the desk was missing.

Once more the contents of the desk drawers had been emptied out. Despite their best efforts, neither Fiona nor Alaya could find any sign of a USB stick or any other storage device.

The last door led to a bedroom and an ensuite bathroom. The mattress had been hauled off the bed and all the soft furnishing cut open; Hill's clothes were dumped in piles. The bathroom was in much the same condition.

'Well, whoever searched this place was very thorough,' Fiona said, as she led the way back to the living room.

'And may well have done so while Mr Hill was on his way to meet us,' Alaya added.

'We're going to have to go through this place with a fine-tooth comb, let's get forensics in first. I'm not hopeful, but maybe whoever did this left behind a fingerprint or some DNA.'

'I'm sceptical too,' Alaya said, picking up a pile of paper from the floor. 'I'd be surprised if anything was missed, it looks like they had plenty of time to remove anything incriminating.'

Fiona took her phone out of the clip holster on her belt and rang Pat asking him to get forensics to the flat as soon as possible. She then started to pick up documents to sort into piles.

There were the inevitable bills, personal correspondence, bank statements and several employment records. Hill's phone, which he'd used to communicate with her on WhatsApp was nowhere to be found.

Fiona was so engrossed in sorting through what had been left behind that she didn't notice the arrival of the forensics team. They got to work immediately, photographing the flat, looking for fingerprints and DNA and searching for any other evidence.

The two detectives followed them around identifying any obvious discrepancies that might need to be sampled. In the bedroom, Alaya moved some clothes and found a photograph album underneath.

Most of the photos were old, after all most people had gone digital by now, but there were some interesting pictures of Hill's time at university that were worth taking with them. If they needed to dig deeper into his past, then identifying and finding some of these fellow students might be helpful.

Just then the police support officer entered the flat and called Fiona over. There was somebody at the door she needed to meet. They walked back down to the porch where a young woman, barely out of her teens, was standing looking frightened and struggling to hold herself together.

'Hello. Can I help you?' Fiona asked,
'I'm Allison Hill, what's going on?'

* * *

She was short, about five feet two-inches tall and slightly overweight. Her round face was dominated by long brown hair and hazel eyes. She was wearing khaki-coloured cargo pants with lots of pockets, a CND t-shirt, a denim jacket and had a large rucksack hanging on one shoulder.

Fiona took her to one side and broke the news about her father. She held her as she broke down in tears and tried to comfort the poor girl

Slowly, she coaxed Allison's story out of her. She'd been staying at her boyfriend's house in Swansea for a few days when she got the news that a friend's father had died.

She'd told her housemates not to tell anybody where she was and was intent on lying low when her father contacted her to say that she might be in danger and to get to London as soon as possible where he could arrange for them both to be protected.

He'd transferred money to her account, sent her a burner phone with some paperwork and told her to leave behind her own phone and any electronic devices. She'd caught the earliest train possible, but she was still too late.

Allison showed Fiona her phone. The only number saved on it was Casey Hill's own burner phone, which the police already had in their possession.

'What will you do now?' Fiona asked. 'You can't stay here. Would you like me to arrange for some accommodation for you?'

'No, please, I'll be okay. I have friends in London I can stay with. I'd like to see my father. Can that be arranged, please?'

'Of course, do you think you're strong enough? We don't have to do it now. You can see him tomorrow if you wish.'

'No.' the young woman was quite firm. 'I want to see him now.'

Fiona asked Alaya to drive them to the mortuary where Casey Hill's body was being stored.

Sitting in the back of the car, Allison was quiet and reflective. Fiona tried to talk to her once or twice but got no response, so they made the journey in silence.

At the mortuary, they watched as she wept over her father's body. It was a scene that both detectives had witnessed far too often and one that they never wanted to see repeated.

When she finally emerged, Allison formally signed off on the identification and sat with them sipping lukewarm tea. Fiona put a comforting hand on the girl's shoulder. She seemed to be having second thoughts about seeking out friends to stay with.

'My father thought I was in danger,' she said. 'What do you think?'

'Is there any reason why you might be?' Fiona asked.

There was no reply. She tried again.

'Were you close, you and your father?'

Allison wiped away a tear and blew her nose on a tissue she had fished from one of her trouser pockets.

'Yes. You know we lost my mother to cancer a few years ago? Now I've got nobody.' She blew her nose again. 'My parents didn't have any siblings and my grandparents are all dead. I'm all alone in the world.'

Fiona put an arm around her and pulled her in for a hug.

'There's no hurry,' she said. 'We can stay with you as long as you like. If you feel unsafe, would you like me to arrange a place where you can stay? Nobody will be able to find you then.'

Allison looked dubious.

'Can I think about it?'

'Of course. Maybe your boyfriend could come down and keep you company. I imagine there will be a lot to do over the next few weeks.'

'Oh no, that's fine. I wouldn't want to drag him into this. He's got finals coming up, he needs to concentrate on them.'

Fiona thought that her answer was a bit hurried.

'Perhaps it would be best if I did stay somewhere else tonight,' Allison said. 'But I don't want to put you out.'

'Don't be daft, it's the least we can do,' Fiona responded. 'Alaya here, will sort something out for you now.'

Just then her phone rang. She excused herself and moved to the end of the corridor to take the call. It was Appleton, seeking an update.

She'd never known a superintendent to be so hands-on, but then it was her first day and maybe he just felt he had to be supportive. Unfortunately, his idea of backing up his officers felt more like micro-management.

Fiona went into a nearby office to continue the conversation. It took the best part of ten minutes to take Appleton through the whole saga of finding the flat trashed, with all the evidence missing, and Hill's daughter appearing as they conducted their examination of the scene.

She explained that their next step was to get Allison somewhere secure, give her time to sleep on it and then interview her in the morning to find out what she knew about her father's activities.

She didn't mention her suspicion that the girl might be holding back information. She'd decided that it was best to be sure before briefing the boss.

Once the call was finished, she returned to the waiting area to find Alaya looking agitated. There was no sign of Allison Hill.

'What's wrong?' she asked. 'Where's Allison?'

'I don't know! I popped out to make a phone call to arrange a hotel for her, and when I came back into the room she was gone. I checked the toilets and the rest of the building but there's no sign of her.'

Fiona was shocked.

'She can't have gone far, surely. Maybe she popped out for a smoke.'

They both ran out of the building, but there was no sign of her. Allison Hill had disappeared.

Chapter Eight

Fiona and Alaya spent the next ten minutes searching the streets around the mortuary to see if there was any sign of Allison Hill. It was not as if she could have disappeared into thin air, they thought. She had no transport, and the nearest bus stop was half a mile away.

If she had help, how had she contacted them. Surely, they would have noticed if she'd made a phone call. Perhaps she'd texted somebody to come and collect her, but if so, who? And why was she hiding in the first place?

She was obviously scared, but hadn't they offered her a safe place to stay? Then again, Fiona reasoned, they hadn't been able to protect her father so why would she think the police could keep her safe?

She was worried too about what Appleton would say about them losing a potential key witness in their investigation. Fiona had a hunch that Allison Hill was important somehow in unlocking this case. She just wasn't sure how or why.

'Did you get the number of her burner phone?' she asked Alaya.

'No, I thought we'd have plenty of time.'

'Bugger. Maybe if we can unlock her father's burner, we'll find it that way.'

Fiona decided that they'd looked hard enough for the missing woman and that they should head back to the office. She rang ahead to give some instructions to Pat as Alaya drove.

As they walked in Appleton was there talking to one of their colleagues. He looked up at them, shook his head in disappointment, and left. Pat had obviously briefed him on Allison's disappearance.

She gathered her team together for an update.

'Our main priority at the moment is to trace Allison Hill,' she told them. 'Pat, can you do a deep dive on her background, please? Speak to Swansea University and the local police, if necessary, we need to trace her friends, any known family, no matter how far removed, an aunt, second cousin, whatever, plus anybody else she might know in London.

'She's obviously gone somewhere; we just don't know where at present. Oh, and do the same for her father. Maybe she's with one of his friends.

'Put a trace on her credit and debit cards and see if we can get a warrant to monitor her bank accounts. You'll have to talk to the Chief Inspector for that. Tell him we think she's in danger and need to trace her whereabouts. Hopefully, that will wash with the judge.'

'What about her email?' Alaya asked.

'Yes, presumably she has a personal email account as well as a university one, get that included in the warrant. We might be able to identify her father's email provider as well from their interactions and see what he was up to before his death.'

She paused to collect her thoughts.

'Have we had anything from forensics yet, Pat? I know it's only been a few hours, but this was flagged as a priority.'

'Nothing very helpful, Guv. No unexpected fingerprints or DNA at the scene of the murder. We did get a mould of the bike's tire track, but the chances are that it was stolen, and the perp has set fire to it by now to destroy any trace evidence.

'They've looked for evidence on the body but again there's nothing, not even a hair. Whoever this perp is he or she is forensically aware and has taken measures not to leave any traces behind.'

Fiona groaned. They were getting nowhere fast with this investigation.

'Okay,' she said, 'let me know when you get the full autopsy report, though I can guess what it'll say. I think it's time we went to Mr Hill's work and sussed out what sort of place it is. What have you found out about them, Pat?'

He handed her a folder.

'There's a full list of all the partners and associates in there,' he said, 'together with their annual turnover. None of the people I identified as working for the company have any sort of record nor do the friends, family, or acquaintances that we know of.

'If you can get me a full list of employees I can see if they have any known criminal connections as well. So far though, it's been a bust.'

'Okay, thanks Pat.' She gestured towards Alaya. 'Shall we go and see for ourselves?'

* * *

The office was situated a few streets away from the main shopping area in Camden Town in a converted three-storey townhouse. A discreet brass plaque fixed to the brickwork next to an imposing red wooden door confirmed that they'd come to the right place... Cutter Associates. A voice entry button and speaker were fixed to the wall above it.

Fiona pressed the button and introduced themselves to the female voice that answered. Seconds later there was a loud buzzing sound followed by the clunk of the door unlocking. She pushed it open and stepped into the lobby.

To her left was a small table covered in neatly piled magazines and a row of half a dozen chairs. To her right was a hatch with a sliding glass panel. Further inspection revealed that the panel opened into a small office, staffed by two women.

Fiona wondered whether news of Casey Hill's demise had reached them yet. It was unlikely given that there had been a news blackout for most of the day, but London was a bit like that, it was difficult to keep anything quiet for long.

A press embargo was in force until 6pm to give them room to work, but that wasn't going to stop a curious journalist contacting Hill's place of work for background information.

A young lady, who looked as if she'd barely left school appeared at the hatch and slid open the glass panel. She had tied-back brown hair and was dressed in a matching knee-length skirt and jacket over a white, frilly blouse. The whole outfit looked ten years too old for her.

'Can I help you?' she asked.

Fiona made the introductions and showed her warrant card.

'We'd like to speak to Mr Cutter.'

'Oh, I'm sorry, did you have an appointment? Mr Cutter is not available at present. He's visiting our Cardiff office. Could I get one of the other partners to speak with you.'

Fiona tried to place her accent. It sounded vaguely west country, but much more refined as if it had been schooled out of her at some posh institution. Yet another debutant, she thought, filling a post offered to her by a friend of the family until a suitable match could be found for her.

She watched as the girl walked back to her desk, picked up the phone and summoned somebody who could talk to them. Even her deportment was classic finishing school.

The two detectives waited for somebody to join them. Time was dragging on, and Fiona was anxious to get this part of the investigation out of the way before the official press conference.

She wondered if Cutter's trip to Cardiff had been planned, or was it just a coincidence that he was one hundred and fifty miles away when one of his employees, a major whistleblower who was going to expose his company as lawbreakers, was murdered?

Just then an officious man in his late fifties appeared. He was thin, with an angular face, balding and wearing an expensive-looking pin-stripe suit. He wore his glasses on the end of his nose as if he were used to looking down at people and walked with a slight limp.

'How do you do. I'm Layton Spenser, a senior partner with the firm. Would you follow me, please?'

He led them into a nearby meeting room that like him, seemed to hark back to an earlier age.

The room was dominated by a large mahogany table

surrounded by matching leather-bound chairs. The walls were completely wood-panelled, there were three glass-door fronted mahogany bookcases stuffed with reference books, while a large chandelier hung from the centre of the ceiling.

Fiona felt her feet sink into the thick brown carpet as she moved to take a seat opposite Spenser. Once they were settled, she got straight to the point.

'Thank you for seeing us, Mr Spenser. We're here about one of your employees, Casey Hill. I'm sorry to inform you that he was murdered this morning.'

Spenser seemed shocked, his mouth hanging open as if he were struggling for something to say. Fiona sensed this was the first time he was hearing about Casey's death. Eventually, he managed to compose himself.

'I'm dreadfully sorry to hear that, Inspector. What terrible news. Casey was a very popular member of staff here. I'm sure that his colleagues will be terribly upset to hear of his passing. Would you be able to tell me what happened?'

'I'm sorry, this is still an ongoing investigation, so I'm not in a position to give you more detail at this time.'

'Of course. I'm sure that there are all sorts of protocols associated with such a crime. What can we do here to assist you?'

'Well, to start with, we'd like to look through any personal effects Mr Hill may have in the office. You understand that even the most innocuous item could provide a vital clue as to motive.'

Fiona was working up slowly to what she really wanted, knowing that it had to be offered voluntarily as she didn't yet have the evidence to secure a search warrant.

'I understand perfectly,' Spenser responded, 'however, it's not possible to provide you access to Casey's personal effects as he resigned from his post this morning and took them all with him.'

Fiona and Alaya looked at each other. This was completely unexpected. At best they'd been hoping to find a notebook, a USB stick or some other clue that might furnish them with the evidence they needed to turn this accountancy firm over.

Spenser seemed to relish their reaction; Fiona noticed. She wanted to arrest him right then and there, charge him with smugness and confine him to a dark cell where nobody would ever find him again. She decided to make one last attempt at getting something useful from this visit.

'Would Mr Hill have a laptop or computer here that we could examine?' she asked.

'I'm sorry Inspector, as I explained, Casey took all his personal effects with him. I'm afraid I won't be able to allow you to examine or remove any items belonging to the company unless you have the authority of a judge to do so.'

Fiona had suspected that the shutters were going to come down in this way. She knew that she wasn't going to get any more out of this man. She still had one more question, however.

'Okay, I understand,' she said. 'Could I ask what Mr Hill's state of mind was over the last few days? Did he appear distracted, depressed, perhaps happy to be leaving his job? Are you aware of any conversations he had with colleagues that might cast some light on why somebody would want to kill him?

'Were you aware if anybody might have held a grudge against Mr Hill, or knew of any threats against him? Was there any conflict at work or in his personal life that might explain why he was targeted in this way?'

Spenser looked affronted, as if he were offended at the idea that he might interact with a junior member of staff at all.

'I'm sorry, Inspector, I confess I barely knew Casey. You are, of course, free to interview his colleagues outside of work hours if you believe that will offer any insight into his disposition in his final hours here.

'When I pass on the dreadful news of Casey's passing to the staff, I will ask them to contact you if they believe that they can offer any help whatsoever with your investigation.'

Fiona had no choice but to accept the crumb that was being offered to her. She handed over her business card.

'These are my contact details,' she said. 'I expect you to tell all your staff to get in touch if they know anything at all, and make no mistake, if I do not hear from you, I will be back and I will line up every member of your staff and interview them one-by-one, and in work hours as well.'

Spenser stood and shook their hands in turn before escorting them back to the reception area. If he was nonplussed by her approach, he wasn't showing it. Fiona made a point of leaving an additional business card with the girl and then left.

'What an appalling place,' she said to Alaya back out on the street. 'I wanted to shove my business card down that man's throat.'

Alaya smiled enigmatically. She unlocked the car and drove them back to the office commenting only to try and calm Fiona down.

* * *

Fiona stormed into the office like a woman possessed. Layton Spenser and his debutant receptionist had really got under her skin. She wasn't sure why.

In her previous job, investigating financial fraud, she'd come across public school Oxbridge graduates all the time, each earning a fortune manipulating stock markets and currency rates.

But none of them had been as standoffish and entitled as the man she'd just interviewed. And if one of their colleagues had been stabbed to death, they would have at least had the decency to appear to be upset.

Alaya maintained her diplomatic silence. Fiona hadn't worked out her new colleague yet, but she did appreciate the sense of perspective the sergeant had brought to the situation on the drive back to the office.

Pat was waiting for them. He'd been unable to trace any other relatives of Allison or Casey Hill living in the London area, but he did have some good news.

'Ma'am, I haven't succeeded in breaking into Casey Hill's burner phone, but I've spoken to South Wales Police... and it turns out they're conducting a murder investigation of their own, one that happens to also involve Allison Hill.

'I've got Casey Hill's email address off them. and the Super has secured a warrant to inspect the account. We're just waiting for the provider to get back to us. I've also had the full post-mortem.'

He handed a print-out to Fiona.

She read it and then put it to one side. It just confirmed what she knew already, there was nothing new there.

The report said that there was some redness around Hill's mouth, which the pathologist speculated was caused by the assailant grabbing him from behind and placing one hand over his face while she or he slashed his throat.

There was though, no foreign DNA in that area, suggesting that the killer had worn gloves.

'I wonder if the murderer might have had some military training. That is the sort of manoeuvre I've seen marines perform on the enemy in the movies.

'Do we have email addresses for Allison Hill?'

'Yes, South Wales Police have passed those onto us. I sent a message but I'm not hopeful. They've been messaging her as well.'

'So, what's South Wales' interest in all this?'

Pat smiled.

'Actually, this is quite interesting,' he said. 'They're investigating the murder of a Cardiff councillor at the Swansea Arena the night before last. His throat was cut by a woman who escaped on a motorcycle.'

'Woah,' Fiona exclaimed. 'That can't be a coincidence.'

'No, and it gets freakier. They've linked this murder to a safe house in Swansea, which was housing trafficked people and which the councillor had stumbled into following a tip-off from, wait for it, Allison Hill.'

'Ms Hill was involved in an asylum seeker group in Swansea and had somehow picked up this information from one of the members, though it looks like her father was also involved somehow.'

'He warned her off, telling her that it was too dangerous.'

'Maybe the group in Swansea was using Hill's accountancy firm to launder their profits,' Alaya said. 'And as soon as Hill realised his daughter was getting involved at the sharp end, he intervened to stop her.'

'That sounds very likely,' Fiona responded. 'Did the Swansea police manage to speak to Allison Hill at all?'

'No. she disappeared. In fact, there's an alert out to look for her, for her own safety,' Pat replied.

'No wonder she's running,' Fiona said. 'I think I need to speak to the SIO in Swansea.'

'I was going to mention that', Pat said. 'They're running it as a joint operation between Swansea and Cardiff because of the politics involved, and because the councillor lived in the capital. That side of it is being led by an Inspector Jennifer Thorne. She wants to speak to you as well.'

Fiona beamed with delight.

'Wow, Jenny,' she gushed. 'They just can't keep us apart.'

Alaya and Pat looked confused.

'I was on secondment in Cardiff last year,' she explained, 'and worked with her on a case. I even went to her wedding a few weeks ago. You'd better get hold of her, Pat, it's time we joined these two cases up.'

Chapter Nine

Jenny got back to her flat that evening feeling tired and disheartened. She couldn't see how she was going to catch this professional killer who'd disappeared without leaving a single clue as to her identity. And now their other leads had vanished too, Casey Hill to the mortuary and his daughter, God knows where.

Even if they did manage to track down the people smuggling gang, and that was a remote possibility, the chances were that they wouldn't have any information that might help in the hunt for Gareth Tresham's killer.

Instinctively, she felt that the employment of a hit woman was above the people traffickers' pay grade, perhaps the work of whoever was pulling the strings on the smuggling operation.

On past experience, it was highly unlikely that those running the safe house on the ground would have any idea as to the identity of their employer. They were being paid to do a job, but the days when the boss handed over a wad of cash in person were long gone, it would all be done electronically to an overseas account, most probably using bitcoin.

Jenny just wanted to have a shower, put on a big fluffy bathrobe, and cuddle up to Dawn with a pizza and a good film on the television. Those hopes were dashed, however, when she opened the front door.

Dawn was home, but she was sitting alongside Jack Chaffont, a large amount of paperwork spread out in front of them. She was wearing her favourite lounge suit, while Chaffont was dressed in his customary blue jeans, a buttoned-up white shirt and one of those western cowboy string ties with an animal head gold buckle holding it all together at the collar. His Stetson hat sat on the sofa next to him.

Jenny thought he looked ridiculous, but then when somebody has his sort of money, she supposed he could dress how he likes and to hell with what other people think.

His long-white hair, tanned leathery face, and thin lips, added to the image he cultivated as a country and western throwback and Clint Eastwood fan. It was not a look Jenny found attractive.

As she entered the room, Chaffont got to his feet, with that half smile on his face which she always found to be sinister. Dawn remained seated, immobilised by the large file that she had open on her lap.

'Inspector, this is an unexpected pleasure,' he enthused. 'I hope that you are well, and congratulations on your recent nuptials. Dawn tells me that you had a most enjoyable honeymoon.'

She threw an accusatory glance at her spouse, who looked away sheepishly. Jenny was quite a private person and wasn't keen on people like Chaffont knowing her personal business.

'Thank you,' she replied cautiously, 'we had a lovely time. I wasn't expecting you to both still be working.'

'I'm sorry, love,' Dawn interjected, 'an urgent matter came up, it couldn't wait I'm afraid. We may be here for a few more hours yet.'

'It's my fault,' Chaffont said, 'A last-minute snag in the legal documentation that needs to be sorted tonight so we can sign all the papers tomorrow. I hope you don't mind.'

Jenny felt that she had no choice, whether she minded or not.

'Of course not. When will your new office be open?' she asked him, pointedly.

'It will be a few more weeks yet, I'm afraid. And then we can get out of your hair.'

Jenny signalled her appreciation with a nod of the head,

'Well, I'd better leave you two to it,' she said, heading for the bathroom. 'I'm going to take a shower to help clear my head.'

A few minutes later she was standing beneath a hot torrent of water, washing away the frustrations of the day, and planning an alternative agenda for her evening. Dawn might be all work and no play now, she thought, but that doesn't mean that I must follow suit.

She dried herself off and crossed into the bedroom, towelling her hair dry as she walked. She found a pair of jeans and a top and pulled them on. A moment in front of the mirror applying some lipstick and she was done.

'I'm off to the pub,' she told Dawn as she re-entered the living room and grabbed a denim jacket from a hook near the front door. 'Don't wait up for me.' She left the flat without waiting for a reply.

It was a good twenty-minute walk from Lloyd George Avenue to the city centre pub where several of her fellow detectives tended to congregate. It was a lovely warm evening, so Jenny didn't mind how long it took, taking her time to explore Callaghan Square properly as she passed through it.

The city had changed massively since she first arrived there, whether that was for the better or not was open to debate. No good can come of standing in the way of progress, she thought.

It was mid-week, but that had never deterred the hard drinkers amongst her colleagues, and as she entered the lounge, she saw that many of them were already present.

She ordered a pint of bitter and a bag of crisps, and joined two detectives at the bar, who were based in her squad room. Predictably, they were bitching about the Super and his lofty ambitions.

Detective Constable Jeff 'Tosh' Overton was in his forties, about five foot ten with a substantial beer belly. His distinguishing features were a thick, black moustache that dominated his rotund face and a pudding basin haircut that petered out some inches above his forehead, which combined to remind everybody of an obscure character from the police drama *The Bill*.

Overton's capacity to hold a grudge was legendary, so much so that colleagues often joked that he still resented ITV for causing the death of Grace Archer nearly seventy years ago.

His colleague, Detective Constable Tim Dillane, or 'Jimmy' as he was universally known, was a few years younger and looked much fitter. A recent divorcee, he'd allowed Overton to lead him astray, but Jenny considered he was not yet a lost cause.

He was clean shaven with curly brown hair, a thin face and long, pointed chin that made him look a bit like the late sports broadcaster, Jimmy Hill, but without the beard, hence the nickname, which wasn't one he particularly liked, but he'd grown accustomed to it. When he wasn't collaring criminals, he was to be found on the rugby pitch, and when he wasn't doing that, he was a player of a different kind in a local theatre group.

The two men greeted Jenny like a long-lost friend, she'd not been a regular in this establishment since meeting Dawn.

'How's love's young dream?' Overton asked her. 'Not with you tonight? Do I detect trouble in paradise?'

Jenny ignored this string of clichés, she knew not to expect any better from these two, it was one of the reasons she'd refused to have them in her team.

'What's wrong, Jeff, are you jealous?'

Overton laughed.

'So, what brings you out here mid-week, Jenny?'

'Your sparkling company, obviously.' She noted that their glasses were half empty and offered to buy them a drink. The gesture was gratefully accepted.

When she returned with the beer, the two men were talking about Brook again and the rumours that he was going to be fast-tracked to Assistant Chief Constable.

'What do you know, Jenny?' Dillane asked, 'You're closer to the seat of power than the rest of us. Spill the beans. Has Brook been cosying up to your mother-in-law?'

She laughed awkwardly. Whatever Brook and the others thought of her, she had never been comfortable with the idea of using her new mother-in-law as leverage in a work situation.

Before she could reply however, she felt a tap on the shoulder. She spun round to see the journalist, Simon Jones behind her, holding a pint of what looked like lemonade.

The stories about him losing weight were true. He looked far healthier than when she'd first encountered him. He still had the John Lennon-style glasses and receding white hair, though now it was cropped short. The beard was gone, and his face was much thinner.

He was wearing a track suit and trainers and was perspiring slightly, as if he'd just been out for a run. Here was somebody who had really turned his life around, she thought.

'Mr Jones,' she said, 'you're looking well. I hadn't realised that you patronised this establishment.'

He grinned.

'How do you think I get my stories? People talk more freely when they've had a few drinks.'

He invited her to join him at a nearby vacant table. She was reluctant but decided that it was better than joining in Dillane's and Overton's office gossip session. As they settled down, Jones launched straight into his interrogation.

'So, what's the news on the Tresham murder? Are you any closer to finding the killer?'

Jenny grimaced.

'You know I can't comment on an ongoing investigation. You're wasting your time if that's what you're after. And it's Swansea police who are leading on this, so you really need to talk to them.'

'You can't blame me for trying,' he said, laughing.

Jenny tried to change the subject.

'What's with the tracksuit? Are you thinking of entering the Olympics.'

'No, nothing like that, but I'm trying to get fitter, and I've even taken to joining in the weekly park runs.'

'Woah, at your age you need to be careful not to overdo it.'

Jones smiled broadly.

'Don't you worry about me. I'm taking medical advice. I plan to be around for some time yet.

'But getting back to Councillor Tresham, did you know him at all?'

'No, I didn't. Aileen and Dawn knew him. They say that he was a decent bloke.'

Jones nodded.

'I've heard that too. Word on the street though is that he was a bit of a vigilante who often took matters into his own hands rather than go to the proper authorities. I'm told he had to be bailed out of trouble on several occasions.'

'Is that so? Well, putting him in charge of community safety was a bit of a faux pas then, wasn't it.'

'Do you think that's what happened to him? That he poked his nose in where it wasn't wanted once too often and paid the price?'

Jenny had to admire Jones's persistence. She could see how others might have caved in and spilt the beans. She was determined that she wouldn't follow suit.

'I really don't know, Simon, and I've told you that I can't comment on an ongoing inquiry.'

Jones straightened up and leaned in towards her as though about to reveal some long-lost secret.

'Shall I tell you what I think happened?'

Jenny knew that whatever she said, he was going to tell her anyway, so she gestured for him to continue.

'I think that the good councillor got wind of a people-trafficking operation in Swansea and decided to investigate it himself. His daughter is at university there, you know.'

Jenny did know, but she wasn't going to validate his argument by admitting it.

'I don't think we'll ever know what happened when he got to that safe house,' Simon continued, 'but he was obviously spotted, and somebody must have decided to silence him.

'Perhaps, he tried to rescue the immigrants himself, maybe they were afraid he'd go to the authorities. Either way, he was an irritant that needed to be scratched out of existence.'

Jones paused to see what reaction his story would generate. Jenny remained stoney-faced. Eventually, she decided to do some probing of her own.

'What makes you think that the safe house that was found in Swansea has any connection to Councillor Tresham?' she asked.

Jones tapped the side of his nose and smirked.

'You know I can't reveal my sources, Jenny, but isn't that the line of inquiry being taken by the police?'

'As I said, I can't comment on that, but let me pose a question to you. Why would the people operating that safe house draw attention to themselves by killing a high-profile public figure, when they could just as easily pack up and take their operation to another property?'

This was a question that had been puzzling her ever since they'd made the connection, and she wondered whether Jones might have a more satisfactory explanation than she could come up with. He couldn't. Instead, he sat there deep in thought.

'Well, you know the minds of these criminals better than I do, Jenny. What do you think?'

'I think you're talking bollocks,' she said as decisively as she could in the hope that this would shut the conversation down.

Jones could see that he wasn't going to get anything out of Jenny, so he switched his line of inquiry.

'Damn, I forgot to congratulate you on your marriage. Did you have a good honeymoon?'

'Very nice, thank you.'

Jenny was happier with this subject, but it transpired that Jones had an ulterior motive in asking this question as well.

'Is Dawn not with you tonight?' he asked.

'No, she's working, apparently the power plant stuff has reached a critical phase, which means lots of meetings and paperwork.'

'Oh, that must be a real letdown.'

'Not really, we don't live in each other's pockets. We do have separate professional lives as well as our own social circles. She's working tonight so I'm having a few drinks with colleagues. On other nights I may be caught up in a case, so she'll go out with her friends.'

Despite this answer, she felt that Jones had rubbed at a sore she hadn't previously been aware of. Had she and Dawn been too busy to really get to know each other? His next point however, pulled her away from that question.

'It must be interesting at work given that your mother-in-law is the police commissioner,' Jones said, trying to open a new line of enquiry.

Jenny was immediately suspicious.

'Why do you say that?'

'Well, I imagine that your colleagues, and your boss in particular would worry about what you might report back to her.'

Jenny laughed.

'Not at all. It hasn't made any difference at all. We're all professionals, we get on with the job.'

'But you do socialise with Aileen Jenkins? In fact, weren't you with her at the Swansea Arena when Councillor Tresham was killed?'

'What's your point?'

'Oh, nothing much. It's just that I'd heard the commissioner had decided not to stand for another term, and I was just wondering if she'd said anything to you?'

'Oh, Simon, you don't give up, do you? It's no good asking me about politics. You'd be better off asking Dawn, or Aileen herself. I really have no idea what my mother-in-law's intentions are. It isn't something that we discuss.'

She looked at her watch. It was getting late, and she had a long day ahead of her. She knocked back the rest of her pint and stood to go.

It's been lovely catching up with you again, Simon. You might have better luck with one of these reprobates though.' She gestured towards Dillane and Overton.

Jones stood up and shook her hand, thanking her for the chat. As she left the pub, Jenny glanced back to see him deep in conversation with Jeff Overton. She shrugged, no doubt there would be a new exclusive tomorrow arising out of that conversation.

It was getting quite chilly, so she buttoned her denim jacket and walked briskly in the direction of Cardiff Bay, ruminating on the conversation she'd just had.

Yes, she and Dawn do have separate lives and many different interests. Did they have enough in common to make this marriage work?

She was annoyed with herself for letting Jones get under her skin and make her doubt her commitment to this marriage. At the same time, she was also irritated at the fact that Dawn had had to work tonight and hadn't made the effort to find time for her.

She dismissed the notion immediately. Hadn't she done the same many times to Dawn? They did have busy jobs and many other distractions, they just had to find a way to make the relationship work.

When she got home, she found Dawn sitting up in bed reading more paperwork. As Jenny entered, Dawn looked up and smiled. At that moment all the doubts disappeared. She was home.

'I'm sorry I was working when you got back earlier,' Dawn said, putting her papers on the floor. 'I'm sure you were looking forward to a quiet night in. So was I, but Jack was insistent that we needed to sort out the bureaucracy straight away.'

'It doesn't matter,' Jenny responded. 'I entertained myself, just as you've had to when I've had to work. I've got news. I'm afraid. It looks like I must go to London for a few days, chasing this killer. I'm sorry to dump this on you so early into our marriage but it can't be avoided.'

Dawn looked disappointed but insisted that she understood.

'As long as you catch Gareth's killer,' she said, 'I'll manage.'

Jenny had almost forgotten that Dawn knew Tresham personally.

'I'll be meeting up with an old friend,' she said. 'There's a related murder that looks like it may have been committed by the same killer. And the man involved was already a person of interest in our investigation. The officer in charge is Fiona Keaton.'

'Oh,' Dawn said, looking a bit taken aback. Jenny recalled that when they'd invited Fiona to their wedding, Dawn was a bit jealous of how closely the two detectives had become during their inquiry into Maga Power Holdings and the subsequent murder.

It was just as well that Dawn didn't know about the kiss on the steps of Fiona's hotel, and how hard it had been for Jenny to walk away without dragging her inside and pulling all her clothes off.

She'd also caught Dawn eyeing up Fiona over dinner and suspected that the attraction was shared. Maybe she should have suggested a threesome. In retrospect it was best that she hadn't, and yet she still regretted not acting on that kiss.

'Don't worry,' she told Dawn, 'I'm not running off with her.'

The remark was made in jest, but both women knew that there was a serious undertone behind it. Maybe Dawn would have been up for that threesome as well. She wondered whether Fiona was into that sort of thing.

'I've got to speak to Brook tomorrow,' she added quickly. 'Just to see if he'll approve the secondment. I'll most probably be going with Pyke or Stoneman.'

Dawn relaxed a bit at this and leaned forward, allowing the covers to fall away from her naked breasts.

'So, are you going to stand there all night,' she said, 'or are you coming to bed.'

Jenny was already turned on by her earlier illicit thoughts. She quickly stripped off her clothes, dumped them on the floor and cuddled up to Dawn's soft, warm, naked body; kissing and making love before eventually falling asleep in each other's arms.

Chapter Ten

It was early the next morning when Jenny arrived at Brook's office. She tentatively knocked on the door. It was never a good idea to bother the superintendent before he'd had his morning coffee, so she had one with her, prepared by his secretary and handed to her as she passed.

He called her in, and she placed the cup carefully in front of him.

'Are you auditioning to be my secretary, now?' he asked, sardonically. Jenny smiled.

'Not at all, just saving her an unnecessary trip, sir.'

Brook sipped from the mug and emitted a loud sigh of relief.

'Good, I feel human again,' he said. 'Now, how can I help you Inspector?'

Jenny outlined what they'd already found out about Tresham's murderer, that the only possible witness who could shed some light on the councillor's movement and motives had likely fled to London, and that the poor girl's father had also been stabbed to death, possibly by the same assailant.

'The whole focus of this investigation has moved to London,' she said, 'where the officer in charge is Inspector Fiona Keaton in their major crimes' unit. You might recall that she was with us last year to assist with the Maga Holdings investigation.

'She tells me that Mr Hill was about to spill the beans on a money laundering operation connected to people trafficking and drug smuggling. Unfortunately, he was killed before he could pass on that information.

'Furthermore, Allison Hill who we've been trying to trace has turned up there and was briefly under police protection. Unfortunately, they lost her.'

'What do you mean they lost her?' Brook asked, incredulously.

'She did a runner while they were arranging a safe house for her. They're still trying to locate her. It was the alert we put out that tipped them off about our interest.'

'I despair,' Brook said. 'Another Met cock-up. I take it that you're making a case to be sent on secondment to London to work with your pal?'

He seemed sceptical, or was he just testing her?

'I think that it would make sense to combine the two operations,' she said.

'And why should I send you and not ask for Inspector Waddingham to go instead? He's still the lead officer on this case, and the murder was committed on his turf, not ours.'

'I think, sir that as I've worked with Fiona before it would make sense for it to be me. More importantly, Simon is also tied up with the associated trafficking case and the death of that poor little boy and would find it difficult to coordinate things from over a hundred miles away.

'And of course, I will continue to liaise with him and keep him up to date with what we find out.'

Brook rubbed his chin thoughtfully. Jenny knew that she'd made a good case for the secondment, it was just a question if it was enough.

'Okay,' he said eventually, 'but I'm not going to send you alone. I want one of your team to go with you. Do you have a preference?'

'Not really, sir. I'm happy for either Pyke or Stoneman to accompany me.'

'Well, in that case it's Stoneman. I need Pyke on Friday night for our Male Voice Choir concert. We're already one baritone down, I don't want to lose another one. Besides, Pyke has a young family, Stoneman doesn't.'

Jenny had always wondered why Pyke and Brook got on so well. She hadn't realised Brook was in the choir too. Or could it be the funny handshake brigade? She quickly discarded the thought.

'That's fine, sir. I'll see if Jane is up for it.'

She left Brook alone with his coffee and headed to the squad room. Stoneman and Pyke were already there working through some of the evidence that had been sent to them by Fiona Keaton.

'Is there anything there that we don't have already?' she asked.

'No, they don't have any DNA or fingerprints either, Guv,' Pyke responded. 'But the picture they have of the killer on the A200 could easily be our woman.'

'What about Allison Hill?'

'Nothing so far. The Met are at a bit of a loss.'

Jenny grinned.

'Well in that case we'll need to go and show them how it's done. Brook has agreed for two of us to be seconded to the major crimes' unit in London. He suggested that you should join me, Jane. Are you alright with that?'

Jane seemed a bit nonplussed at the suggestion, which she clearly hadn't been expecting.

'Yes, of course, Ma'am. I'll need to clear it with my husband. When are you proposing that we go?'

'First thing tomorrow morning. I can't see us being there for more than a few days, but as you know it will take as long as it takes.'

'No problem,' Jane said. 'I'll get myself organised.'

Just then Jenny's phone rang, it was Waddingham.

'We've found the van,' he said. 'It was abandoned and burnt out up by Tythegston Tip. I've got forensics on the way there now. You interested?'

'Absolutely, send me a pin and I'll meet you up there.' She turned to her colleagues. 'Pyke you're with me. They think they've found the van used to transport the refugees.'

She paused to think a minute.

'It's interesting that they felt that they had to dispose of it. The appeal could have spooked them. But there was no way that they knew we had the number plate and a search area,' she said.

'It was most probably Waddingham telling the whole world that we'd sussed what they were using to transport the live bodies,' Pyke said.

'Yes, you're right, of course. It's just that from what we know here and what happened in London, they seem to be always a step ahead of us. I'm just being paranoid, I suppose.'

Pyke grabbed the keys and led the way down to the cars. 'We'll see,' he said.

* * *

Dawn looked at the paperwork in front of her and groaned. She was used to all the bureaucracy, of course, but there were times when it seemed never ending. It would be nice, she thought, just to get outside for once and see it on the ground.

She was confident that she'd done everything humanly possible on the power plant planning application. It was now just a matter of the relevant minister signing off on the Inspector's decision.

But she also had to get an environmental permit from Natural Resources Wales and that had proved to be an expensive and time-consuming nightmare. She'd got the process underway as soon as she'd started the job but there were still months of meetings ahead of her.

Fortunately, this would not unduly delay the build as Chaffont was still working on the finance. She had a projected timeline in mind and believed that, provided all the agencies played ball, she could meet it.

This was a new experience for her. As a planner, she was used to working on large projects, but this was the first time she'd had the opportunity to take one all the way, from gestation to implementation. She was really looking forward to the cutting of ribbons, though that event was still some years off.

She couldn't wait either for the new office to be ready. At least then she could separate her home and work life and get out from under Jenny's feet. It would also make the house move that much easier.

Just then her phone rang, but where was it. She picked up pieces of paper carefully, trying not to get things out of order, and eventually found it beneath a file currently occupied by Myrddin, her black and white cat. He'd miss her once she moved out to an office to work.

The caller was Chaffont, and he was so excited he could barely get his words out.

'I've just had a tip-off,' he said. 'The Welsh Government is about to announce planning consent for the plant. We're to expect a press release later today, embargoed for nine-o-clock tomorrow morning and the paperwork is in the post, or at least on email.'

Dawn felt a frisson of excitement. At last, they were making some progress. The group of Nimbys put together by the late Morgan Sheckler would be incandescent. She could imagine Gerald Rebane's fury when he heard the news.

Rebane had picked up the baton when Sheckler had been killed and had brought his customary military efficiency and business acumen to the protest group. He was a tough opponent, but he was fighting a losing battle.

Chaffont too, was keen to get on with things.

'I think we need to move our own operation forward now,' he said. 'I know that there are other consents to get in place, but let's work on the assumption that they're imminent and start to plan things on the ground. That way I have something to show to the moneymen.

'I've arranged to meet some surveyors on site in an hour's time to start staking it out and to talk through the construction process, so I'll pick you up in ten minutes. Is that okay?'

'Yes, of course. Can you give me fifteen?'

Dawn was wearing a tracksuit and a bathrobe as she hadn't anticipated having to attend any meetings that day.

Quickly, she pulled on some warm clothes and a pair of Doc Martens and grabbed her Barbour wax jacket. When she got to street level, Chaffont was already waiting for her in his white Range Rover.

She'd never quite understood why anybody should choose white as the colour for what is an off-road vehicle. If the owners used the car as intended, then they'd spend hours in the car wash every week.

She settled into the cream-coloured leather passenger seat and buckled up as Chaffont sped away in the direction of the Gwent Levels. He was wearing his Stetson and had one of Ennio Morricone's soundtracks playing. He turned the music down so that they could talk.

'This is all very exciting,' he said. 'Have you actually been to the site before?'

Dawn was mildly offended by this question. Of course, she'd been there, many times. She'd led the project in the regional mayor's office. Did he imagine that they all sat around drinking tea and put together these proposals from artists impressions?

'Yes, I've been several times,' she said, 'but not for a few months now.'

'Well, you may find that there have been some changes,' Chaffont said. 'We had to put up a security fence as you know, and since then some of the protesters have taken to camping out by the entrance.

'There's normally only one or two of them at a time, and they work it on a rota basis, but they have a very efficient bush telegraph and at the first sign of activity are able to increase their numbers.'

'Are we expecting any trouble?'

'Oh, no. They're quite a civilised bunch really, and Gerald keeps them in order. It's not like when I was a student. Some of the anti-apartheid protests I went on were wild.'

Dawn was having a problem thinking of Chaffont as a student radical, even fifty years ago. She couldn't think of anybody who was more establishment minded than him, except for Rebane. She would put money on it that they even belonged to the same London clubs.

The idea of a long-haired, unshaven Chaffont in ripped jeans, a cheesecloth shirt, denim jacket and university scarf throwing insults, and possibly missiles, at a police crowd-control team or digging up rugby pitches, was hard to imagine.

As they pulled up to the site, Dawn could see a group of half-a-dozen men and women carrying banners next to a small encampment by the entrance. As she watched two more vehicles drew up alongside them and three men got out.

The gate was open, and a small team of surveyors were already inside with measuring equipment. They were all wearing yellow hi-vis vests and safety helmets.

As she looked closer, she could see two or three others hammering stakes into the ground. It may have been early in the process, but the fact that something was happening at all was thrilling.

The land itself had been taken over by shrubs and weeds. It sloped away to her right towards a small copse, trees that she had already established were not valuable enough to have a protection order imposed on them.

Nevertheless, the scheme did involve substantial landscaping work and the planting of dozens of trees on the boundary, which, she thought, should keep the environmentalists happy.

It was such a big site that there was potential for a lot of mitigating measures, all of which she'd written into the planning application and would be conditioned in the consent. Even the need for substantial drainage measures and the protection of watercourses had been covered. These proposals would now involve months of work by specialist engineers to implement the scheme.

Chaffont drove straight onto the site and parked near to a portacabin that had been placed there as a temporary base for the initial survey work. Once building started there would be a virtual village of such buildings surrounding this lone structure.

As she left the car, Dawn could hear chanting coming from what was now a sizeable demonstration. It was clear that they too had had advance notice of the planning consent being granted and had gathered on the site to make their displeasure known.

If that was the case, she thought, then the media wouldn't be far behind and no doubt it wouldn't be long before they were joined by Gerald Rebane as well. She wondered why Chaffont had not thought to employ some security guards to protect the site and those working on it.

Admittedly, there was little there to damage but demonstrations of this nature could get out of hand and the last thing they needed was a sit-down occupation preventing work from getting underway. Chaffont seemed to have read her mind.

'I've got a security team starting work tomorrow,' he said. 'Now that we have an active site with planning and with the environmental consent pending, we need to protect it. We'll be installing security cameras and security guards with dogs twenty-four seven.'

Dawn watched as a large group of protesters moved closer to the entrance.

'Do you not think that those measures should already be in place?' she asked. 'Things are looking a bit tasty out there. At the very least you should remove your Stetson, you're offering them an easy target for their protest.'

Chaffont laughed.

'They're harmless, nothing to worry about. They're not going to do anything while we're here. Now. Let's get down to business.'

He started to outline the talks he'd had with some of the big energy companies, who were prepared to put up the money to get the power plant built.

He was also hopeful of getting a decent government subsidy on the price they could sell the electricity for because of the jobs that would be created both in the plant and in the associated businesses that would be attracted to the area by the prospect of cheap power.

Just then they were joined by one of the surveyors. Chaffont shook hands with him and introduced Dawn. They set off on a tour of the site with the surveyor pointing out where various features of the plant would be built.

As they got closer to the gates the chanting grew louder. Suddenly, one of the men shouted out Dawn's name. She turned to look, thinking that it might be somebody she knew.

However, the heckler was not trying to attract her attention, he was highlighting her presence to the other protesters. A small group started chanting 'murderer' in her direction and the crowd began to surge through the gate.

Without warning, the man who had initiated the chant was standing in front of Dawn, staring down at her with ill-concealed malice. He was a full six feet tall, in his mid-thirties with a mop of brown hair that looked like it had never been combed.

'You and your boyfriend murdered Morgan Sheckler,' he shouted, spit landing all over her face. 'You should be in prison, not lording it over the rest of us with this monstrosity.'

Other demonstrators started to join in, pushing forward towards Dawn demanding that she be held accountable for Sheckler's death. Concerned for her safety, Chaffont and the surveyor tried to intervene, but they were pushed aside by the crowd, with her boss ending up on the ground.

There were now half-a-dozen men directly confronting Dawn, shouting at her, chanting slogans and in some cases spitting on her. She tried to step back out of their way, but they kept moving with her.

The original protester was now red in the face with anger. As Dawn tried to move around him, he grabbed her and punched her in the face.

She fell over, dazed, blood pouring from a cut in her upper lip, her whole mouth numb. The man stepped towards her again, but before he could act somebody intervened, stepping between her and the protesters. It was Gerald Rebane.

'What the fuck do you think you're doing?' he shouted at the crowd. Dawn had never heard Rebane swear before. 'This is meant to be a peaceful protest. How dare you assault a helpless woman. Have you taken leave of your senses?'

He pointed towards the fence where a television crew had taken up position and were filming the entire incident. And then addressed the blond man directly.

'As for you, congratulations, you've just committed actual bodily harm on a woman on national television. You're no longer welcome in this group. I don't want to see you at meetings or any future protests. Now get out of my sight.'

The man started to walk sheepishly back to the entrance, followed closely by his mates, all the time being filmed by the camera operators who had turned up to report on the protest.

Rebane offered Dawn his hand, which she took, and he helped her to her feet. She rubbed her mouth ruefully. It had started to sting and was still bleeding.

Rebane took out an expensive looking cotton handkerchief still folded from being laundered and ironed and handed it to her. She applied it to the cut lip and looked around.

Chaffont and the surveyor were back on their feet, staring murderously after their assailants. Dawn still felt dizzy and started to fall again only to be caught by Rebane.

'I can't leave you like this. I need to take you to be checked over. Is that your car?' he asked pointing at the Range Rover.

Dawn started to laugh at the absurdity of the question, but it hurt too much.

'No, that belongs to Jack.'

'Right, we'll go in my car then. Are you able to walk?'

She mumbled that she could, conscious that her mouth had started to swell. Nevertheless, Rebane supported her as they picked their way through the field. As they got to the car, Dawn had a sudden thought.

'Would you mind ringing Jenny?' she asked. 'Let her know what happened and where I am.' She handed him her phone.

'Of course, that's no problem at all,' Rebane responded, finding the number in the address book and pressing the green button.

As he spoke to her wife, Dawn looked back towards the development site. Chaffont appeared to be no worse for his ordeal. He'd picked up his Stetson, dusted it off and was proceeding with his guided tour, happy that she was in safe hands. She shrugged. Nothing could faze that man.

Chapter Eleven

Jenny and Pyke had arrived at the site of the abandoned van to find Waddingham and his team already there. A forensics officer was photographing the interior of the burnt-out vehicle, while another was scouring the area around it for any clues.

Waddingham walked over to them smoking a cigarette while Rhodri Quinn continued to organise the search.

'The vehicle's a write-off,' he said. 'I'm surprised they didn't see the fire from police HQ.'

'Well, it's about five miles away as the crow flies,' Pyke said, 'and we're on a hill so it is feasible, I suppose. They could have had other things on their mind.'

Waddingham stared at him in disgust. He hadn't expected to be taken literally and wasn't quite sure if Pyke was being sarcastic. Jenny jumped in before relations between the two men could deteriorate.

'They chose this site well,' she said. 'I believe the tip's been closed for some time and we're surrounded by trees. I'm surprised we found it at all.'

'Passing motorist saw the smoke and rang the fire brigade,' Waddingham said.

Jenny went and walked around the now-derelict vehicle, looking for anything that might be of use. She wasn't expecting to find something that the forensics team had missed but a fresh pair of eyes was always useful. Waddingham joined her.

'The question is, how did they get back to their safe house once they burnt the van,' Jenny said. 'The whole area is a nightmare for us urban dwellers – narrow country roads, lots of trees, miles from civilisation. There must have been a second vehicle. I don't suppose there's any CCTV around here.'

Waddingham laughed.

'Not likely. The cameras in the recycling centre were decommissioned some time ago. Assuming they were heading back to Porthcawl, and that's only a guess mind you, the first set of traffic cameras are not until you get into the town centre, unless that is they triggered the speed camera in Newton.'

'I thought so,' Jenny said resignedly. 'Have we found any tyre tracks for a second vehicle?'

'No, I assume that they parked their getaway on the road and walked back to it. We haven't even got any useful boot prints. The ground is too dry.'

'So, a dead end then.'

'It certainly looks that way.'

Jenny walked back to the road, to where she believed the traffickers would have parked their second vehicle. As she did so she spotted what looked like a cigarette butt. She put on a latex glove and carefully picked it up.

'Is this one of yours, Simon?' she shouted.

Waddingham quickly joined her.

'No, you don't think I'm going to drop fag ends in a crime scene, do you?' He examined the butt carefully. 'I think this is a Camel, a very popular brand in Turkey. You can just make out the camel silhouette above the filter. I'll get it checked for DNA.'

He bagged it.

'Thanks, Jenny.'

'Is this a common brand in the UK,' she asked him.

'No, but I think most tobacconists sell them.' His eyes lit up. 'Ah, I see where you're going with this.'

He called Quinn over and handed him the bag.

'Can you get that examined for DNA, please, and can we get officers to call on every shop that sells cigarettes in a five-mile radius from here. I want to identify any that sold Camel cigarettes in the last five days. If they find any, get me some CCTV.'

Quinn took the bag and pulled out his phone. Waddingham turned back to Jenny.

'I hear you're heading down to London.'

'Yes, going tomorrow morning. You're not jealous, are you?'

'God, no. You're welcome to it. Besides, I've got my hands full here.'

'Yes, that's what I told my Super.'

'I bet your other half is thrilled. How long have you been married? A couple of weeks?'

Jenny smiled. She was used to this type of banter. Why was it that her fellow officers always thought they could stick their nose into her affairs? Was it worse because she was a woman?

It often felt that way, though she reckoned she could give all the men on this force a run for their money at any activity they felt like naming.

'Don't you worry about me, Simon, Dawn's got her hands full anyway with the new power plant proposal. Just be grateful that I've helped keep your marriage together by not asking the Super to send you instead.'

Waddingham grinned.

'Touché,' he said.

Pyke joined them. He'd been working alongside Quinn and the forensics team to scour the area.

'Apart from that cigarette, it's been a complete bust,' he said. 'I've arranged for some officers from our end to give a hand canvassing newsagents and supermarkets. You never know your luck.'

'Thanks Darren. We'd better get back.' Jenny turned to Waddingham. 'Keep us up to date on anything you find. While I'm with the Met, Darren will be coordinating from the Cardiff side.'

Waddingham lifted his arm in acknowledgement.

'Enjoy,' he called after them.

'As they approached the car, Jenny's phone rang. It was Dawn, at least that's who she was expecting to hear. She stood and listened to what Gerald Rebane had to say.

'What? Is she alright? I mean, how badly hurt is she? What happened?'

She listened again, with mounting anger.

'Tell her that I'll be there as soon as possible.'

Jenny ended the call and turned to Pyke.

'Get me back to the office as soon as possible, please. Dawn is hurt and I need to get to A and E.'

As they drove off, she thought of what Rebane had said to her.

'Where the fuck is The Grange?' she asked.

* * *

Gerald Rebane was ex-military, a colonel in the Royal Logistical Corps. He was used to taking charge. In his mid-fifties, his family had moved to the UK from Estonia and settled in South Wales. He now worked as a finance manager for a large manufacturing company headquartered in Cardiff and had his finger in several other business ventures as well.

A tall well-built man, with thick blond hair, a full moustache, an angular face and deep-set brown eyes, he and his family lived in a five-bedroom detached cottage on the outskirts of Magor complete with wood burners, an aga oven and extensive gardens.

Dawn knew this because she'd read it in a magazine feature published during Rebane's run to succeed Morgan Sheckler as regional mayor. What she hadn't expected was his car, a white, brand new Mercedes E-class cabriolet with cream leather seats.

What is it about white cars, she thought. She ran her hand across upholstery, stopping suddenly to clasp Rebane's handkerchief closer to her cut lip.

'Are you okay?' he asked, 'handing her phone back to her.'

'Yes, I was just worrying about bleeding all over your very expensive car,' Dawn mumbled through her swollen mouth.

Rebane laughed.

'Don't you worry about that, just try not to talk for a bit.'

It was a sunny day, so Rebane had the roof down as he drove to the new hospital at Llanfrechfa. Dawn wished that she had a hat; her hair was going to be a complete mess by the time they got there.

Personally, she would rather that Rebane had taken her to accident and emergency in the Heath in Cardiff, but she understood that The Grange was nearer to the incident. She was also beginning to wonder whether she really needed to go to hospital at all.

'Isn't taking me to hospital for a few bruises an overreaction?' she mumbled, trying her best to be comprehensible.

Rebane seemed to be having difficulty understanding her. It wasn't just the fact that she couldn't form words clearly but that the wind from the open roof was sweeping anything she tried to say away from the car altogether. She decided to give up arguing.

It was her first time at the new hospital in Llanfrechfa. It was a large modern building, six or seven storeys high with white cladding on the outside. A long glass-fronted section dominated the entrance.

Rebane parked up and helped her into the Emergency Department where she registered her presence and began the long wait. From her political connections, she knew that the target waiting time was four hours, but many people waited twice, sometimes three times that long to be seen, and as she wasn't an emergency she anticipated being there for some considerable time.

She turned to Rebane, he may be feeling guilty that a member of his protest group had assaulted her, but it wasn't his fault, and he shouldn't feel that he had to stay with her.

'Look,' she said, 'you don't need to wait with me. You must have a lot of other things to do. I'll be fine and besides Jenny will be here soon.'

Rebane demurred.

'Absolutely not, I won't hear of it. I'm not going to abandon you here. You wife would never forgive me and there's no way I'm incurring the wrath of your mother either.'

Dawn would have laughed if it didn't hurt so much.

'You're quite a decent bloke really, aren't you?'

Rebane chuckled.

'It's nice of you to say so,' he said sarcastically. 'We may not agree politically, but I'm not a devil in disguise.'

'No, no. I didn't mean it like that,' Dawn said backtracking furiously, only to be stopped in her tracks by the sight of Rebane laughing at her.

'Ha' ha, very funny. Seriously though I do appreciate you looking after me.'

'It's the least I could do in the circumstances.'

Just then Rebane's phone rang. He excused himself so that he could answer it and went outside to speak privately. Dawn took the opportunity to take in her surroundings.

It may only have been early afternoon, but the waiting area was packed. Many of those keeping her company seemed to be in a much worse state than she was. Once more she felt guilty for imposing herself on this vital service with what were comparatively minor injuries.

Perhaps she would get Jenny to take her home rather than hang around. She didn't feel concussed, which was Rebane's main concern. She could always present herself at her local doctor's surgery if she could get an appointment.

She reflected that although she was a strong supporter of the Labour Party, they had hardly covered themselves in glory in the twenty-five years they'd run the Welsh health service. She decided that on this at least she and Rebane were likely to see eye to eye.

She looked up as her protector and guardian returned to join her. He looked a bit flustered.

'Is everything alright?' she asked.

'Yes, yes, fine. It's only business. I've got to go to London tonight for some meetings tomorrow. I was hoping that I could postpone the trip until next week, but it didn't prove possible.'

Now Dawn felt even more guilty.

'Gosh, you're busy. Seriously. You should go and get on with your work. I'll be okay, honest.'

'No, it's fine. I really don't mind.'

Just then there was a small commotion by the entrance and a figure came hurtling towards them. It was Jenny.

As she got there, she embraced Dawn gently, still struggling to get her breath back. She had obviously run all the way from the car park.

'Are you okay?' she asked,' standing back to examine Dawn's face. 'My God, that bruise is a beauty. Does it hurt? Are you going to tell me what happened?'

Dawn beamed, and then quickly reverted to a more normal face because of the pain.

'If you give us a chance then of course we will.'

Jenny embraced her again and then turned to Rebane.

'I regret to say,' he said, 'that a member of our group got carried away when he saw Dawn at the power plant site and verbally and physically assaulted her. I intervened and thought it best to bring her here for a check-up in case she was concussed.'

Jenny was livid.

'I knew this was going to happen,' she said. 'You need to keep your people under control. Who was this bloke? I'm going to throw the book at him.'

Dawn put a hand on her arm to try and calm her down.

'To be fair,' she said, 'Gerald faced the man down and looked after me. You shouldn't take it out on him.'

Rebane handed her a piece of paper.

'I've written down the name and address of the man who hit Dawn,' he said, 'I'm more than happy to act as a witness to the assault if you want to press charges. As I told him, I'm not prepared to tolerate violence or law-breaking in my group.

'We believe in protesting peacefully and will always keep within the confines of the law. Anybody who is not prepared to accept that is not welcome and will be ostracised by my campaign.'

This little speech had calmed Jenny down. She took the paper.

'We will certainly be pressing charges,' she said. 'I will be onto the Gwent police with a request that they arrest this thug. Thank you again for looking after Dawn.'

They both shook hands with Rebane who made his excuses and left them alone. Jenny turned to Dawn and kissed her softly on the unbruised cheek.

'How are you feeling?'

'Sore, but fully compos mentis. We really don't have to wait here. I'm sure I'll be fine.'

'I don't know,' Jenny said thoughtfully, 'we should let the doctor have a look at you. I think that lip is going to need a stitch or two.'

Dawn moaned. She knew when she was beaten.

'Listen,' Jenny said. 'I can't go to London tomorrow and leave you like this. I'll get Jane to go on her own and catch up with her in a day or two.'

'Don't be daft. I'll be fine. It's just a few bumps and bruises. I'm not going to stand in the way of you doing your job. You should go.'

Jenny looked dubious and was going to protest further when a familiar figure appeared in front of them...

'Mr Jones,' she said sarcastically. 'What brings you to this far-flung hospital? Are you lost, perhaps?'

Jones smirked.

'Actually, I was looking for you. I went to the power plant site to cover the protest and heard what'd happened. I figured Mr Rebane might bring Dawn to this hospital, so I took a chance.'

'Well, you've found us,' Jenny said. 'Don't you think that following an assault victim to A&E might be considered as stalking? Maybe I should arrest you.'

Dawn placed a hand on Jenny's arm to calm her down. She was more used to the media and their tricks than her spouse, and knew not to upset them too much, especially when her power plant project needed as much good coverage as it could get.

'It's fine, Jenny,' she mumbled. 'What do you need, Simon?'

'I was hoping for a reaction to the protest and, of course, the assault on you. Will you be pressing charges?'

'Yes, we will be pressing charges,' Jenny intervened. 'I have the name of the assailant and witnesses to the incident. This sort of behaviour is completely unacceptable. I hope you are going to hold the protest group to account for this violent assault.'

'Don't worry,' Jones responded, 'I managed to grab Mr Rebane as he was leaving the hospital. He's given me a statement and has apologised for what happened.'

Jenny seemed satisfied.

'On behalf of the company,' Dawn said, 'we recognise that building this power plant has provoked strong emotions within the neighbouring communities, but we are committed to working with our neighbours to minimise any nuisance and hope that we'll be able to offer some concrete benefits to them by sponsoring improvements in the local villages.

'I believe that this power plant will act as an economic catalyst, and will bring jobs and prosperity to the area, which is why we're persisting with it despite some opposition locally. I am confident that we can bring people around to our way of thinking in due course.'

Jones wrote all this down. He looked happy that he had his story. Jenny was still annoyed with him for doorstepping them in Casualty. Conversations in the pub were one thing, but there were places like hospitals where journalists should respect people's privacy.

'I hope that you've got what you want,' she said. 'I don't suppose you'd like to do a story on excessive waiting times in Accident and Emergency departments.'

'I'd love too,' Simon replied, 'except that it's no longer news. It's part of everyday life now, more's the pity.'

As he left, Dawn grasped Jenny's hand.

'Thanks for not arresting him,' she said with a wicked glint in her eye.

Chapter Twelve

Jenny hated early morning train journeys. It wasn't just the unearthly hour that she had to drag herself out of bed and away from Dawn's warm body, but the fact that she often had to share the experience with commuters all jostling to grab the available seats.

Dawn had still been sore that morning after an unsettled night. They'd waited nine hours in Casualty for a nurse to put a couple of stitches into her lip and hand her a small box of pain killers. As a result, they were both exhausted by the time they got back to the flat.

They ordered pizza, which was consumed in bed and then fell asleep in each other's arms. When their alarm went off Dawn pulled Jenny towards her, stroked her hair away from her face and kissed her gingerly on the lips.

She flinched slightly as Jenny pressed her mouth harder against hers, forgetting in the moment about the bruising, but then relaxed as they explored each other's bodies with their hands and lips before making love.

They continued their love making in the shower - a goodbye present for Jenny to take to London, as Dawn put it - and then had to drive quickly to the station to avoid missing the train. They kissed once more before Jenny sprinted to Platform Two where Jane was waiting for her.

The detectives settled into their reserved seats, surrounded by commuters in formal work clothes heading for their jobs in Bristol and London. The journey time to the capital of two hours and twenty minutes had been reduced considerably by the electrification of the mainline, but there was still time for Jenny to go to the buffet car to pick up breakfast.

At Paddington Station they caught a taxi to their budget hotel in the centre of London. Jenny's room was a basic ensuite with a double bed and few frills. There was a television mounted on the wall, but it only provided access to Freeview channels. She was going to have to find her own entertainment after work.

She quickly unpacked, grabbed her shoulder bag containing her laptop and some case files and then walked with Jane to the office where Fiona Keaton was based. They produced their warrant cards at the desk and had to wait ten minutes while temporary ID cards were provided for them that would enable swipe access to the inner sanctum.

They were just beginning to lose the will to live when Fiona appeared. She was even more attractive than Jenny remembered and given that at their last encounter they were both dolled up in their glad rags at the after-wedding party, that was quite a feat.

Fiona had worn a short skirt and was showing off a pair of legs that a top model would envy. And it wasn't just her who'd noticed, Dawn had also commented favourably on their friend's appearance.

Fiona greeted Jane, who'd also been at the wedding, like an old friend and then embraced Jenny.

'Welcome to civilisation,' she said, beaming.

'Don't you bloody start,' Jenny scolded. 'You know very well we have running water and electricity in Wales; we've even got the internet.'

The three women walked up stairs to the major crimes' squad room chatting and laughing. As they walked into the door, Appleton was waiting to welcome them. They each shook his hand while Jenny told him that she appreciated being able to work with his team. Appleton looked at her askance.

'That's a bloody funny accent, you've got there, Inspector. It ain't Welsh, would it be Devon by any chance?'

'It certainly would, sir, and I don't think you're in much of a position to find my accent funny.' Jenny responded, half seriously.

There was an awkward silence for a few seconds and then Appleton burst into laughter.

'Ha-ha, you'll do, Jenny. I'll leave you to it.'

As he walked away, he turned towards Fiona.

'I like that one, just make sure you look after her.'

And with that he vanished into his office.

Fiona quickly introduced the two South Wales detectives to Alaya and Pat and then brought them up to speed on the case.

'We've been focusing on trying to trace Allison Hill,' she said, 'and so far, haven't had much success. We have the burner phone that her father had in his possession when he was killed, but his actual smart phone, laptop and any other devices have vanished. We believe that they were stolen from his flat either before or shortly after he was killed.'

Pat took up the explanation.

'We managed to get access to Hill's phone. There wasn't a great deal of info on it, but we did get a number for Allison we didn't have before, possibly also a burner phone. And yes, that's switched off as well.

'As you know, we've been unable to contact her by email. We've not been able to secure a warrant to access her email account nor her bank accounts, and I believe you've had the same negative response, Inspector Thorne.'

'Unfortunately, yes. Our magistrate was not convinced by the safeguarding argument and of course, she hasn't committed any offence. We've also been unsuccessful in gaining access to her lodgings in Swansea.'

'She told us that she left her phone and laptop in those premises before coming to London, so if there is any other way in there, it might help,' Fiona said.

Jenny shrugged.

'I'll talk to Waddingham again. What about Casey Hill's financials?

'No unusual activity, very much as you'd suspect' Pat said, 'Credit cards and overdraft up to the limit, there are no unusual payments. I don't know how principled he was, but if he'd been offered a large sum of money to stay schtum, he might have accepted it and still be alive today.'

'And his email account?'

'Nothing much there either. Any information he had must have been on his laptop, the missing USB stick, or on his work computer, which we cannot get our hands on, and which may even have been wiped clean by the firm, anyway.

'There is one thing, however. I've been trawling the email conversations between Mr Hill and his daughter, and he mentions a man called HAL, all capitalised, who he says used to work for GCHQ.

'I've put in a request to them for anything they might have on such a person, but honestly, it's a bit of a leap in the dark.'

'Do you think they'll even respond?' Jenny asked.

'Who knows,' Fiona said, 'but if we don't get a break soon, we might as well all go home. What do you have, Alaya?'

Alaya hit some key strokes on her computer and watched as the contents of her monitor appeared on the white board in front of them. A list of names and addresses appeared.

'I've been trawling Companies House,' she said, 'and the HMRC Chartered Accountant Directory, and I've come up with a list of the partners, senior partners and associates working for, or who have a stake in Cutter Associates.

'I've cross referenced them all against our databases, and none of them have a criminal record or known associates. Ideally, I'd like a list of employees as well, but so far, we've been unable to obtain that information.'

'What about clients?' Jane asked. 'Presumably, any criminality will originate there. Do we have any way of finding out who they're working for?'

'I was rather hoping that the USB stick that Casey Hill had for us would give us that,' Fiona responded.

'So, we're no further forward,' Jenny said. 'Maybe we need to pull the lot in and then interview them one by one.'

'If only we had reasonable cause,' Fiona said, but Jenny was studying the list on the wall.

'Hey, I know him,' she said, pointing at the screen. 'Gerald Rebane stood for regional mayor in Cardiff. I can't believe that he's up to anything dodgy. I don't know a more upright bloke. What's his role in the firm.'

Alaya grabbed her keyboard and pressed a few keys.

'It says here that he's a consultant partner. What does that mean?'

'Maybe we should ask him.' Fiona said. 'I'm sure Pyke can get his number. In fact, I came across him only last night and he said he was going to be in London. If anybody is going to cooperate, it will be him.'

She hoped that she was right. What if Rebane had a secret criminal life she didn't know about, she'd look a right idiot vouching for him in this way. And now she had to work out a way to get his mobile number.

He'd rung her on Dawn's phone so that wasn't going to help. Would Dawn have his contact details? She thought it unlikely. Then it occurred to her that candidates tended to swap this sort of information in case something came up and they needed to discuss it, so perhaps she'd ask Byron Harris, the winner in that election.

As it happened, she had Byron's number stored in her phone from the election, Dawn had insisted in case there was an issue. Why hadn't she done the same for Rebane?

She popped out of the office and dialled his phone. She was a little taken aback when Dawn's mother answered.

'Aileen,' she said, 'it's Jenny, I was trying to get hold of Byron.'

'Oh, no worries, dear. He's just popped out; he'll be back in a second. Is everything okay?'

'Yes, it's all fine. I was just wondering whether he had Gerald Rebane's mobile number. I need to speak to him urgently.'

'Of course, dear. I'm sure he must have it. Is there a problem?'

'I'm sorry Aileen, you know I can't discuss an ongoing inquiry, but don't worry I just need some information.'

'Here he is now, dear.'

She passed the phone over to Byron, who was happy to oblige without inquiring too closely as to what Jenny needed it for. Jenny rang off wondering what exactly Byron and Aileen were up to closeted together, answering each other's phones.

A few minutes later she was speaking to Rebane.

'Gerald, it's Inspector Jenny Thorne, I hope I'm not disturbing you.'

'Not at all. I hope that Dawn was alright after her little escapade.'

'Yes, thank you for intervening and taking her to hospital, it's much appreciated. When I spoke to you in the hospital, you said you would be in London today. Are you still there.'

'As it happens, I am, and it's likely I will be here for the rest of the week. Why?'

'Well. I'm here on a case and we were wondering whether you would be able to assist us.'

'I certainly will if I am able. What does it concern?'

'If it's okay with you I'd like to leave that until we can talk face-to-face, but it chiefly relates to what you can tell us about Cutter Associates. You may be aware that one of their employees was murdered recently and we're just trying to get background.'

There was a brief silence as Rebane absorbed this information.

'Yes, there was a company email about that. More than happy to tell you anything I can to assist your inquiry, though I didn't know the poor man. Would 10am tomorrow be convenient?'

Jenny went into the squad room to report back. Fiona was pleased. She asked Pat to enter it as a task on the HOLMES 2 system and assign it to her and Jenny.

'We could get some of the others to come in as well. Alaya, can you track down phone numbers for them and see if any are willing to come in voluntarily?'

Jane was deep in thought.

'I know we're asking GCHQ about this HAL character,' she said, 'but should we also ask Mr Rebane as well, and anybody else we can get in here. I just have a feeling that he or she is significant.'

Fiona agreed. They were interrupted by the sound of Jenny's phone ringing, it was Pyke.

'Afternoon Guv, I was just ringing to catch you up on what's happening back here. Your idea of trawling all the tobacconists has paid off.'

'Great, what do you have?' Jenny was pleased that at least one part of this investigation was coming together.

'It turns out that the Co-op near Trecco Bay holiday park has been doing a roaring trade in selling Camel Gold fags. The shop assistant even remembered who she sold them to, an eastern European.

'We pulled up their security footage and ran it through face recognition, even checked out with Interpol, and it turns out that our guy is a well-known member of a people-trafficking gang, a Bosnian Serb who goes by the name of Gavrilo Princip. We don't know his real name, That's an alias.'

'How do you know?'

Pyke laughed.

'Google it,' he suggested. 'Princip was the man who started World War One.'

Jenny quickly changed the subject.

'So, we have a rough idea of where they moved the migrants to, then' Jenny said.

'We do, and we have a car registration number from external CCTV. I've got the local Bobbies going door-to-door down there now, and we're checking the holiday camp cameras to see if the vehicle has gone into there.'

'Good work. I bet Simon's pleased. There is one thing that puzzles me, however, why burn the van? They knew we were looking for it, but there are a lot of similar vehicles out there. They can't have known we had the index number; it doesn't make any sense unless they were tipped off.'

'Beats me, Guv.'

Jenny decided to park the question for a while, it was yet another development that didn't add up for her. Perhaps it would all come together when they'd caught them.

'Okay,' she said, 'So, what's their next move? Let's put ourselves in their shoes.' They've had to move to a secondary safe house, and in doing so have been forced to dismantle all their cameras and other monitoring equipment.

'Let's suppose they must reinstall all that on the new property. That part of Porthcawl is much busier than the area around the house they were using in Blaenymaes. Any unusual activity is bound to attract attention. Something else for the team to look out for when talking to residents.'

'Okay, noted,' Pyke said.

'And what happens next?' Jenny asked. 'They've got a house full of migrants, all of whom need to be passed on to whatever sweat shop they've got planned for them, but they've got no van.

'They can't very well move them in the car, they'll need to replace the vehicle they burnt out like-for-like or get some other means of transport. Where are they going to get it from?'

'They could steal one.'

'Yes, and then they'd need to change the number plates, or it'd be picked up on camera, especially if they're using the M4.'

'Perhaps a second hand one, then.'

'That might do the job. Get onto all the dealers in that area and look through the sales ads online and in whatever rag serves Porthcawl and see if that throws up anything. And do a check for reports of stolen vans.

'I really feel that we've got them cornered here, we just need to reel them in.'

Jenny specialised in mixed metaphors when she was in full flow. Pyke seemed oblivious.

'I'm not sure it's that simple, Guv, but I do feel we're making progress. How are things in the Metropolis?'

'Give us a chance, Darren, we've only just got here. They're not making much progress from what I can see though there is one interesting connection… Gerald Rebane.'

'Really? He never struck me as dodgy.'

'No, but he is involved with the company that Casey Hill was going to blow the whistle on. He's coming in tomorrow to answer questions. Hopefully, he can help, though I'm not counting on it.'

They ended the call and Jenny turned back to face the team. It was now late afternoon, and she was very hungry.

'Shall, we call it a day?' she said. 'I'm starving.'

They left Pat and Alaya chasing up various bits of background information and headed to a nearby pub. Pat was working through Casey Hill's email account looking up any contacts that might be referred to in there. Alaya was still doing background on partners in the accountancy company and seeing if any of them were prepared to talk to them about their deceased colleague.

It was just early enough to miss the rush from office workers having one quick pint before they headed home. The pub itself was a typical old style London establishment, cavernous, with a solid oak bar, polished brass, and lots of pictures of various celebrities on the walls. The only unwelcoming aspect of it as far as Jenny was concerned were the prices.

'How do you afford to live here?' she asked Fiona. 'The price of beer is extortionate, and the food is not much cheaper.'

Jane agreed. Although there were now two salaries coming into her household following her recent marriage, she was still struggling to pay her mortgage at Cardiff prices. If she and her partner had lived in London, they could never have afforded to maintain their present standard of living, even with the London allowance.

The three of them ordered some basic pub grub; fish and chips for Fiona and Jane, pie and mash for Jenny, and got down to discussing the case.

'I think Allison Hill is the key to unlocking this,' Fiona said. 'I don't know why; I just have a gut feeling.'

'I agree,' Jenny said, 'but I can't explain it either. She didn't witness either crime, she's had no dealings with the accountancy company or with the traffickers, other than to tip-off poor Councillor Tresham about the safe house, and yet the very fact that she's avoiding us implies to me that she has something very valuable that the perps want.'

'She's not much good to us if we can't find her,' Jane said.

The three of them lapsed into silence as they ate their food, before moving onto more trivial matters.

'So, how is Dawn?' Fiona asked. 'Are you enjoying married life?'

'Yes, it's been good so far. We're in the process of buying a house, so the stress of moving is ahead of us. If we survive that then we'll get through anything.' She laughed awkwardly.

'Oh, and before we get into the interview tomorrow, you need to know that Dawn was assaulted by a demonstrator yesterday at the power plant site. She's got quite a bruise on her face and a badly cut lip.

'Anyway, Gerald Rebane was there, and he took her to hospital. So, I've had recent dealings with him. Just so you're aware.'

Jane looked shocked.

'I didn't know that' she said. 'So that's where you disappeared to yesterday. I'm so sorry. I hope that Dawn is okay.'

'Yes, I think so,' Jenny said in a matter-of-fact way. 'I did offer to delay coming down here and send you on your own Jane, but she insisted. So here I am.'

Fiona put her hand on Jenny's sympathetically. It was warm and comforting, sending a tingling sensation through her body. Fiona must have felt something too as she quickly disengaged.

Jenny looked down self-consciously and fiddled with her wedding ring. If this was a test of her fidelity, she was failing it badly. She could feel Fiona's eyes on her so decided that she'd better change the subject.

'If it's not too late,' she said, 'I'd like to see your crime scene. I know it's all been fully processed and I'm not going to add anything to it, but it'd be useful just to get a feel for what happened and how it differed from the Swansea Arena killing.'

Fiona agreed and offered to drive, Jane though, decided that she needed to get back to her hotel and speak to her husband. She told them that it had been a long day and she wanted to be fresh tomorrow.

The two Inspectors drove through London and across the Thames in silence. Jenny was still thinking about the way she'd felt when Fiona touched her hand. She hoped that her companion was doing the same.

She had to pull herself together. She was a married woman, at work, any sort of flirtation was both inappropriate and dangerous. She fixed her eyes onto the road and was relieved when the warehouse came into view.

There was still police tape at the entrance, but the area was no longer guarded. Fiona led Jenny into the building and over to the office where they'd found Hill's body.

'According to the pathologist,' she said, 'Mr Hill was grabbed from behind, the killer placed a gloved hand over his mouth, pulled his head back and slashed his throat.'

'That's identical to what happened to Councillor Tresham. It sounds like we're dealing with the same killer. I also understand that our two pathology labs have compared the wounds and believe that there is a good chance they were caused by the same weapon.'

She turned away, having seen enough.

'Thanks, this visit has been really helpful.'

* * *

Back at her hotel, Jenny unpacked her laptop, logged onto the hotel wi-fi and then skyped Dawn, who answered immediately. The bruise on her face had now turned a strange shade of purple and her mouth looked swollen and painful, but at least her enunciation was better. Jenny couldn't help smiling.

'What's so funny?' Dawn demanded.

'Nothing, honest. It's just you look so hot with that bruise and your cut lip. If I were there, I'd jump you straight away without a second glance.'

Dawn was not amused.

'It's bloody painful, you know, especially when I eat. Besides, if you didn't want to jump me before then I'd worry.'

'So, what's been happening. Did you lodge a complaint with Gwent Police?'

'I did, you could have warned me that they'd be interrogating me as well.'

'Why, what happened?'

'I had to give a complete statement of everything that happened up to the assault as well as describe how he came to hit me. You'd think I'd provoked *him*. And then they made me pose for photographs.'

'Good, that means they're taking it seriously. Have they arrested the guy?'

'Yes, I had a phone call from the detective earlier to say that he was in custody and was being processed. They've rung Gerald and arranged for him to come in a make a statement, and they're interviewing other witnesses as well. Gerald gave them some names. They've also asked for the video footage from the TV company that was there.'

Jenny was pleased at the speed with which the case was being dealt with. Perhaps, they knew who Dawn's mother was.

'I'm really missing you,' she said.

'Me too. How much longer are you going to be down there?

'I don't know, not too long, I hope. I promise I'll get back to you as soon as I can.'

They finished the conversation and Jenny climbed into bed. She suddenly felt very tired. She hoped that they'd make more progress on the case tomorrow so she could get back to Dawn and away from temptation.

Chapter Thirteen

When Jenny woke the next morning, she was temporarily disorientated. The layout of the room was unfamiliar, and the bathroom was on the wrong side of the bed.

She adjusted herself quickly, remembering her conversation with Dawn the night before and the brief flirtation with Fiona prior to that. She suddenly had the urge to speak to her wife again. She wasn't sure if her desire for a conversation was because she was feeling lonely or whether she wanted to assuage her guilt at being attracted to somebody else.

She looked at her mobile phone, it was just 6am, Dawn would still be asleep, or would she. Perhaps she was taking advantage of being alone in the flat to start her day earlier. She decided to risk it.

She got out of bed, put on a dressing gown, and dragged a brush across her hair. Dawn had, of course, seen her in all sorts of dishevelment but she knew she'd feel more comfortable with at least a token effort.

She booted up her laptop and initiated the video call. The ringing tone sounded for a few minutes before Dawn answered. She looked half asleep, her hair plastered onto her face, the bruise, and the cut lip more prominent without any make-up to cover them.

Jenny smiled, seeing her spouse like that had cheered her up and cast out any memory of the spark that had been reignited with her Fiona a few hours earlier.

'What's up,' Dawn asked, 'are you alright? Has something happened?'

'No, not at all.' Jenny was beaming now. 'I just wanted to see you.'

'But we spoke last night. Are you going to ring me every few hours?'

'I might.'

'Huh, you're missing me then?'

'More than you can imagine.'

Dawn sat up in bed exposing a breast on the camera.

'You see, it was worth it just to see you naked,' Jenny said.

Dawn smiled.

'You can see more if you wish.'

'Hmmm, go on then.'

And Dawn did.

* * *

By the time Jenny got to the hotel's dining room at 7am, Jane was already there with a full English breakfast in front of her.

'How can you eat that at this time of day?' Jenny asked, grabbing a dish of grapefruit and a black coffee from the buffet table. 'I feel like I've put on two pounds just looking at it.'

Jane cut a piece off a sausage, speared it on her fork and held it near her mouth.

'Just enjoying the break,' she said. 'I never have time for a cooked breakfast at home, so I thought, why not. Did you sleep okay?'

'Like a baby. Do you have any thoughts on this Rebane interview?'

Jane chewed on her food thoughtfully.

'What have you told him so far?'

'Just that we want background on the accountancy firm.'

'Mmm, perhaps we shouldn't mention the link to the Swansea Arena killing at this point. It may muddy the waters.'

'I thought the same. I don't think Mr Rebane is involved in anything nefarious, but he might be able to give us some insights on the company.'

'Who's doing the interview?'

'That's up to Fiona of course, but I'd like to be in on it. You can monitor remotely. We need to explore exactly what he has access to in the company. It's not cleat from Pat's background work whether he's senior enough to get us what we need from them?'

'Hopefully, he is.' Jane said. She had finished her breakfast and was preparing to go back to her room. 'Shall we meet in the lobby at 8am?'

Jenny agreed. She fetched herself another cup of coffee as Jane left the room. She'd have the full breakfast next time.

It was a warm, sunny day, which in London always translates as sweltering heat. The walk to the police station was a short one, but they got caught up in the rush hour crowds so it took twice as long as it should have.

'We should leave earlier tomorrow,' Jenny said as they signed in. 'Let's hope that our witness can get here in good time.'

Fiona and Alaya were already in the office going through the detailed background work on the partners. Pat was beavering away at his computer.

'Do we have anything?' Jenny asked.

'Not really,' Fiona responded. 'We need some new insights if we're going to get under the skin of this firm. Mr Rebane might be able to help.'

Jenny was about to reply when her phone rang. It was Pyke. She moved into a quiet office to take the call.

'Morning Guv, I hope you're enjoying the delights of the big smoke. I thought I'd bring you up to speed on the hunt for the illegal immigrants.'

'You're making progress, that's great.'

'Well, it was Inspector Waddingham who made the big breakthrough. He met up with the PCSOs for the area and the local councillors and they went through all the empty properties street by street. It took most of yesterday.'

Jenny was impressed.

'Great idea, did it work.'

'Well, yes and no. They found the house they were looking for on the northern edge of Porthcawl. Whoever is scoping out these safe houses for them clearly knows what they're doing. If we hadn't been looking, we'd never have stumbled across it.

'Anyway, they set up a raid this morning, police, and immigration together. Got it all signed off at Chief Super level, all properly logged and everything. When they got there, they found all the immigrants, but the traffickers had gone.'

'What, seriously?'

'Yep, all the cameras and other equipment, including the server ripped out overnight. It's almost as if somebody tipped them off.'

'They couldn't get the immigrants out of there, so they cut their losses?'

'That's pretty much it, Guv. Waddingham was spitting feathers, his Super wasn't too pleased either.'

'What about the immigrants, were they able to help identify the traffickers?'

'We've hardly started processing them. Immigration brought some translators with them and will start conducting interviews in a few hours' time once we've got the health checks out of the way.

'Hopefully, we'll be able to confirm the identity of the little boy we found dead in the Blaenymaes house as well. But as for the traffickers, well they're in the wind.'

'I don't like this,' Jenny said. 'It seems that whoever is pulling the strings is one step ahead of us all the time. The bad guys have either been very lucky, they're working with a psychic, or else they have a source in the department. And not just in South Wales.'

'I agree,' Pyke said. 'Even Inspector Waddingham is coming around to that way of thinking. It's been kicked upstairs for now so that the bosses can carry out a full review of procedures and look at the case through fresh eyes.

'No doubt you'll be interviewed when you get back, though given what's happened in London with a key informer being killed just as the police were going to scoop him up, I wouldn't be surprised if the review takes in the Met as well.

'All the action has moved to London now so it's down to you lot to get to the bottom of this. Good luck with that.'

'Thanks Darren,'

Jenny ended the call. She was starting to feel as if she was banging her head against a brick wall. Every lead, every avenue they tried was coming to nothing and, yes, there appeared to be a leak contributing to that.

She went back to the squad room to brief the others. They were looking just as despondent as she felt. Superintendent Appleton joined them, looking for an update.

He listened as Jenny outlined the saga of the illegal immigrants and took especial note of a possible review of the case at a senior level.

'I suppose I'd better talk to my opposite number in Swansea, then,' he said. 'Get our story straight. We need to put this whole investigation on a need-to-know basis. If we make a breakthrough, and I assume you will make a breakthrough,' he said looking directly at Fiona, 'I don't want anything leaking out. Is that understood?'

There was silence for a few seconds, though to those in the room it felt like an hour before Fiona spoke up.

'Absolutely, sir. We're keeping all information limited to this small group only. All data on HOLMES 2 is restricted access for us and yourself only. That includes operational matters and records. When we get this killer, we're not going to allow her to slip through our fingers.'

'Excellent. Make sure Swansea and Cardiff are operating the same protocols.'

'Already on it,' Jenny said.

Appleton turned on his heels without acknowledging this last contribution, stopping only to turn back again to pass on a message.

'By the way, there's a Mr Rebane in reception for you. I understand he's early, so I thought it didn't matter if he waited for a few minutes.'

Rebane was dressed in what for him was casual dress, a beige, lightweight suit, blue linen shirt, and brown Oxford brogues. As Alaya led him to the interview room, Fiona turned to Jenny.

'He's very much a patrician, isn't he?' she said.

'Really, he isn't even from English stock.'

'Okay, Estonian aristocracy then.'

Jenny was impressed.

'Wow, you've done you've homework.'

'We've done a lot of background reading on all the characters associated with this firm.'

They followed Rebane to the interview suite. Alaya was already ensconced in an observation room. As they entered Rebane stood and shook each of their hands in turn.

'Jenny, it's good to see you so soon after the last time,' he said with just a hint of irony, 'I'm glad Dawn is recovering. And you must be Inspector Keaton. I'm pleased to meet you.

'As you know, I'm always happy to help the police with anything they need, however, I'm not sure what it is you want of me with regards to Cutter Associates. I would say from the outset, though that I've been waiting forty-five minutes and need to get to another appointment shortly.'

'I understand, that's no problem, and I apologise for the delay in starting this interview,' Fiona said. 'Do you know why we've asked you to come in today?'

'I believe so. You want background information on Cutter Associates. I'm aware of the death of Mr Hill - the whole firm mourns his loss, but I'm not sure how information on his employers can advance your inquiry.'

Fiona invited him to sit and then took her seat alongside Jenny.

'Can I start by thanking you for coming in, today. We will of course, try to explain the relevance of our request to see you during this interview. Could I start, though, by asking how long you've been associated with Cutter Associates?'

Rebane sat thinking for a minute before answering.

'Oh, I would say at least ten years. You see I sat my accountancy exams with John Cutter, so when he struck out on his own, he asked me to come on board as a consultant.

'I'd left the army by then and was happily settled in South Wales with my family and a finance director's job in manufacturing, so it seemed perfectly natural to expand my horizons a bit professionally.

'I actually hold a number of consultancy roles so the request was not unusual for me, and of course I get to come to London regularly, where I can stay at my club and catch up with friends.'

Fiona gave her fellow Inspector a knowing look at the mention of a club. Jenny smiled, Rebane certainly didn't disappoint in giving out information about himself.

'Thank you for that,' Fiona said. 'What we're trying to do here is to establish a motive for Mr Hill's death. We believe that he had information, which he was prepared to share with us about some illegal activities that may or may not have a connection with the firm.'

Rebane looked outraged.

'Are you suggesting that the company is involved in criminal activities?'

'No, we're not saying that, however Mr Hill may have stumbled across such activities in the course of his work and that might have got him killed.'

'Good grief, that is terrible.'

Rebane looked genuinely shocked at the scenario being presented to him. Jenny took up the story.

'Our problem, Gerald, is that when we searched Mr Hill's home it had been ransacked. Any electronic devices had been removed and there was no sign of the information he had promised to pass onto us.

'Naturally, we approached Cutter Associates to see if he'd left any clues at his place of work, but they were less than helpful.'

'Ah, I'm beginning to see where you're going with this,' Rebane said. 'You do know that I'm a non-executive director and have no power to direct staff or to remove anything from the premises without authorisation.'

'Yes, we do,' Jenny said. 'However, we were hoping to prevail on you to talk to Mr Cutter and ask him to cooperate with our inquiry.'

Jenny knew that this request was meaningless in the context of their inquiry. They didn't want to alert Cutter that his firm was under suspicion at this stage and Cutter wouldn't volunteer anything that might incriminate himself or his firm, so they were reduced to finding incriminating evidence indirectly.

The impression they had was that Rebane knew nothing about the money-laundering, so introducing an element of doubt into the firm by having him ask questions might elicit a response. She just hoped that it wouldn't prove fatal.

'Well, I'm more than happy to do that,' Rebane said. 'I'm surprised that John hasn't already volunteered to do so. What exactly do you need?'

'Initially,' Fiona said, 'we'd like to examine Mr Hill's work computer and any other electronic devices he may have used in the office. It hasn't been possible to get a search warrant to do that, so some co-operation from the company would be appreciated.

'We know that Mr Hill removed all his personal effects when he resigned from his position shortly before he was murdered, but he may have left some clues on whatever machines he left behind in the office.

'Of course, you can be assured that we'll respect any proprietary or sensitive commercial data that may be stored on the computer, but you will understand I hope, that we just need to eliminate the faint possibility that there may be a clue there to why he was murdered.'

Rebane seemed to understand what was being asked of him.

'I'll certainly do my best,' he said.

'Tell me.' Fiona asked, 'when you've been in the office, have you noticed any suspicious activity or come across any files or information that you believe don't look quite right.'

'I don't believe that I have. Are you now saying that the firm may be complicit with this alleged wrongdoing?'

'No, but it's possible that some of their clients may be, and that, unwittingly at least, the firm's services may have been…er… misappropriated.'

'To be frank, Inspector, my role doesn't involve day-to-day management, nor do I have direct contact with clients. I serve on the board in a non-executive capacity, and I offer advice on investments and risk management.'

'Do you have a relationship with any of the other directors apart from John Cutter?'

'Well, I meet them professionally, but socially, no. John and I have of course met up outside of work. Our families have been on holiday together and he's a member of the same clubs as I am, but that's it as far as I'm aware.'

He looked at his watch.

'I'm afraid that I have another appointment. If that is all, then I really must leave.'

'No, that's perfectly okay,' Fiona said. 'We're very grateful for you coming in to talk to us.'

'That's no problem, I will report back to you on my attempts to obtain access to Mr Hill's computer.'

Rebane stood as if to leave, but as he did so Jenny thought of one last question.

'I'm sorry,' she said, 'but there is one more thing, has John Cutter ever mentioned somebody called Hal to you?'

Rebane paused, as if trying to dredge up some distant memory.

'I'm sorry it doesn't ring any bells, but I'll have a think and get back to you.'

'That's no problem. I thought I'd ask on the off chance. Thanks again for your help.'

'I'm pleased to assist in whatever way I can, Jenny. But please, give my regards to Dawn, I hope that the Gwent police are pressing charges against the man who assaulted her.'

'Oh, don't worry, they are.'

Fiona handed Rebane over to Alaya to escort him out of the building and then turned to Jenny.

'Well, what do you think?'

'Obviously, he has no idea what's happening at the firm, or that they're laundering money as Casey Hill suggested. However, it was useful background and when he goes in and asks about that computer it might provoke a reaction.

'But let's face it, we're fishing. Even if the computer did contain anything incriminating, it will have been wiped clean by now. The hard disc may even be sitting in several pieces at the bottom of a landfill site. We've got nothing.'

Fiona shrugged.

'You're right, but we've got to keep probing until something pops up, even the smallest clue might help to unlock this case.'

'Yep, been there many times,' Jenny said resignedly. 'Sometimes you've got to wait for the bad guys to make a mistake.'

'If only we knew who the bad guys were?'

As they approached the squad room, Alaya joined them, on the way back from seeing their visitor out.

'How was he?' Fiona asked.

'He seemed fine. Very upbeat, happy to help and really posh.'

They all laughed.

The squad room was empty other than Pat and Jane who were standing side by side, inspecting a computer screen. The former looked up and gestured for the three detectives to join them.

'Have you found something?' Fiona asked.

'Well, Jane has.'.

She looked up from the screen.

'I thought I'd have examine all the background information you'd gathered while you were interviewing Mr Rebane,' she said. 'It doesn't do any harm to have a fresh set of eyes look it over.

'Anyway, I noticed that when John Cutter left university, and before he qualified as an accountant, he ran a computer software company. So, I did some digging. His partner in that venture was a Harold McQueen, full name Harold Anthony Lawrence McQueen. The initials of his Christian name spell HAL.

'It just seemed too much of a coincidence, so we ran the name on the system, and this is what we got.'

She turned her computer screen around. It stated that the information is classified.

'So, how do we get our hands on this guy's file?' Jenny asked.

'I'll need to clear it with the Super,' Fiona said, 'but I guess we'll have to approach one of the intelligence agencies. He'll know who to ask.

'Given the reference to HAL in Casey Hill's email, though, it looks to me that this is somebody we need to talk to.'

'And the email said that the HAL character used to work for GCHQ as well,' Pat said. 'That will explain the classified block on his file.'

'Right, I'll get hold of Appleton now. I believe we've already put in a request to GCHQ. Now we know who this HAL is, we can refine it.

'What do we have on Cutter?'

Pat pulled up another file on his computer.

'Public school boy, graduated from Cambridge with a degree in computer science, started up that computer software firm Jane mentioned, which he sold for a tidy profit after two years and then went back to college to do a chartered accountancy qualification. Worked for some of the big accountancy firms for fifteen years and then started his own company. Lives in a big house in Kensington, married with three kids.'

'Good, I think we need to get this man under surveillance. Can you arrange that, please. Alaya?'

Fiona was about to head to Appleton's office when he appeared in the doorway looking very grave.

'I've just had the front desk on to me. They tell me that shortly after Mr Rebane left the station he was attacked in the street, in broad daylight. I've spoken to the officers who attended the scene.

'Witnesses say that the assailant was a woman wearing a hoodie. She had a knife. He's still alive and on his way to hospital.'

There was a stunned silence. Eventually Jenny spoke up.

'Bloody hell, the contract killer again. How the fuck did she know he was talking to us, and at that specific time?'

'Those are the million-dollar questions, Inspector. Something is wrong here and I'm going to get to the bottom of it. I've called internal affairs and asked them to review our investigation.

'I'm not accusing anybody you understand, but we need a fresh pair of eyes to see if they can work out what's going on.

'Jenny, you know this man, can you get your office to notify his family please?'

'Of course, I'll speak to Darren now.'

'In the meantime, Fiona, brief me on the interview and anything else you've uncovered today.'

Chapter Fourteen

At the hospital Fiona and Jenny caught up with the police officer who'd been first on the scene. He'd summoned the ambulance and travelled with it to Accident and Emergency.

Jenny was shocked at how young he looked or was it just that she was getting older. PC McPherson was just twenty years old, had joined the force straight from school and was already an old hand.

He stood a good eight inches taller than both women, a fact that started to give Jenny a sore neck after just a few minutes of conversation.

'Shall we go and sit down,' she said, in an attempt to communicate on level terms.

They grabbed some seats in the waiting area, where McPherson outlined what he knew about the attack.

'I'd just left the station and was walking towards the high street when I saw a commotion ahead of me. I rushed to the scene where I found a man barely conscious and bleeding profusely from the chest. A woman in a dark hoodie was moving away from me at some pace, but I decided that my priority was to tend to the victim.'

'Did you notice anything at all about this woman that might help us identify her?' Fiona asked.

He consulted his notebook.

'Slim, about five foot two, wearing jeans, trainers, and a hoodie, which was pulled up over her head. That's about it, I'm afraid, she had her back to me, so I had no chance of identifying her.'

He paused.

'Oh yes, she was carrying the knife at her side, in her right hand, possibly a six-inch blade. It looked like she had white PVC gloves on, but they appeared torn as there was a red stain. She may have been bleeding herself, though the blood could have been that of the victim.'

Jenny was impressed. She knew scene of crime officers would be scouring the area as they spoke and would pick up any blood that didn't belong to Rebane. They'd also be collecting CCTV images so there was a chance they'd get a look at the woman's face.

'Has anybody interviewed the witnesses,' she asked.

'Oh, yes,' McPherson replied. 'I called it in straight away and two detectives arrived on the scene together with some other uniformed officers. They were gathering statements as we were leaving for the hospital.'

'That was Pat and Alaya,' Fiona said to Jenny. 'They'll be taking over this investigation, Constable.'

'Yes. Ma'am.'

'Where is Mr Rebane now?'

'He's being operated on; he was unconscious when we got here so they took him straight in.'

'Good. I want you to stay here and keep an eye on him until I can arrange a twenty-four-hour guard. If the assailant thinks he's still alive then she may come back to finish the job.'

She handed McPherson a card.

'And I want you to ring me the moment he is out of theatre, and again when he recovers consciousness, do you understand?'

'Yes, Ma'am.'

'And pass these instructions on to whoever relieves you.'

She left him to report to his sergeant and walked with Jenny back to reception where she produced her warrant card.

'I'm here about Mr Rebane, who was brought in half an hour ago with a knife wound. Can you please find somebody to gather his clothes together and place them in a bag for me? I need to take them to forensics.'

Fifteen minutes later, they were walking out to Fiona's car, carrying a sealed plastic bag containing Rebane's clothes.

'It's such a shame,' Jenny said. 'It was a lovely suit as well. They'll never get those blood stains out.'

Despite her best efforts, Fiona laughed.

'You're starting to sound like an old married housewife already,' she said.

Back at the station Fiona gathered the team around her to catch up on what they'd been able to glean from the scene of the crime. Appleton was observing on the periphery of the group.

''I've been going through the witness statements, which have now been entered on HOLMES 2.' Alaya said. 'A couple of ladies had a very good view of the attack but unfortunately not of the attacker's face.

'They say that she approached him from behind and was about to plunge the knife in his back when he turned towards her. They think he may have seen her reflection in the shop window.'

'So, Mr Rebane may have seen her face?' Fiona asked.

'Possibly. Anyway, he managed to parry the blow with his hands, a move which I believe left some deep cuts, but she ducked to one side and stuck the knife into the right side of his chest.

'You understand that I'm filling in blanks in the statements using information based on observation of Mr Rebane by officers before the ambulance took him away.'

'I did wonder,' Jenny said. 'I've never known a civilian witness able to remain collected enough to take in that much detail before.'

'Despite, extensive questioning of all those who saw the woman,' Alaya said, 'we still haven't been able to find anybody who can provide a usable description.'

'Is there any useful CCTV footage?' Jenny asked.

'There's plenty of it,' Alaya responded, 'but she seemed to be aware that many of the shops would have cameras and deliberately kept her head facing away from them.

'Pat has started reviewing all the footage, so there's a chance that we'll find something usable. It might take a few more hours yet.'

'What about DNA?' Fiona asked. Constable McPherson told us that he believed that the assailant cut herself during the attack.'

'Yes, a small pool of blood was found a few feet from the scene, which we are assuming is hers. Samples have been sent to forensics with a request that it is processed urgently.'

'I've also handed Mr Rebane's clothes to forensics. McPherson said that she was wearing gloves so it's unlikely that we'll get much, but you never know.'

'Good,' Appleton said from the back, 'what about the victim's family?'

'I spoke to Sergeant Pyke on the way back here,' Jenny said. 'His wife and kids have been notified and are on the way to London.'

'I've also arranged for two officers to guard Mr Rebane while he's in hospital twenty-four-seven,' Fiona added. 'What we need to find out now, is how a professional hit could have been arranged in the time it took to contact Mr Rebane, bring him in here and interview him, a time period of just under sixteen hours.'

'As I mentioned earlier, I've got internal affairs coming into the station in an hour or two to assist with that,' Appleton said. 'They'll want to take statements from you all and seek to establish who knew what and when. They'll also be looking at Casey Hill's murder in the same way.'

Fiona groaned.

'Yes, I know it's not pleasant and that you've all got better things to do with your time,' Appleton said in response, 'but I've got to cover my back and your collective arses as well. We must do things by the book, so that when questions are being asked, we have all the answers.'

He strolled out of the office, leaving the team to work through the statements in detail. Just then Fiona's phone rang. She moved to a quiet area to take the call and then returned to the team.

'That was McPherson, Mr Rebane is out of surgery and has been moved to intensive care. He has a collapsed lung as well as other more superficial injuries, mostly on his hands and arms. He's stable and on a ventilator but they have him in a medically induced coma to help him recover so we can't talk to him yet.

'Two uniformed officers have arrived to take over guard duty, so McPherson is coming back to the station to give a formal statement. Jane, can you meet him and handle that, please?

'Alaya can you please arrange for a forensics officer to go to the hospital and look at the knife wound? We need to establish if it's compatible with those on Casey Hill and Councillor Tresham. I'm sure it is but let's document everything for when we eventually bring charges.'

'*If we're* able to bring charges,' Jenny muttered to herself.

Fiona gave her a disapproving look, which she acknowledged. She had to learn to keep her scepticism to herself. There was a small commotion behind them as a man and woman entered carrying a document case. Each had a laptop holder draped over their shoulder.

'Internal Affairs are here,' Fiona said as the two newcomers moved towards Appleton's office. 'Are they setting up in Cardiff and Swansea as well?'

'Only a matter of time,' Jenny replied. 'You'd think they'd let us conclude this case first. They're only going to get in the way.'

'Unfortunately, I think the Super's right. If we're leaking like a sieve, then we're never going to get anywhere.'

Fiona surveyed the room.

'Okay, thinking caps on everyone. Let's work this through. What's so valuable that it's deemed necessary to knock off anybody who might offer even the smallest threat to their people smuggling, money-laundering scam?

'Just how big is this operation that whoever is directing it is prepared to take lives to protect it? Are we talking about an organised crime group? And if we are, who's running it?

'I want information on all known people smugglers, organised crime groups, anything that seems relevant. I want you to contact Customs and Excise, Immigration, the National Crime Agency, and the UK Border Force. I want all their latest intelligence. And can somebody chase up GCHQ? Tell them it's urgent that they respond to us about this Hal bloke.'

Pat, Alaya and Jane went back to their desks and started work, only to be interrupted by Appleton's secretary calling Pat in to see Internal Affairs. Jenny took her mobile phone to a quiet area and rang Pyke.

'What's happening down there, Darren? We've got internal affairs crawling all over us here.'

'Us too, Guv, it's chaos. They've taken all the records for the Councillor Tresham murder and the immigrants and are going through them with a fine-tooth comb. Inspector Waddingham's pulling his hair out in Swansea, or he would be if he had any hair.

'Rhodri tells me that he's shot off to the smoking shelter with a packet of fags to get away from it all. They've finished interrogating the immigrants, you'll be pleased to hear.

'As you'd expect they're all from Albania, came over in a container lorry which mysteriously didn't get inspected at customs.'

'Do you think somebody's on the take?'

'Looks like it. Either that or they were lucky to come through at a time when everybody was on a break.'

'Almost as if they had details of shift patterns and day-to-day operations,' Jenny said thoughtfully. 'Do you think Border Force has a leak as well?'

'Nah, it'll be somebody feathering their nest,' Pyke said. But Jenny was already processing an alternative theory.

She finished off the call and went back to talk to Stoneman.

'Do me a favour, Jane. Can you speak to Immigration and Customs and Excise and ask them for details of any operation in the last year that's gone tits-up at the last minute.

'I'm looking for any unexplained change that allowed the bad guys to get away when they thought they had them bang to rights, anything that led them to suspect that there was a leak in their department.'

'Sure thing, Ma'am,' Jane said picking up the phone. 'Are you onto something?'

'Just a hunch. Don't say anything to anybody else for the time being, I may be barking up the wrong tree. '

She walked over to Alaya and asked her if anything had come back from forensics.

'Not yet, Guv, but I'm expecting the DNA results any minute. They're really pulling all the stops out down there.'

Fiona returned from speaking to Internal Affairs. She was looking flustered.

'They haven't got a bloody clue,' she said to Jenny. 'They really think we've got a bent copper among us feeding information to an organised crime group. I told them I could vouch for all my team and that if their theory was correct then whoever it is will be operating across three cities.'

'So, you pointed them in my direction?' Jenny said half-seriously.

'No, no, absolutely not. I told them that all the officers working this case are above reproach. No doubt, you'll be called in soon, but there must be another explanation.'

'I wonder,' Jenny said. 'It may not be just the police.'

'Really?'

'Yes, I spoke to Pyke earlier and he said that the immigrants Waddingham picked up in Porthcawl had effectively sailed through customs. It was as if somebody there were turning a blind eye.

'He's convinced that one of the customs officers has been paid off, but what if it's something bigger? I've asked Jane to speak to the other agencies to get a list of any operations that have failed due to some sort of leak.'

Fiona looked thoughtful.

'Bit of a long shot, but it might take the pressure off us,' she said. 'I'm just at a loss to understand how these people are staying one step ahead of us all the time.

'Listen, I've had a quick word with the Super and he thinks we may need to tool up the next time we follow up on a lead. He's concerned that one of us may get injured and, of course, the best way to disarm somebody coming at you with a knife is to shoot them. Are you or Jane firearm trained?'

Jenny thought back to the fateful moment she'd unloaded a gun into Morgan Sheckler's face and shivered. She pulled herself together quickly. It didn't do to give anything away in front of Fiona.

'No, we're not, though as you know, I have used a gun recreationally with Dawn at a gun range in Cardiff. She was brought up in the country where guns are more commonplace to control vermin.'

'Yes, I remember you telling me when I was in Cardiff. Unfortunately, that isn't going to cut it for the Met. Training involves knowing when not to fire a gun as well as testing your marksmanship.

'You're lucky, I've had the training and had to use a gun twice now on active service. It's not something you want to do, shooting somebody, even in self-defence. It took hours of counselling to come to terms with it.'

'Was it fatal?' Jenny asked.

'I'm afraid so. I don't really like to think about it. What about you, have you used a gun outside the range, maybe, like Dawn, shooting vermin on the farm in darkest Devon?'

Jenny hesitated. It hadn't been a serious question, but it'd hit home with her conscience, nevertheless. She knew that her hesitation was going to throw doubt on whatever she said next.

She decided to swallow her guilt as best she could and laugh it off.

'I don't believe I've killed anything or anybody,' she said smiling.

'Surely, you'd know if you had,' she insisted.

'Well, not being firearm trained like you, the opportunity hasn't arisen yet.'

Fiona grimaced and then laughed out loud.

'We're not all gung-ho in the Met, you know, but fine, maybe you should do the training. In the meantime, we'll make do with tasers.'

She left it there, but Jenny wondered what it was Fiona thought she knew that had led her to phrase her question in that way. She'd certainly asked some awkward questions about Morgan Sheckler's shooting when she'd been posted in Cardiff last year.

Maybe it was nothing. Perhaps it was her own guilt causing her to read things into conversations that weren't there. Either way she knew that she needed to be doubly careful in future when in Fiona's company. The woman was too sharp for her own good.

She was suddenly conscious that Alaya had joined them.

'We've just had the DNA results back,' she said. 'It's the same as one of the many samples taken at the Swansea Arena, but there's no record on our system to match it. Forensics say that she's female and likely of north African origin.'

'So, a possible terrorism link,' Fiona said. 'Have you approached other agencies such as Interpol?'

Alaya looked insulted that there might be any doubt that she'd done so.

'I put a request into Interpol immediately. I'm waiting for them to come back to me.

'What do you think?' Fiona asked Jenny, 'do we need to involve the National Crime Agency?

'What, and have the case taken off us? We know that this isn't terrorism, until evidence becomes available that says differently, we should hold onto the case.'

'We *think* we know it's not terrorism,' Fiona corrected, 'but what if the proceeds of these crimes are funding terrorism?'

'We don't know that.'

'No, we don't, but as the SIO I can't take that risk. I'm going to have to run this past the Super to see what he thinks we should do.'

Jenny was disappointed. All their hard work looked like it was going to be handed over to somebody else, and just when she felt that they were getting somewhere.

'Will you be making a recommendation?' she asked.

'Too bloody right, I will. I want to hold onto this case as much as you do. I'll suggest that we ask the NCA to have a watching brief at this stage and that we keep it out of their mucky paws as long as possible.'

There was a cough behind them. The three detectives turned to see a uniformed officer trying to attract their attention.

'My apologies, Guv, I didn't mean to interrupt; however, you have a visitor.'

Chapter Fifteen

The man who was subsequently escorted into the squad room was tall and blond with a hint of moustache that had clearly not been given time to flourish, if it could establish itself at all.

He wore a black suit with a white shirt and a thin black tie. A pair of dark rimmed, over-large glasses dominated his face.

'My name's David Cornwell,' he said, showing Fiona and Jenny his identification, 'and I'm with one of the government intelligence agencies.'

Jenny struggled to suppress a laugh.

'Couldn't you have chosen a better pseudonym,' she asked. 'And have you written any novels recently?'

The man looked bemused. He obviously hadn't expected such a reaction to his name. Fiona though, seemed confused.

'Sorry, I don't understand.'

'David Cornwell is the real name of John le Carré,' Jenny explained patiently, and then, blushing a little as if she'd given too much away, 'I do a lot of reading.'

She wondered what his colleagues thought of having to work with somebody with an ego big enough to adopt such an alias. He must have a very thick skin.

As if to confirm this judgement, Cornwell ignored her question and got down to business.

'I'm responding to your requests for information about Harold McQueen, or HAL as he prefers to be known, after his favourite computer.'

They all looked blankly at him.

'*2001: A Space Odyssey*,' he said, 'look it up. McQueen was obsessed with it for reasons that will become apparent shortly.

'Firstly, I must stress that everything I tell you is classified and should not leave this room. For that reason, there are several details which I will not be able to divulge to you.'

'Great,' Fiona said under her breath but audibly enough for others to hear.

'Secondly, before I tell you anything, I must know your interest in Mr McQueen.'

Fiona hesitated. If he wasn't going to be frank with her, she didn't see why she should cooperate with him.

'Mr McQueen's name has come up twice in a murder investigation, and we need to speak to him to exclude him from our inquiries,' she said.

Jenny jumped in.

'At this stage we don't know if he's involved or not, but he's one of the few leads we have, and he may well provide us with information that could shed light on motive and possibly allow us to arrest the murderer.'

Cornwell accepted these explanations.

'Okay, Harold McQueen is a former employee of GCHQ. His speciality is computers and in particular artificial intelligence. He's a widely acknowledged genius who fell out with management when they refused to give him the budget to develop what he described as a sentient computer.'

'Wow, is that even possible?' Alaya asked.

'No, I don't think it is, at least not for some considerable time, but McQueen believed that he could make significant progress towards developing the sort of self-aware and independent computer that Arthur C Clarke wrote about in *2001: A Space Odyssey*. And let's face it, he was years, possibly decades ahead of his time.'

'Preposterous,' Pat said.

Fiona was inclined to agree, especially as Pat was the most tech-savvy of all of them and knew a little bit about AI.

'Isn't AI prohibitively expensive to develop and uses up a huge amount of power?' Pat continued.

'Yes, which is why the big tech firms are leading the way - they're the ones with the budgets; we're barely holding on to their coat tails, unfortunately. That is why the director at GCHQ at the time vetoed his research.'

'So, what happened?' Jenny asked impatiently.

'McQueen resigned in disgust. He went off to the private sector, and that, unfortunately, was when we lost track of him.'

'You're saying that he just dropped off the grid?' Fiona asked. 'I thought you lot kept a close watch on your former assets, especially ones who have knowledge of sensitive systems.'

'We do. And yet McQueen was able to slip quietly into obscurity without us noticing. That's not to say that we don't have our suspicions.

'We've had intelligence to say that subsequent to his employment, he involved himself with hostile players.'

'Foreign powers?'

'Oh, good grief, no. We'd never have tolerated that. I meant criminal elements who would benefit from his expertise. We believe that he took the work that he was doing for the private sector and used it to enrich himself. It was at that point that the agency lost track of him.'

'I have to say that I'm a little surprised at that,' Fiona said. 'It strikes me that a former GCHQ employee who was consorting with known criminals would ring so many alarm bells that you'd be tearing London and the rest of the country apart to find him.'

'I absolutely agree, and I have no explanation for our apparent lapse of protocol and judgement. All I can say is that this happened before my time at the agency and that when I made inquiries yesterday, I was told that there'd been changes of personnel and that for some reason our systems started to throw up different priorities that led us to lose focus.'

'You're saying that McQueen actively intervened to prevent himself from being tracked?' Jenny asked.

Cornwell looked impressed.

'How remarkably perceptive, Inspector. Yes, it certainly looks like that happened, but I have no explanation as to how he achieved this other than to suggest that his previous access to our systems meant that he was aware of their vulnerabilities, and he exploited that.'

'Another dead end then,' Fiona said.

'I'm sorry, I wish I could have brought you better news. I can assure you that my superiors are as anxious to talk to Mr McQueen as you are.'

He stood up to leave and then paused as if a further thought had occurred to him.

'Tell me, who was murdered? Knowing might help me make some connections, which in turn could assist you.'

'There have been two murders, Councillor Gareth Tresham, a prominent Cardiff councillor and an accountant called Casey Hill,' Fiona said. 'In addition, there's been the attempted murder of a south Wales businessman called Gerald Rebane. In all three cases, we believe that the perpetrator was a female professional, paid to kill these men.

'There also appears to be a connection to a people smuggling operation that was unearthed in Swansea, though at present we can't definitively establish what that connection is.'

She stopped as Cornwell had gone pale and was struggling to support himself. She rushed to provide a chair for him to sit on and sent Pat off to get a glass of water.

The five detectives watched as the spook sipped the water and some colour came back to his cheeks.

'Are you alright?' Fiona asked. 'I thought you were going to faint then.'

'No, no, I'm fine. It was just a bit of a shock, that's all. Can I ask was the Casey Hill you referred to an accountant with Cutter Associates, based in Camden Town?'

'Yes, he was.'

Cornwell took another sip of the water.

'I may need something a bit stronger than this. I knew Casey, he's a good friend of mine, or should I say he was a good friend of mine. We were at university together, I was best man at his wedding, and I'm godfather to his daughter, Allison.

'Blimey.'

Fiona pulled up a chair next to him and then sent Pat to get tea for them all. This was going to be a longer session than she'd anticipated.

'When was the last time you spoke to Mr Hill?' she asked.

'Well, that's just it, not for some months. We've both been very busy. We were going to catch up at the college reunion but in the end neither of us could make it. I only emailed him last week saying we should go for a drink and a curry but didn't get a reply.

'I hadn't thought much about it, he never was one for keeping on top of his emails. I suppose I would have phoned him at the weekend if I'd thought about it, but that's not going to happen now, is it?

'Oh, God, how is Allison? How is she taking it? I must speak to her, give her a hand with the funeral arrangements Is she in London?'

Fiona let him talk himself out and then handed over the mug of tea. It was strong and sweet, designed for somebody in shock. Cornwell gulped down a mouthful.

'I'll try and answer your questions, but I'm going to need you to focus,' Fiona said. 'Do you know where we might find Allison?'

'You mean you haven't seen her? Does she know that her father's dead?'

'Yes, she knows. She was on her way to London when he was killed. We were in Mr Hill's home trying to find key evidence when she showed up.

'I took her to identify the body, but then she disappeared. We're concerned for her safety, and we believe she may be able to help us shed light on her father's death. We need to find her.'

Cornwell seemed confused.

'I think you'd better start from the beginning,' he said, pulling himself together.

'Mr Hill was offering us evidence that his firm of accountants was operating a money-laundering operation, but he was stabbed to death before he could hand it over to us. Somehow, the killer got wind of the handover and beat us to it, grabbing the evidence in the process.

'When we went to search his home, it had been ransacked, all electronic equipment had been taken. Naturally, his employers were less than cooperative. We believe his death is linked to the murder of the Cardiff councillor who stumbled onto a safe house in Swansea full of illegal immigrants.

'Allison was involved in identifying that property and we have messages between her and her father indicating that she may have known about the money laundering as well as the people smuggling.

'She came to London at the request of her father so she could go into protective custody with him. In retrospect, when she found that her father had been murdered, she was obviously scared for her own life and fled. That's why we need to find her.

'What if this killer is after her too? What did her father tell her? It's important that we find her and protect her.'

Cornwell put his head in his hands.

'Oh my God, Casey, what did you get yourself involved in?' he mumbled to himself, and then looking up: 'You're right of course, Inspector, we need to find Allison and keep her safe.'

'Would you know where she might have gone to?'

'I may have some ideas, but we're going to have to tread carefully. We don't want to frighten her off. Let me get onto it. I'll do my best to find her and bring her in.'

Fiona acknowledged the offer. She knew that she wouldn't be able to find Allison Hill alone. Now at last there was some hope, this case was getting somewhere after all.

Cornwell stood up. He still looked shaken, but his expression was a determined one as if he were intent on revenging the death of his friend.

'I'll be in touch,' he said. 'I'll also do more digging on McQueen, I'm sure there must be people still in the agency who were around when he went off the grid.'

'And we'll keep you updated on anything we find out,' Fiona said.

As he left, she turned to her team.

'What do we think? McQueen is the only lead we have, is he the key to unlocking this investigation?'

'Well, if he is, we still have to find him,' Jenny said. 'And if the spooks have lost him then things don't look so hopeful.'

Fiona grimaced.

'Ah well, we'll keep him on our radar, and remember, the spooks aren't proper police officers like us. They're too busy breaking into people's homes and setting up surveillance cameras, to understand the basics of an evidence-based investigation.'

'Any ideas then?'

'Not now, but we'll get there. McQueen himself looks like a dead end, so let's work this from the bottom up. So far, his name has popped up twice in our inquiries, firstly in a conversation between Casey Hill and his daughter, and secondly as a past colleague and friend of John Cutter, the man who owns our target company.'

'What do we have on the surveillance of Mr Cutter? Has he been meeting any suspicious computer geniuses recently?'

Alaya opened a file on her computer.

'The latest report was from just a few hours ago,' she said. 'Nothing untoward. In fact, if you thought that the life of an accountant was boring, this surveillance would reinforce that prejudice tenfold – work, home, client, work, home. That's all there is. Even the client is in the clear, it's a government agency.'

'What we're trusting the Government now,' Fiona said sarcastically. 'We need to mix things up a bit, throw him off his game and see where that gets us. Let's bring him in.'

'On what pretext?' Alaya asked.

'For a start, we can ask him about Casey Hill, make him think that he gave us the evidence after all. More credibly, let's tell him that we're looking for his mate, Harold McQueen in connection with alleged criminal activities, focus on their relationship, maybe imply that we have more than we do, shake the tree a bit and see what falls out.'

Jenny agreed.

'We've got nothing else, so let's give it a go,' she said. 'But he's bound to lawyer up. We need a strategy to get past that, scare him into ignoring his lawyer's advice to stay schtum.'

'Let's raise the stakes a bit,' Jane suggested. 'Look at who he is, a white-collar accountant with a spotless record, that maybe… is… laundering money for an organised crime gang. What's his motive?

'Have they got something on him? Is he doing it for McQueen, a lifelong friend? Or is he doing it for the money? Maybe he thinks it's a victimless crime.'

'Of course,' Jenny said, 'he has no conscience because he thinks he's not harming anybody. So, let's show him what he's helping to finance, the ten-year old boy, the two murdered men. He's effectively an accessory after the fact. Let's see how tough he is when we're trying to pin two murders on him.'

Fiona nodded.

'Let's do this,' she said. 'Alaya, can you please arrange to pick him up? I take it that he'll be at the office.'

'Well, if he isn't we won't have many problems finding him. I'll speak to the surveillance detail.'

'Good. Pat, please update the file on HOLMES 2. We've got to do this by the book and that means keeping our records bang up to date. Jane, would you mind going through the research on Mr Cutter and see if there are any more weak points we can exploit. This is all or nothing now, if we screw this up, we may not have a second chance.'

As she spoke, Fiona's phone buzzed. She grabbed it off her desk. It was a text. She read it twice and then passed the phone to Jenny, who gasped.

'I don't believe it,' she said. The others looked at them expectantly.

'It's a text from Allison Hill,' Fiona said. 'She wants to come in and talk to us.'

She quickly keyed and sent a reply. A minute later the phone buzzed again.

'Miss Hill doesn't feel safe coming here,' Fiona said, reading from the screen. 'She wants to meet at a local shopping precinct. She says that it will be more public and safer and that I'm to come alone.'

Jenny was incredulous.

'It's a set-up' she said. 'How naïve do these people think we are? For a start how does she think that Allison Hill got your number?'

'Oh, that's easy, I gave it to her, but I think you might be right,' Fiona responded. 'However, maybe we can turn this to our advantage. If this hit woman is trying to lure me into a trap, then we should play her at her own game.'

She turned to Alaya.

'Hold off on picking up John Cutter for now. With a bit of luck, we'll have a more interesting guest in our interview suite tomorrow morning.'

'What if it really is Allison Hill?' Jane asked. 'After all, if this is a set-up, it's transparently so, a child would see through it.'

'In that case, we move forward with her. This is win-win,' Fiona said, 'but I don't believe in gift horses in the middle of murder investigations. Whatever, happens we proceed with extreme caution and let's not put anything on HOLMES 2 for now.'

'Really, why?' Alaya asked. 'What happened to doing things by the book?'

'Just a hunch,' Fiona said. 'There's too many things going wrong around here, and now it looks like we may be up against a computer whizz kid. We'll update the record tomorrow. I don't want information about this operation to be made available to anybody outside us five, and that includes the Super and the bloody computer. Do we all understand.'

'Yes, Guv,' they all said in unison.

'Right,' Fiona said, 'I'm going to go in with Jenny. I want you three in an unmarked car a minute away. We stay in touch by radio on a secure channel. Break out the stab vests and the tasers.'

She sent another text.

'We're meeting her in an hour, whoever she is.'

Chapter Sixteen

It was late afternoon as they pulled up at the entrance to the shopping centre. Dark rain clouds were gathering above them, and the light was fading. Jenny worried that the impending darkness and possible bad weather might give an advantage to their target and help her get away.

The centre consisted of two rows of five, single-storey, bunker-style shops, arranged back-to-back with an access road in front of each row, running at right angles to the main road. It was a mix of retail and light industry. Occupants included an MOT centre, a ceramics shop, a jewellery outlet, and an engineering supplies business.

Although most of these businesses were still open the estate was quiet with virtually no traffic and only one or two people working there. Jenny assumed that most of them would be winding down for the weekend.

Between them Jenny and Fiona carried out a quick assessment of the terrain, noting that the two roads were joined by narrow passageways separating the units, an ideal place for somebody to lie in wait.

Although there were streetlights, one had been vandalised and the remaining lamp posts appeared inadequate to successfully illuminate the whole area. When the light further faded there would be dark patches, not least in the alleyways, which seemed to be mostly used to store refuse.

'This looks like fun,' Jenny said. 'This place is purpose-built for ambushes.'

Fiona agreed. She unhooked her phone from her belt and made a call, it went straight to answerphone. She clicked the red button and turned to her colleague.

'Well, if Allison Hill is here, she hasn't got her phone switched on. I don't see the point of leaving another message, this is almost certainly not her.'

'Agreed.'

Fiona spoke into her radio.

'We're going in Alaya. We'll keep the channel open so you can hear everything. We have our body cams attached to the stab vests and switched on.'

She pressed a button on the portable camera stuck on the chest plate of her protective clothing. Jenny followed suit.

'Are you ready?' Fiona asked. 'I'll take the road on the right, you go left, if you see anything at all call out. '

'One day, just one day, I'd like these encounters to take place somewhere more civilised, like a pub or something,' Jenny complained.

'You and me both.'

They advanced together taking care to spin in turn, right and left, to avoid anybody taking them by surprise. Both had their hand on their tasers, ready to draw it at any time and fire.

Jenny moved towards the first unit. It was open. Inside two men were working on a car, a third was on the phone in an office. They glanced up at her and resumed work. There was no sign of anybody else.

As she passed the unit, she came to the first alleyway. It was stacked with empty plastic oil containers, and a dozen black bin bags making it impassable. She relaxed and moved onto the second unit.

A large sign over the doorway announced this was a tanning salon. She tried the door, it was locked. A notice stated that the business was closed for a few days due to a family crisis.

The next alleyway was clear of any debris, and Jenny could see daylight at the far end. She wondered how much progress Fiona was making on that part of the estate. There were still three more units and three alleyways to go.

The plumbing supplies business in the third unit was open. There were two cars parked in front of a large display window containing samples of piping, bathroom and kitchen fittings and an entire bathroom display.

There were three customers inside carrying on a vigorous conversation with a fourth man standing behind a counter in tan-coloured overalls.

She moved cautiously towards the next alleyway. It seemed narrower than the others and was pitch black. She shined her torch into the void, briefly illuminating an empty space, then relaxed again.

As she approached the ceramics shop in the fourth unit, a door opened in front of her, and a man stepped out quickly. Jenny jumped back, pulling out her taser. The man looked even more startled than she was.

'Jesus,' he said, 'you gave me a fright.'

She looked him up and down. He was wearing blue overalls stained with white clay. His hands were dusted with a white powder that had somehow transferred itself to his face.

'Is this your business?' Jenny asked.

'Yes, can I help you?'

She showed him her warrant card and put a finger to her lips to indicate that he should remain quiet, while gesturing that he should continue whatever he was doing. He did as he was asked and walked to his car where he proceeded to take a heavy-looking box out of the boot.

Jenny glanced into the premises quickly. There was no sign of anybody else there, so she moved onto the alleyway. It was dominated by two large metal dustbins full of broken pottery. If there was anybody hiding behind those bins, she concluded, they'd struggle to get past them and certainly wouldn't be able to do so quietly.

The final unit was a wholesale pet food supplier. It also had a display window and a protective metal shutter for after hours. Inside were sacks of animal bedding, large boxes of cat and dog food, kilogram bags of various food stuffs and a selection of toys and rubber balls for those long walks in the park with your canine companion.

There were three or four vehicles parked outside, all empty, the occupants were inside purchasing goods for their pets. On second glance, Jenny could see that one of the car windows was partly open so that a large golden retriever didn't get too hot. The animal looked at her with doleful eyes. She grinned at it and moved on.

At the end of the estate was a tall fence and a final alleyway. She checked it out quickly and then turned to make her way back to the car. She could see Fiona walking towards her, about a hundred metres away. She raised her hand to signal that her road was clear.

Then suddenly, Fiona was calling out her name over the radio and gesturing at the area behind her. Jenny turned quickly, just in time to deflect a knife onto her stab vest. The impact caused her to lose her balance and she fell heavily to the ground, banging her head on the concrete kerb.

As consciousness drained away, she was aware of a woman in a hoodie leaning over her, poised to cut her throat, she could hear the dog barking loudly and the fizz of a taser and then nothing.

When Jenny awoke, she was lying in an ambulance with a paramedic leaning over her. Her ribs were sore, and her head was throbbing. Fiona was standing close by, looking very anxious.

Jenny touched her head but quickly withdrew. It felt wet and was sensitive to the touch. She looked at her hand, it was bloody. The paramedic told her to relax as he applied a dressing to the wound.

Everything was fuzzy. She looked over to Fiona, who in the fog of semi-consciousness looked almost angelic. She reached out towards her fellow Inspector, who took her hand.

'What happened?' Jenny asked.

'Thank God, you're okay, you had me worried for a moment. You hit your head and knocked yourself out.'

Jenny tried to respond again but found it difficult to speak. The fog grew thicker, and she lapsed back into unconsciousness.

When she woke again the ambulance was speeding towards the hospital. Fiona was seated beside her, holding her hand, it was warm and comforting.

'Hey,' Fiona said, 'you're back with us.'

Jenny tried to move but couldn't push hard enough against the momentum of the ambulance to sit up straight. She reached up to her head again and gingerly fingered the bandage that was now wrapped around it.

'You were telling me what happened,' she said. 'Where the fuck did that woman come from, anyway? I'd checked out that area.'

'You got careless; it looks like she was hiding underneath one of the vehicles. Luckily, your stab vest took the force of the knife, but she wielded it with some force so you may have a nasty bruise on your body where she struck you.

'She was just going to finish you off with the knife when I got into taser range and was able to paralyse her. Pat, Alaya and Jane were there in minutes and helped me to secure her. She's on her way to the cells now.

'We're going to leave her to cool her heels overnight before questioning her tomorrow. How are you feeling now?'

'Bloody awful, but I'll recover. You'd better expect me there in that interview room tomorrow.

'I think we need to let the doctor decide that. I've no intention of explaining to Dawn why you had a relapse by trying to do things too quickly.'

Jenny was about to respond but was interrupted by the ambulance coming to a stop. The paramedic helped her into a wheelchair and pushed her into Accident and Emergency.

A doctor came over to look at her. There was no way they were going to keep a serving police officer with a possible concussion waiting. He flashed a light into her eyes to test her reaction and examined her head. A nurse was summoned to apply more appropriate dressings.

'Well, you've got a lovely bruise on your back,' he said, 'and quite a cut on your head. I want to keep you in overnight just to make sure that you're not concussed.'

'Absolutely not,' Jenny said. 'I'm fine, it's just a few bumps. I'm perfectly fine to go back to my hotel and resume work tomorrow.'

The doctor looked doubtful and looked to Fiona for support.

'Really, Inspector I must insist. You cannot be alone tonight. You lost consciousness twice and that is a major warning sign, Concussion can be very dangerous, if we don't catch it quickly it could lead to serious brain damage or even death.'

Jenny sat up with difficulty.

'Look doc, I'm fine. I promise to take it easy, but I'm not going to spend the night in a hospital bed in the middle of a murder investigation.'

The doctor sighed.

'I understand that you feel you're okay now, but concussion can creep up on you. I strongly advise you to avoid being alone for the next forty-eight hours. Somebody needs to keep an eye out for any symptoms.'

Fiona could see that there was an impasse developing between her colleague and the doctor.

'Would it help if she stayed with me?'

The doctor looked relieved at the offer and addressed Jenny directly.

'Are you experiencing any nausea or dizziness at the moment?'

'No.'

He put his finger in front of her face, moved it from left to right and asked her to follow it with her eyes.

'Good, you seem alright for now. Staying with your friend might be a suitable compromise, providing she monitors your condition.' He looked at Fiona. 'I'd need to tell you what to look for.'

He sent a nurse to get a suitable leaflet.

'I want you to wake her every few hours. If she starts to exhibit any sign of dizziness, nausea, confusion, sensitivity to light, or blurred vision I want you to get her to a doctor. Is that understood?'

'Of course.'

'There's more detail in this leaflet. In addition, she can take pain killers but avoid Aspirin, at least before consulting a doctor, and I'd advise her not to drink alcohol either.'

'Bloody hell,' Jenny said, 'do you want me to move into a nunnery as well?'

'That would help, Inspector,' he said with a straight face, before walking away, smiling.'

Jenny got to her feet slowly and with Fiona's help walked out of the hospital to a nearby taxi rank. Alaya had taken Fiona's car back to the station.

'So, you've caught me,' she said, playfully putting her arm around Fiona's waist, 'and you're taking me back to your lair. What are you going to do with me there?'

'Are you sure you're not concussed? You sound like you're losing it.'

She removed Jenny's arm.

'You're right, I'm sorry. The bump must have loosened my inhibitions a bit. Look, I'll come back with you but on one condition. You're not to tell Dawn what happened. I'm not going to have her worrying about me without reason.'

'If that's what you want.'

'Oh, and I'm buying the wine.'

'You're not meant to be drinking.'

'Oh, I'm fine. These doctors go over-the-top. If I don't have a drink to ease this headache, I'll lose it.'

Forty-five minutes later they staggered into Fiona's flat clutching a bottle of wine each. Jenny took in the scene in front of her.

Fiona lived in a first-floor one-bedroom flat in a converted three-storey house. It was nicely decorated with lots of framed prints and cushions. There were several bookshelves, stuffed with the sort of popularist novels sold in airports and railway stations, as well as some more serious tomes. Several magazines were strewn on the coffee table.

'Very nice.' Jenny said.

She quickly explored the various rooms, starting with the kitchen, which was astonishingly neat. There were no dirty dishes in the sink, everything was put away in cupboards and a cat's litter tray sat in a corner looking as if it was cleaned out regularly. One of the fitted units was stacked high with cookbooks.

The bedroom was dominated by a large double bed covered in a pink bedspread, more cushions, and several cuddly toys. She picked up a pillow. It smelt of camellia and orange which was the scent of Fiona's shampoo, as she discovered, when she went into the bathroom.

She walked back into the living room where Fiona was pouring a couple of glasses of wine and started to browse through the fiction on the bookshelves. They were filled with blockbuster romances and thrillers, one or two classics by Austen and Dickens, some biographies of female celebrities, a few self-help books, a couple of books on police procedure and half a dozen travel guides.

A tall stack of vinyl records, mostly classical but also some early punk and Seventies and Eighties chart music were piled next to a turntable. And sitting next to them was a large ginger cat, patiently waiting to be fed. She scratched his ears.

'I see you've met Rufus,' Fiona said, 'handing her a glass of white wine. 'I'd better go and feed him.'

The cat followed her into the kitchen. Jenny pulled out *Reggatta de Blanc* by The Police and set it to play. She sank into the sofa as the dulcet tones of Sting echoed through the flat singing *'Message in a Bottle'*. Fiona plopped down next to her and started to fiddle with her phone.

'I've just ordered pizza; I hope that's okay.'

'Totally, thanks. I love your flat,' Jenny said. 'It's so cosy, and I love the retro music. Such a change from Taylor Swift.'

'Is that who Dawn is into?'

'No, she prefers classical music and heavy rock. It's a bit of a contrast I know but each to their own.'

'How is married life?'

Jenny laughed.

'Oh, it's far too early to tell,' and then more seriously, 'it's a bit claustrophobic if I'm honest. Maybe that's a reaction on my part to being tied down to one person for the rest of my life. I'll get used to it, I'm sure.'

'Is that what the play acting was about outside the hospital?'

Jenny felt a bit embarrassed.

'I'm sorry, that must have been the bump on the head, though maybe subconsciously I was making a pass at you.'

She turned her body so that they were leaning into each other, ignoring the pain as she did so, and moved some hairs off Fiona's face.

'I still think about that kiss outside your hotel in Cardiff, you know.'

Fiona put her hand on Jenny's waist and kissed her on her cheek.

'Me too, but that's history. You're married now, we've got to move on.'

Jenny leaned in and kissed her on the lips. Fiona didn't resist at first but then pulled away.

'What happens in London, stays in London,' Jenny said.

She moved to kiss her again but the voice entry buzzer sounded, breaking the mood. It was the pizza. They ate in silence, moving on to the second bottle of wine as they did so. As she finished her food, Jenny suddenly felt tired.

She felt that the romantic moment had passed and that was most probably for the best. Now, she just needed to sleep. She struggled to suppress a yawn.

'I'll sleep on the sofa,' she said.

'You will not!' Fiona replied indignantly. 'You can have the bed; I'll sleep out here.'

They were at an impasse.

'Okay, compromise,' Jenny said. 'We'll share the bed and I promise to behave myself.'

They went into the bedroom where Fiona offered her a pair of pyjamas. Jenny preferred to sleep naked but took them out of politeness. She changed quickly and turned to get into bed.

Fiona was standing, still dressed, watching her. Jenny smiled and got under the covers and watched intently as her host removed her clothes. She made no attempt to put on any nightwear. Instead, she climbed into bed, turned towards Jenny and kissed her.

'I hope you're not too tired,' she said.

Jenny quickly pulled the pyjamas off and returned the kiss. She was still sore, and her head was pounding a bit, but all of that was forgotten, as was her vow to behave herself.

Afterwards, she lay looking at Fiona as she slept, the covers pulled partly away to reveal their nakedness. She knew that she had to sleep as well, they had a big day ahead of them, but she couldn't stop thinking about what they'd just done.

She thought that she should feel some guilt or shame at having betrayed Dawn, and yet there was only relief, a release of sexual tension, and a sense that the bonds of fidelity were no longer suffocating her.

Maybe she needed this last fling to help her come to terms with her marriage. She knew that didn't make any sense. She wanted to commit to the relationship with Dawn, but there was something nagging at her, as if it was too safe, too secure.

It was as if she needed to take risks, to put everything on the line just to feel alive. It wasn't something that Jenny could easily come to terms with.

She stroked Fiona's back, carefully positioned herself into a spooning position and fell into a troubled sleep.

Chapter Seventeen

As it turned out, it was not the restful sleep Jenny needed. Her bruised body made manoeuvring difficult, even in the larger five-foot-wide bed, while the trauma of the knife attack triggered yet another dream about Sheckler.

This time she was on the motorbike driving around Cardiff looking for him. He was always just out of reach. The gun was in her hand, the safety off, pointing towards the late mayor as he ran from her.

Suddenly, he stopped and turned towards her, a large hole in his head, blood and brain matter oozing from the wound. He had her gun in his hand and was pointing it at her head. He fired. She shouted 'no!', waking suddenly, covered in sweat.

The cat was lying asleep at the bottom of the bed as if nothing had happened. Fiona was sitting upright, her brow creased with concern. She pulled Jenny towards her and kissed her forehead.

'Hey, you were dreaming and talking in your sleep, it sounded a scary one at that. Are you okay?'

Jenny realised that she was crying and buried her head in Fiona's shoulder. The warmth of her lover's body was comforting and helped calm her.

'I'm sorry,' she said. 'I get these bad dreams, often after traumatic incidents.'

She wondered if she'd said anything incriminating, or that might arise suspicion.

'It sounds a bit like PTSD to me, you should get some counselling,'

'Oh, I have, and it's much better now, thanks.'

The closeness of their bodies was now having more than a soothing effect. Jenny eased her hand down between Fiona's legs causing her to groan in pleasure. Fiona reciprocated and started to explore Jenny's body with her lips. It was a nice way to start the morning…

Afterwards, they showered and dressed quickly, and grabbed some coffee and a piece of toast.

'I'm not sure I'm going to be able to concentrate on this interview,' Fiona said over their frugal breakfast. 'Perhaps we should avoid being in an enclosed space together for too long when we're in the office.'

'You'll be fine,' Jenny said. 'We'll keep it professional.'

She felt the bump on her head. When she had inspected it in the mirror earlier, it had not been too noticeable, but now it seemed to be getting bigger and it hurt like hell. She hoped that Dawn wouldn't spot it when they skyped later; camera angles would be important.

They took the Tube into the office, as Fiona's car had been left there the previous day. The team were anxious about Jenny's welfare and looked pleased that she seemed alright. Appleton though, was not so accommodating.

He appeared as soon as they entered the squad room and summoned them to his office.

'What the hell did you think you were doing going ahead with this operation without my sign-off,' he demanded of Fiona. 'Anything like that - and I mean anything that could involve a possible danger to officers under my command - needs me to okay it.

'And where's the paperwork? There's nothing on HOLMES 2, no record of the intelligence, no operational plan, no risk assessment. Did you even do a risk assessment? You both could have been killed.'

'I'm sorry, sir,' Fiona said. 'We had an hour to get the operation together if we were going to catch this woman. I took the decision to keep details within the narrowest possible group considering the leaks we've been experiencing.

'And yes, I did conduct a risk assessment, that's why we were all wearing stab vests, had tasers and had back-up nearby. We also ignored the request to go alone, so both of us went in, and we had open radio mics to keep in touch.'

'You just felt that you couldn't tell me, because you felt that I'd leak it, is that right?'

'Absolutely not, sir. I understood that I am the senior officer in charge of this inquiry and believed I had the authority to go ahead with the operation without further reference to a senior officer.'

'Well, you were wrong, but as you're new here and obviously are not up to speed with how I do things, I'm going to overlook it just this once. In future, you run all operations like this past me first, do you understand? And you get your paperwork in order.'

'Yes, sir.'

He turned to Jenny.

'I heard you took a bit of a fall, are you fit enough to continue today? No sign of concussion at all?'

'Thank you, sir. I'm a bit bruised but I'm fine and raring to go.'

'Good, now go and talk to this suspect. But get your paperwork in order first.'

They walked back into the squad room.

'Right, let's get this show on the road,' Fiona said. 'Pat, can you update HOLMES 2 with details about last night's operation, please?'

'Already done, Ma'am. Sergeant Chopra and I did it first thing this morning.'

'Great, what can you tell me about our prisoner?'

'She's not talking at present, but we've done a bit of digging,' Alaya said, 'I've spoken to Interpol and the National Crime Agency, and I believe we've identified her.

'Her name is Rachel Abadi, she's 35 years old and she's a British citizen, born and brought up in north London with Syrian parents.

'Jane has spoken to the Army Personnel Centre and has confirmed that she served ten years in the special forces before leaving and, according to the very thin records held by the Foreign Office became a freelance mercenary, serving in Africa and other trouble spots.

'Interpol has no record of her fingerprints or her DNA, but they do have a slim file on an unknown assassin for hire whose weapon of choice is a knife and who fits the profile. We've been able to access her phone and from that the presence she has on the dark web where she advertises under the pseudonym of Falcon. We believe, from what Interpol tells us, that she can be linked to several murders on the continent.'

'The information on her phone tells us that she receives her instructions by text. It was remarkably low-tech, actually,' Jane added.

'The good news is we've found texts ordering the assassination of Councillor Tresham, Casey Hill, and Gerald Rebane. The bad news is it's not been possible to trace the source of those texts.'

'We'll have to ask her then won't we,' Fiona said. 'We need to find out who hired her and why.'

'There is one thing that puzzles me,' Jenny said, 'surely, she understood that killing so many people in such a brief time was bound to cause us to focus in on her. She must have been very confident she could get away with it.

'But the last job, the contract to kill you, Fiona, it's almost as if she wanted to get caught. The set-up was so obvious, you were bound to bring back-up, and there's no way an experienced police officer was going to go into a situation like that on her own.

'She doesn't strike me as being either naïve or stupid. Was she set up? Or was it the person giving the instructions who was naïve?'

'I agree,' Fiona said. 'We need to move quickly in getting some answers. If Abadi's client finds out that she has failed and is in custody, then they may find somebody else to do the job. They may even go after *her*.

'Which reminds me, Alaya, can you please check on Gerald Rebane and make sure that he still has protection. In fact, double it. Thanks'

Jane stopped them before they could leave the squad room.

'I've just had Abadi's service record sent to me,' she said. 'It's the uncensored version, thanks to David Cornwell's intervention. He's added a few notes as well. It may be worth having a quick look before you go in there.

'She left under a bit of a cloud, not a dishonourable discharge but close to it. Her Sergeant caught her torturing a prisoner in Afghanistan, along with other members of her team, she tied the prisoner up, cut him with a knife half-a-dozen times and threatened to castrate him. Her commanding officer described her as reckless and unhinged.

'David said that the members of her special forces team used to psych each other up and take it out on the prisoners. Abadi was particularly susceptible to this provocation and took it too far.

'Fortunately for her, the army was in delicate negotiations with a couple of the local tribes, so they covered it up to avoid a scandal. Instead, they sent her, and others involved home and discreetly sacked them two months later.

'There are also incidents recorded here where she put her troop at risk on excursions to take out key enemy positions. By all accounts, her colleagues were glad to see her go.'

'Mad and dangerous then,' Jenny said, scanning the documents. 'That could explain a lot.'

Before they started the interview, Jenny and Fiona took a proper look at their assassin on the camera feed. She was about five foot three inches, wiry with tattoos on bare arms that showed well-developed muscles.

Her brown eyes glittered with defiance beneath a crop of short, black hair. A team had raided her home shortly after she'd been arrested and found a dozen wigs, several combat knives and a laptop, which was currently being analysed by a police specialist.

Two police officers watched her as she sat handcuffed to the desk, which in turn was bolted to the floor.

The two detectives entered the room and sat down opposite her. Fiona asked the officers to wait outside, activated the tape machine, announced the names of those present for the tape, told Abadi that the interview was being filmed and read out her rights, just to make sure.

'You've told officers that you don't require a solicitor, can I confirm that is your wish? We can arrange legal representation if you want?' Fiona asked.

The question was met with a sullen silence.

'I am going to take your silence as an indication that your previous decision stands and that you do not require a solicitor. If I'm wrong, please say so now.' She paused for a response, but there wasn't one. 'Good, then we'll proceed.'

Jenny opened a tablet and placed it on the table where all three of them could see it. She opened a screenshot of a series of texts.

'These messages were taken from your phone. They are instructions to you to commit a series of murders. This first one instructs you to kill Cardiff councillor Gareth Tresham, a crime you committed six days ago in the Swansea Arena. There is a photograph of him attached to the message. Do you have anything to say about that?'

Again, there was silence. Fiona showed the next one.

'This text is an instruction to kill Casey Hill, an accountant working for Cutter Associates. It tells you where to find him and when and offers to pay twice your usual rate if you can commit the crime before he is able to speak to us.

'Can you tell us how that information was obtained by your client? Can you confirm that you killed Mr Casey four days ago?'

Once more Abadi refused to reply, sitting there with her hands flat on the table and an expression of blank defiance on her face.

'Okay,' Fiona said. 'Let's try this one. This is a picture of Gerald Rebane, and the accompanying text instructs you to ambush him yesterday morning outside this police station. Unfortunately for you, Mr Rebane survived that attack and is likely to be able to identify you.'

She eyed Abadi's bandaged right hand.

'You also cut your hand during that assault and left blood behind which has enabled us to get a match with your DNA. There is clear evidence that links you to that incident in addition to these instructions.

'You will be charged for all of these crimes, but we want to know who your client is, and why you were willing to take so many risks for him or her, risks that eventually led to you being caught?'

For a moment it looked like Abadi was going to respond but she obviously thought better of it and stayed silent. Fiona slammed her fist on the table in frustration, causing Jenny to jump in surprise. Abadi just smiled.

'This isn't the bloody army now,' Fiona said angrily, 'there's nobody here to cover up your crimes. You messed up then and you've messed up now. As far as the army are concerned, you're an amateur, a savage who was given too much responsibility. Well, you've finally got your comeuppance.'

Abadi snarled, rattling the handcuffs that secured her to the table, and gave them both a look that said she would have liked to cut their throats then and there, but she didn't rise to the bait.

Jenny showed her the next screenshot.

'This is an instruction to attack and kill Inspector Keaton here at a local shopping centre not far from here. It links to earlier texts sent to the Inspector purportedly from Allison Hill, which asked her to go alone to that venue.

'Did you send those texts? What do you know about Allison Hill? Why did you think that an experienced police officer like Inspector Keaton would follow the instructions she was sent and walk into an obvious ambush alone? How stupid are you?'

This last insult caused Abadi to flush in anger, her nostrils flared as she leant forward to respond.'

'Don't you call me stupid. I'm paid a lot of money for what I do, and I've avoided being caught for over ten years. You'll see from the instructions that it doesn't identify the target as a police officer. If it had I would never have accepted the assignment.

'It was only when I saw your stab vest with Police on it that I realised I'd been set up. I attacked you, even though you weren't my target, to escape capture. I hadn't realised you had back-up nearby.'

'Oh, you draw a line as to who you will kill do you?' Fiona asked.

'No, I will kill anybody if the money is right. I was offered £50,000 to kill you. But as you've pointed out, to have accepted a job like that in full knowledge of who I was being asked to kill and considering you were already looking for me for previous jobs would have been bloody stupid.'

'You're telling us that your client let you down then, that he or she screwed you?

Abadi had clammed up again, but it was obvious that this was exactly what she thought. Fiona leant forward and raised her voice.

'We need you to tell us who your client was. Why did he or she want you to kill all these people? You may as well tell us; you're going down for them. You're going to prison for the rest of your life.

'But if you cooperate with us, we might be able to make things a little easier for you.'

Abadi refused to respond. She leant back in her chair defiantly and placed her hands flat on the table again. Jenny decided to have a go.

'Look Rachel, you're being thrown to the wolves here. Your client doesn't care if you go down for this. They're going to walk away from these murders as free as a bird while you rot in a cell in a maximum-security prison.

'Do you know what sort of people end up in those prisons, even the women's prisons?'

'I can look after myself.'

'Yes, I'm sure you can, but while your employer remains free, he's going to worry that at some stage you'll give him up. He might decide to come after you. The only way you're going to be safe is if we lock him up as well.'

Abadi remained unmoved.

'Don't you think that you need to protect yourself by giving up your client? Don't you think that he deserves to be in prison for the way he's treated you?'

Abadi sat thinking for a few minutes and then looked straight at her.

'You're right Inspector, he does deserve to pay for what he did and if I ever get my hands on him, he'll die a very slow and painful death. But I have no fear that he'll come after me because I'm not a threat to him.

'You see, I have no idea who my client is. I have no clue about his motives or what it is that he's trying to protect by killing all these people. I do my job, take my money, and ask no questions. That's why people hire me. I think this interview is over.'

Jenny and Fiona gathered their things and left the room, sending the uniformed officers in to keep an eye on their prisoner. Alaya emerged from the observation room.

'Book her, please will you Alaya,' Fiona said. 'Two counts of murder, attempted murder, assaulting a police officer and grievous bodily harm. Throw the fucking book at her.'

She stormed off with Jenny trailing behind.

As they entered the squad room, Appleton was waiting for them.

'Back to square one then,' he said. 'What's your next play?'

'I don't know. Give me some time to think about it. We need to wrap up the case against Abadi first.' She looked across the room. 'Any joy on her laptop, Pat?'

'Yes, just got it back from ICT.'

'Great, I'll be there now.'

Appleton took the hint and left her to it. Fiona and Jenny marched over to Pat's workstation.

'We've got access to the admin side of her website on the dark web, but it's set up to delete any cookies. There's a list of IP addresses for those who've visited it, but they're going to take a bit of time to work through, and even then, there's no guarantee that any of those users actually paid for her services.

'Here's the interesting bit though. She has an overseas bank account. Presumably, all the payments go into that. We're going to need them to cooperate with us so we can trace where those payments came from.'

'Fortunately, that's my speciality,' Fiona said. 'I'll get onto some former colleagues. I guess we'll also want to get a court order at some stage in the relevant country to recover those funds as proceeds of crime.'

Jenny knew that Fiona wasn't going to let this go, if anybody could recover the money, she could. She turned to see Jane approaching them.

'I've just heard, Gerald Rebane has woken up. He's still weak but we can talk to him. We'll need his statement for the case against Abadi. Do you want me to do it?'

'No, that's okay,' Jenny said. 'We'll do it together; I owe him for looking after Dawn when she was assaulted. You can come with me. Is that okay, Fiona?'

'Yes, that's fine. I've got more than enough to be getting on with here. See if you can find out if he knows anything about Harold McQueen, the more information we have on him the better. I'm convinced our former ICT spook is involved in this somehow.'

She paused as if trying to work something out.

'It looks like Abadi is a dead end as far as finding the person who hired her. What do you say that we go back to plan A and bring John Cutter in?'

'I think that's an excellent idea,' Jenny said.

Fiona turned to Alaya, who'd just returned after charging Rachel Abadi.

'Can you arrange for Mr Cutter to be picked up, please, Alaya? It's about time that he came face to face with the consequences of his little scheme. Let's not put it on HOLMES 2 for now. I suddenly find myself distrusting that system.'

Jenny was pleased. It finally looked as if they were getting somewhere. She grabbed her bag, stuffed some files into it, and joined Jane who was already on the way out and heading to the hospital.

'Just how far away is this place?' she asked.

'Don't worry. Alaya's got me a car,' Jane said, waving the keys in her face.

Chapter Eighteen

Jenny settled into the car with some difficulty. Her bruised back was feeling a little stiff, while her head was tender to the touch. She knew that she'd been lucky, that if it wasn't for the stab vest she would've been severely injured, maybe even killed, but that was little comfort at present.

Perhaps she deserved to die. She'd taken a man's life in the most horrible way, and it was haunting her. She'd betrayed her wife within weeks of the wedding. What was she doing? It was almost as if she was living on the edge as a means of justifying her continued existence.

Jenny was so deep in thought that she hadn't realised Jane was speaking to her.

'I'm sorry, I wasn't paying attention,' she said apologetically.

'I was asking how you were feeling,' Jane said. 'Perhaps you should have taken the day off to recover.

'No, no. I'm fine, just a few bumps and bruises.'

Jane looked sceptical.

'I hear that Inspector Keaton took you home last night, to ensure you didn't slip into a coma or something.'

Jenny shrugged, trying not to look too guilty.

'On doctor's orders. They were threatening to tie me to a hospital bed or something. He insisted that somebody kept an eye on me.'

'Oh, is that something we need to be briefed on? I can't have you conking out on me in the car.'

Jenny laughed.

'You've got no worries on that score. I'm fine. I think if I were concussed it would have shown itself by now.'

Jane steered the car into the hospital grounds and found a parking space. They walked into the building and followed the directions of a receptionist to Rebane's private room. Two armed police officers were standing outside.

The detectives showed their warrant cards and made their way to Rebane's bedside. He was sitting up sipping on a cup of tea, while a male nurse adjusted his dressings.

'Inspector Thorne,' he said cautiously, 'how nice to see you again. You've just missed my wife and kids. They've decided to go and spend some of my money in Harrods.'

It was obvious that he was in some pain. Jenny could see through the half-open pyjama top that his chest was heavily bandaged, and he was holding an oxygen mask in his hand to assist with his breathing.

Jane introduced herself and sat down on the opposite side of the bed with a pad and pen. She switched her phone to record to ensure she didn't miss anything.'

'I'm glad you're feeling better, Gerald,' Jenny said. 'I believe it was touch and go for a short while.'

'Yes, so I'm told. I'm telling you, if I hadn't glanced into a shop window and seen that woman coming at me with a knife, I would've been a goner.'

'I was hoping you'd be well enough to give us a statement,' Jenny said. 'Do you mind if Jane records it and takes notes? We'll get it typed up then for you to sign.'

'Of course, no problem at all. I seem to be helping the police with their inquiries a lot these days. First Dawn and now this.'

Jenny smiled.

'Can you tell me what happened?'

'I'll do my best, certainly. Now let me see... Oh, yes. I'd just left the police station after talking to you and that other Inspector. I set off towards my next appointment when I turned my head to look at a sale notice in one of the shops.'

He put the oxygen mask to his mouth and breathed in before continuing.

'As I did so I just caught sight of a woman in a hoodie bearing down on me with a large knife. I turned quickly and tried to parry her blow, but she slipped under my arm and stabbed me in the chest.

'She tried to stab me again, but this time I deflected the blow and knocked the knife out of her hand. She must have realised the game was up because she picked the weapon up off the ground and fled. I believe that she may have cut herself in the process.'

Another intake of oxygen.

'It was at that point that I realised she'd done some real damage. The next thing I know I was waking up here after an operation.'

'Would you be able to identify this woman?'

'Do you know what, I think I could. I got a good look at her face.'

Jenny opened her bag and took out a set of six photos. She presented them to Rebane who looked thoughtfully and then pointed at the image of Abadi.

'That's the little minx,' he said. 'She looks a right handful doesn't she. Do you know where she is?'

'Yes, we arrested her last night. She's ex-military and a killer-for-hire, goes under the name of Falcon apparently.'

'Do you mean that somebody paid to have me bumped off?'

'It does look that way. We think that they may have been worried that you'd expose some illegal activities at Cutter Associates.'

'But that's preposterous,' Rebane spluttered. 'I don't know anything about such activities.'

This time he had to spend longer breathing from the mask. Jenny paused until he'd finished before responding,

'We know and that's what's worrying us. The chances that any of the files you promised to get us could have advanced our inquiries were slim, but at the time it was the only lead we had. Now we're wondering what exactly is going on at the firm that justifies killing somebody, and not just you, Casey Hill too.'

Rebane looked thunderstruck.

'Do you know, they told me not to go into accountancy. Now I know what they meant.'

He tried to laugh at his own joke but grimaced in pain instead, and took more oxygen in.

'Sorry, graveyard humour, something you get used to in the armed forces.'

Jenny could see that Rebane was still trying to process what he'd been told, but she decided to press on.

'Can I ask, have you ever come across a Harold McQueen while working as a consultant for Cutter Associates?'

Rebane sat impassively for a few minutes as he worked through all the contacts he'd had with the firm.

'Do you know, I think I might have met him once, at a social event hosted by the company. John Cutter may have introduced us. They're friends I think and a major client.'

'Do you have any knowledge of the work the company do for Mr McQueen.'

'No. I'm afraid I don't. It's not an area of work I have any dealings with. Why, do you think this McQueen character is dirty? Is he the one who hired this Falcon woman to bump me off.'

'We don't know. We're just trying to piece things together at present.'

A nurse arrived with some food. Jenny and Jane stood up to leave.

'Thank you once again for your help, Gerald. We'll be in touch with the statement for you to sign and we may need to ask you to do a formal identification at some stage.

'Although we have the woman who attacked you in custody, we're going to leave the police officers outside your room for now. Better safe than sorry.'

They each shook hands with Rebane and headed back to reception. Jenny felt that she should let Dawn know what had happened to him; after all, he'd been so good to her.

She realised then that she hadn't spoken to her wife for some time. Hadn't she promised to ring every day? Dawn would wonder what had happened to her. She wasn't going to elaborate.

* * *

Alaya was waiting for them as they walked into the squad room. She had a big smile on her face.

'We've found Allison Hill,' she said. 'She's just got here. Mr Cornwell, our spook, brought her in.'

They followed her into the squad room where Cornwell was sipping on a cup of coffee. Allison Hill was sitting next to him, a glass of water in her hand, looking scared and bewildered. Fiona called them over.

'Mr Cornwell was just about to explain to us how he found Allison,' she said.

'It wasn't that difficult. Allison contacted me. She'd been staying with an old school friend whose parents persuaded her that hiding wouldn't solve anything. Luckily, Casey had given her my number and said to contact me if she were in trouble, I brought her here as soon as I could.'

They looked across to Allison who was clutching a large file of papers.

'How are you, Allison?' Fiona asked. 'Can we get you anything to eat?'

'No, thank you. Uncle Jeff says I can trust you to look after me,' she said.

Fiona looked confused.

'That's his real name,' she added, nodding her head in the direction of the spook.

Cornwell shuffled uncomfortably, but Allison had moved on.

'Just before I left for London, my father sent me this file. He said it was insurance in case anything happened to him and that I was to give it to the police. However, there was a condition…

'I'm to insist that there is to be no record of my presence here or of my giving you this file on police computers.'

Fiona protested.

'If I don't record where the paperwork came from then the chain of evidence will be broken and I might not be able to use it to catch your father's killer.'

'I'm sorry, but that's my condition and it's final. My father believed that Hal, whoever he is, has access to all your computers and if that's the case then I won't be safe.'

Jenny whistled, if that was true, then it would explain a lot, but it didn't seem possible.

'Are you saying that he has somebody on the inside?' she asked.

'I don't know. I'm just repeating what I was told. I'm not prepared to go the way of my father and I'm sure Uncle Jeff will back me up in that.'

She turned to look at Cornwell, who confirmed his agreement.

'We'll find a way around chain of evidence,' Jenny said to Fiona, who agreed. Allison handed the file over.

'Alaya here, is going to take you to the canteen to get you something to eat after which Mr Cornwell, er…Uncle Jeff has promised me that he's going to find you somewhere safe to stay,' she said,

They waited until the three had left the office and then swooped on the documentation.

Fiona was ecstatic. The paperwork contained everything she'd hoped for. They were joined by Cornwell, who'd obviously felt able to leave Allison with Alaya for the time being.

'This is it,' Fiona said. 'There are details here of systematic money laundering by Cutter Associates on behalf of an unnamed client referred to only as HAL, and we know who that is, don't we.'

'What about the accusation that McQueen has access to our computers?' Jenny said. 'Do we think that he has an insider on his payroll?'

'Or maybe he's hacked into them,' Cornwell suggested.

'Impossible,' Appleton said as he entered the room.

'Do you really think so?'

'The police national computer is one of the most secure on the planet.'

'And Harold McQueen is a genius. If anybody can do this then he can.'

'Okay,' Fiona said, 'let's not take any chances. I told Alaya to keep the operation to pick up John Cutter off the books, no tasking on HOLMES 2. It helped us catch Abadi, let's see if it works this time. I didn't want him tipped off or killed before we got to him.'

Appleton indicated his approval.

'Once I've settled Allison at home, I'll head back to the office and see what else we have on McQueen,' Cornwell said. 'Allison is family, as was Casey. If he's responsible for orphaning her then he's going to pay.'

'Thanks,' Fiona said. She turned to Jenny and Jane. 'Do you fancy getting something to eat?'

* * *

The three of them ate in silence. Jenny was itching to get Fiona alone so she could discuss what had happened last night.

She could see that her lover was feeling awkward as well. Perhaps when Fiona suggested they go to the pub for food she hadn't anticipated this scenario.

'You do know that you're not meant to drink with suspected concussion?' Jane said, eyeing Jenny's large glass of Pinot Grigio accompanying her lunch.

'I think I'm in the clear by now, don't you?' Jenny replied, grinning.

'Perhaps you should have warned us about that last night,' Fiona said.

'Oh, you mean you two had a secret party last night, and I didn't get an invite? I'm offended!' Jane said, half-joking.

'What? Well, there wasn't an opportunity...' Fiona started and then stopped herself, as if realising that she'd already said too much, her face going bright red with embarrassment.

The three of them ate in uncomfortable silence, but Jenny's mind was loud with questions... like, what Fiona felt about last night. She seemed just as awkward about it as Jenny did. Now in the confines of the pub, seated side by side, their bodies touching, Jenny's appetite was for something more satisfying than food.

She noticed Jane glancing at them between mouthfuls, as though trying to figure out what was going on. Surely it wasn't that obvious that the two senior officers had had sex less than twenty-four hours earlier.

It seemed to her as if Jane was about to raise her suspicions when a familiar voice cut through the tension. Jenny looked up and was stunned to see Dawn walking towards them.

She stood to greet her, not knowing what to say or how to react. Eventually, she found the words.

'What are you doing here?' she asked, kissing her wife. They embraced for what seemed an eternity. Dawn broke away first.

'What happened to you?' she asked, anxiously, noting the cut and bruise on Jenny's forehead.

'I asked first,' Jenny replied, noticing that Chaffont was standing awkwardly by the door.

'We had meetings with potential power plant investors in the City and I thought I'd surprise you. We went to the police station, and somebody called Pat told us you were here.'

Dawn turned to Chaffont and invited him to join the others.

'Jack, you may remember Fiona and Jane from the wedding,' she said. 'This is Jack Chaffont, my boss.'

Chaffont greeted them awkwardly and then went to the bar to buy a round.

'So, what happened to your head?' Dawn demanded.

'Oh, it's nothing. I had a fall while apprehending a suspect.'

'Is that why I couldn't get hold of you last night? I tried several times.'

'Yes, I went back to the hotel and fell asleep. I'm sorry. I was going to ring you this morning, but I slept in and was in a hurry to get to the station.'

She could feel Jane's eyes burning into her as she told the lie.

Dawn kissed her again, and then tentatively fingered the area around the cut. Jenny flinched.

'We've got matching wounds,' Dawn said gleefully.

Jenny ignored the remark, her attention was on Jane, who was looking at her suspiciously, no doubt wondering why Jenny had just lied about her whereabouts the previous evening. She willed herself to focus on her wife instead.

'Are you staying the night?' she asked.

'No, I'm sorry, we only have time for one drink. I had to twist Jack's arm as it is. We've got to catch a train in an hour. We both have an early meeting tomorrow morning that can't be missed, on a Sunday of all days. But, yay, I get to see you.'

Jenny smiled. Despite the awkwardness, she was happy to see Dawn. She wasn't so sure about Fiona, who sat in silence, observing and smiling as best she could.

Jane eyed the two with growing comprehension, the crease in her brow deepening with disapproval.

As they all settled into their seats, Dawn pressed the three detectives for news about their investigation.

'I heard Gerald Rebane was attacked, is he okay?'

'He is now,' Jenny said. 'I've just seen him, sitting up in bed in the hospital. It was a close one through.'

'Oh my God, have you got the attacker?'

'Yes, it was the same one who killed Councillor Tresham.'

'Wow, thank fuck you've got her off the streets.'

'We're still trying to unravel it, but if you can pass on the news to your mother, I'm sure she'd want to know.'

'I will do. Does this mean that you're ready to come back to Cardiff?'

Jenny looked to Fiona.

'We still have a bit more to do yet,' Fiona said, 'we may have the killer, but we still have to catch whoever it was who paid her. Hopefully, I'll be able to get your wife back to you in a few days' time.'

Dawn beamed.

'Well see that you get her back in one piece.

'I'll do my best.'

Jenny and Dawn sat arm-in-arm as Chaffont briefed Fiona and Jane on the power plant project. After half-an-hour had passed he looked at his watch and gestured to Dawn.

She pouted and then kissed Fiona.

'We have to go,' she said. 'We can't afford to miss this train. Much as I'd like to.'

Jenny accompanied them outside where she and Dawn embraced as Chaffont looked on impatiently.

'I'll call you,' Dawn said as she got into the waiting taxi. Jenny blew her a last kiss and walked back into the pub. As she approached her colleagues, she noticed that the atmosphere was more tense. Jane was shoving her coat on, looking furious.

'I need to get back to skype my husband,' she said pointedly. 'Will I be seeing you for breakfast, Ma'am'.

Jenny could feel the disapproval in her colleague's voice.

'You might do, Jane. If not, I'll see you in the office.'

As she was about to leave, she turned back to look directly at Jenny.

'And I had such high hopes for you and Dawn,' she said, almost inaudibly.

Before Jenny could respond by telling her to mind her own business, she'd walked out of the pub. She turned to look at Fiona, who was sitting open-mouthed.

'Wow, that was really uncomfortable,' she said. 'What are the chances of that? We have sex and then your wife appears in person. What are you going to say to Jane? I'm not sure she has your back.'

Jenny shrugged; she was too stunned to respond. Fiona though took the opportunity to air her own doubts.

'This is a real fucking mess, isn't it? More for you than me, I have to say.'

'What do you mean?'

'Well, it isn't the ideal situation, is it? How do you think I felt watching you paw each other, and what exactly is going on with you?'

Jenny was flabbergasted. She hadn't been expecting an interrogation. Fiona continued.

'You seem distracted, you're getting careless, is that what marriage does to you? And then, just a matter of weeks after you tie the knot, you're shagging around. It's as if you're looking for some sort of validation.

'I knew you were a risk-taker, but this really takes the biscuit.'

She waited for a response, but Jenny was still trying to process the evening's events. Eventually she managed to squeeze some words out.

'You've got me there,' she said. 'If you want answers I don't have them.'

She struggled to hold back tears, dabbing at her eyes with a tissue as Fiona put her arms around her.

'I've got so much going for me, a beautiful wife, a good job, a great life and yet I feel trapped. Maybe I *am* trying to validate my existence. I really don't know.'

'It does seem as if you're suffering some form of PTSD. Has there been a traumatic event recently that might have set that off.'

Jenny was tempted to tell her but knew that she couldn't. How could you admit to a homicide detective that you're struggling to hold onto your sanity because you once blew a man's head off at close range?

She would if she could, but it wasn't just about her. There were so many lives and careers dependent on what really happened to Sheckler remaining a secret, not least Dawn's, her mother-in-law's and the Cardiff region's Mayor, Byron Harris.

Instead, she decided to parse out the truth.

'It started with Morgan Sheckler,' she said. 'I just can't get the image of his corpse out of my head, most of his face was missing, it was horrendous, and then with every subsequent murder I've been involved with it's got worse.'

Jenny struggled to hold back tears as she spelled out half-truths. She had to keep control somehow. Fiona pulled her in closer and kissed the top of her head.

'Perhaps you need a break from homicide and to sign up for more counselling.'

'Yes, I think that might help. I'll do it as soon as we've got this wrapped up, I promise, but I can't get distracted. I've always worked through these problems, and I'm going to do so again.'

Fiona kissed her once more.

'You can't live in denial. You must get help.'

Jenny acknowledged the sentiment. There was no way that she could get help, not without confessing to her crime, but she wasn't going to tell Fiona that. Instead, she was silently chastising herself for this moment of weakness, telling herself that she needed to do better.

She pulled herself together and struggled to reassert herself as the tough no-nonsense detective she projected to the outside world.

'I'll think about it,' she said. 'In the meantime, I can't be alone tonight.'

Fiona looked sceptical.

'Seriously? We're talking about sex now. Do you even have a conscience, don't you feel guilty about betraying Dawn?'

'Of course, I do, and I didn't mention sex. I just need to be with somebody. I'm so confused.'

Dawn's sudden appearance had thrown her completely, but Jenny's new-found lover was not so sure that she could offer what was needed.

'Last night was great,' Fiona said. 'But we got carried away, the booze was a factor, but also, I was selfish, I wanted the experience.

'I've only been with a woman once before. I had no idea I'd enjoy it so much. But we must show some restraint. You're married, we're working together. We've already upset one of your colleagues and maybe Dawn suspects as well. I don't want to hurt her.

'Oh yes, and I don't believe in taking advantage of someone who's having an emotional crisis.'

Jenny took Fiona's hand, squeezed it and then held her.

'I'm sorry, I thought I was taking advantage of *you*, but if that's what you want then I'll respect your wishes. It looks like I'll be seeing Jane in the morning after all. That'll make her happy.'

They finished their drinks and walked back towards the station car park where Fiona had left her car. As they reached the entrance she turned to face Jenny.

'Well, I'll see you tomorrow then.'

Jenny moved closer to her and kissed her on the lips. Fiona hesitated and then committed herself fully to the embrace. They fumbled with each other's clothes before realising where they were.

Fiona stood apart, took Jenny's hand and walked with her to the vehicle.

'Maybe I could manage breakfast after all,' she said, 'but this is the last time.'

Chapter Nineteen

They woke the next morning with their bodies still entangled after the previous night's lovemaking.

For once, Jenny had slept soundly with no nightmares. Perhaps the conversation with Fiona the night before had done some good, or maybe it was just a case of waiting for another trigger event.

They dressed quickly, ate a quick breakfast, and then made their way to the station in Fiona's car. It was too late to worry about what their colleagues thought so they were quite relaxed about walking into the squad room together.

Jane was already there, bent over a computer screen with Pat looking on, commenting on some aspect of the case. As Jenny approached, she looked up.

'Missed you at breakfast,' she said, pointedly, and then went back to work.

Jenny glared at her, told her to mind her own business, and walked over with Fiona to talk to Alaya, who'd already fulfilled the order to pick up Cutter. He'd been cooling his heels in a cell most of the night and was now in an interview room waiting for his solicitor to arrive. He wasn't happy at all.

She suggested that they go through the files gifted to them by Allison Hill one more time before plunging into the interrogation. She'd made copies of the key documents and laid them out on a desk for ease of reference as they strategised.

Just then Appleton walked in accompanied by Cornwell. They were deep in conversation. Appleton broke off the conversation as he approached them and grinned.

'Mr Cornwell has just been briefing me about his goddaughter. He's got her stashed away safely and has had permission from his superiors to assist with our case. I'll leave you with him.'

Fiona pointed Cornwell to a nearby chair and continued with the strategy meeting.

'I suggest that Jenny and I carry out the interview,' she said, 'while Alaya and David observe. We'll both have an earpiece, so any suggestions or observations you may have please let us have them.'

She looked over to Pat, who gave a thumbs up to indicate that Cutter's lawyer had arrived and was consulting his client. He then left with Jane to join other officers who were carrying out a pre-arranged raid on the premises of Cutter Associates.

'Okay, let's do this,' Fiona said.

A full head of grey hair sat atop the heavily jowled, beak-nosed face of John Cutter, immaculately dressed in an expensive-looking pin-stripe suit and wearing what appeared to be hand-stitched leather shoes. He was about five-ten and in his early fifties. Beside him sat a lawyer, Michael Suderman, twenty years his junior, whose Armani suit, Jenny concluded, gave Cutter's a run for its money in the style stakes.

Suderman adjusted his dark-rimmed designer glasses before reaching into his jacket for his pen. As he did so, she noted that his shirt had the initials 'MS' embroidered on the breast pocket, and the plain blue tie he wore was held in place by a gold pin. The whole ensemble was completed by gold cufflinks and a Rolex watch. He looked like he was a walking advert for a gentleman's gift catalogue.

Fiona settled herself down opposite the two men, read Cutter his rights and introduced all those present for the benefit of the tape. She explained that the interview was also being filmed and that other officers were observing proceedings. remotely.

With the preliminaries out of the way, she started by asking Cutter to tell her what role Casey Hill had in his company.

It was a simple enough question but as soon as he heard the name Cutter froze. Jenny thought that he looked terrified. Fiona repeated the question.

Instead of answering, Cutter entered a prolonged and whispered discussion with his lawyer, who intervened on his behalf.

'Mr Cutter has requested that before we proceed with this interview that you provide an assurance that his presence here and anything that is said is not recorded on the police's computer system.'

Jenny and Fiona looked at each other knowingly.

'I'm sorry, I couldn't possibly accede to that request,' Fiona said. 'But could Mr Cutter explain why he would want us to abandon our usual recording methods?'

Suderman looked at his client, who started to rock back and forth muttering what sounded like 'he'll know' repeatedly. Fiona looked on, trying to keep her poker face intact despite the agitated display.

'I think you need to get your client in order, Mr Suderman,' she said, suspending the interview and taking Jenny with her so that the two men could consult in private.

When they returned Cutter seemed calmer. He apologised for his behaviour, saying that he'd been under a lot of strain. Fiona restarted the tape and repeated her question.

'Mr Hill was a valued employee,' Cutter said. 'The whole company was devastated to hear about his death. He was an accountant working on several client accounts.'

'Good,' Fiona said. 'Before Mr Hill was murdered, he came to us with allegations that your company is involved in money laundering for various criminal enterprises. Do you know anything about that?'

If she was expecting Cutter to be flustered by the question, then the calm denial that followed was unhelpful. It was though just the opening gambit. Fiona proceeded to lay out a series of documents in front of Cutter and his lawyer.

'These documents show that over the last few years your firm, Mr Cutter, has been systematically laundering money on behalf of one of your clients. Would you care to comment?'

Cutter went bright red and became agitated once more.

'Where did you get these documents from?' he demanded. 'They're fakes.'

Suderman placed a hand on his shoulder to quieten him.

'What my client is asking is whether you have verified the origin of these documents,' he said.

'We're confident that they are genuine,' Fiona said, 'and based on the information contained in them officers are, as we speak, executing a warrant to seize all relevant records and computer equipment from Cutter Associates.'

Cutter looked devastated.

'So, can you confirm that you were involved in this money laundering activity?' Fiona repeated.

'No comment.'

'We will be challenging the admissibility of these documents, which have clearly been stolen from my client's company,' Suderman said. 'I will also be arguing that as it was based on stolen property, the warrant to seize material from Cutter Associates should be struck out and that any evidence obtained through it also be deemed inadmissible.'

'Well, that's an argument for another day,' Jenny said, 'but your client should know that money laundering is the least of his problems.'

'Perhaps you should enlighten us,' Suderman said.

'We believe that the money that is being laundered relates to people smuggling and possibly drugs as well. One operation we can link the money to led to the death of a ten-year-old child. How does you client feel about having that on his conscience?'

She could see Cutter go pale.

'But the real problem for Mr Cutter lies in the effort made by his client to cover all this up, leading to two murders, including Casey Hill, and an attempted murder. This is not a matter of conscience but of him being implicated in those deeds, conspiracy to murder, maybe even going as far as commissioning the killer.'

Fiona chipped in with more detail.

'We have access to the killer's bank account, we'll be able to trace the payments to her back to the source, and once we open the routes used by Mr Cutter to wash the money, I believe that we'll find that some of that cash was used to hire her.'

Jenny could see that the series of assumptions they had laid out were hitting home. Cutter started to bluster.

'I had nothing to do with those murders,' he said. 'You can't pin them on me.'

'Oh. I disagree,' Jenny said. 'My colleague here is an expert on these things, we're already halfway to tracing the money back to you, and once we have all the records from your company, we'll have all the proof we need. You're going down for a very long time.'

Fiona knew they were stretching things a little in terms of what solid evidence the team had secured, but equally she knew that she had to push this man as hard as she could.'

A look of sheer panic crossed Cutter's face; it was obvious that he hadn't signed up for any of this. Suderman was trying to calm him down and persuade him to revert to a 'no comment' interview, but his pleas were having no effect.

Fiona decided to press home their advantage. She poured a glass of water and offered it to Cutter. He took it gratefully and gulped a large mouthful.

'Perhaps you could help yourself by telling us what you know,' she suggested.

Cutter stared at them, trance-like. Jenny wondered whether they'd triggered some sort of breakdown. She wanted to shake him back into consciousness, but was saved the trouble by Suderman, who gently placed his hand on his client's arm and whispered in his ear.

'We would like a break so I can consult my client,' Suderman said.

Fiona agreed, stopped the taping, and walked out to join Alaya and Cornwell in the observation room. Alaya had already switched off the sound so that they couldn't hear the conversation between their suspect and his lawyer.

'I hope you can back up all these claims,' Cornwell said.

'Oh, don't worry, I think we've got him bang to rights,' Fiona responded. 'What we need to do now is get him to admit to it and give us some names.'

'I think you're almost there,' Jenny said. 'He knows the game is up, now we just have to offer him an incentive.'

Before they could discuss it further Suderman passed them a message that he and Cutter were ready to resume and that his client wanted to make a statement. They settled themselves back into their seats and restarted the tape.

'Before we commence,' Suderman said, 'I want to know what's on offer to my client if he gives you the information you want. For starters any charge relating to these murders must be off the table. Mr Cutter was not involved in these heinous acts.'

'If he can give us the person who hired the killer, then I will certainly make that recommendation,' Fiona said.

Suderman prompted Cutter to proceed.

'As you have said, I have been running money given to me by an old colleague through my company's accounts,' he said, 'with the purpose of legitimising it. That money has then been transferred to various offshore banks. I will of course help you to identify where it has ended up once you have all my records.'

'And can you tell me where that money has come from?' Fiona asked.

'My client is…er, a facilitator. He has a unique skill set that he uses to create an environment in which others can safely commit crimes.'

'I think you're going to have to explain that one,' Jenny said.

'Essentially, he has used his ICT knowledge to access your computer systems and that of Customs and Excise, and is able to monitor ongoing cases, get advance details of raids and take advantage of weaknesses in your systems to send you on wild goose chases.'

'Preposterous,' Fiona said. 'I'd be prepared to believe that he'd paid somebody off to provide that information, but there is no way he could get into those systems without us knowing about it.'

'We're not talking about any old ICT expert here; my colleague is a genius. I believe that if you actively look for the trojan then you'll find it.'

'Okay, let's suppose we believe you,' Jenny said, 'what exactly is your colleague doing with this information?'

'As I said, he is passing on information about Customs and Excise rotas and operations to assist others to bring contraband into the country. He's informing his clients of police operations that might compromise their activities, and he's finding safe houses and storage facilities for them, which he is able to protect with remote surveillance and other measures.'

'Like having people who stumble onto one of his safe houses killed, for example?' Jenny intervened.

'I know nothing about that," Cutter responded. 'My role was confined entirely to legitimising and banking the fees he got for that work.'

'Some of that money was used to pay a hired assassin,' Fiona said. 'Perhaps you'd like to give us the name of this so-called genius.'

'I'm sorry – really, I am, but that's more than my life is worth.'

Cutter was looking terrified again, which underlined the calibre of criminal he'd been dealing with.

'Okay,' Jenny said, 'the documentation we have refers throughout to somebody called Hal, would that be Harold McQueen, and is he the client you have been referring to?'

Silence.

'We know that you once ran a software company with Mr McQueen, that you were friends at college, and we have a witness who tells us that he's been at social events at which both of you were present. So can you confirm that McQueen is the so-called mastermind you've been referring to?'

Cutter dropped his head and muttered an almost inaudible 'yes'.

'Louder, for the tape, please. Mr Cutter.'

'Yes, Harold McQueen is the man I've been laundering money for.'

'Thank you.'

'I think you've got everything you want now,' Suderman said.

'No, I don't think we do,' Fiona replied. 'If your client wants this deal, he needs to tell us how we can find Mr McQueen, and of course we'll want all this in a written statement, and an undertaking that he will give evidence at Mr McQueen's trial.'

Cutter looked beaten, resigned to his fate. He nodded his consent.

'I don't have an address for him. In fact, I doubt if he even goes by his given name anymore. However, when I want to meet him, I know that I will find him in a small café just off Leicester Square.

'Hal conducts all his business there. He is there from 10am to midday every Monday, Wednesday, and Friday. That's where you'll find him.'

Fiona noted the information and finished the interview. She told Suderman that they would not be charging Cutter yet but would do so the next day once she'd had a chance to consult with the CPS. She confirmed that the charges would relate to the money laundering.

Alaya entered the room to escort Cutter back to the cells. Fiona, Jenny, and Cornwell headed back to the squad room where Appleton was waiting for them.

'Do you believe any of this nonsense?' he asked.

'I don't know,' Fiona said, 'but it would explain a lot.'

'I certainly believe that McQueen is capable of something like that,' Cornwell said.

Appleton nodded.

'Okay, I need to let the Commissioner know, and we'll somehow have to find somebody as clever as our Mr McQueen to undo all the damage he's done.

'In the meantime, let's keep everything as close to our chests as we can and just keep paper records.'

'I have somebody who might be able to help,' Cornwell offered. 'I'll need to clear it with my superiors but given that we're talking a hack that could...has compromised the whole security of the UK, I'm sure he'll be happy to help out.'

'Good, get him to liaise with the Commissioner's office. In the meantime, it's a Sunday for God's sake, you've all been at it seven days solid, take a break and come back tomorrow refreshed and ready to close this case once and for all.

'I, for one, am missing my Sunday roast.'

He left them to wind things up for the day, passing Pat and Jane on the way out. They were weighed down with evidence bags containing files and equipment. There were more computers on a trolley behind them.

'Well. That's going to keep you busy for a bit,' Jenny said.

'Is that the stuff from Cutter's office?' Fiona asked.

Pat confirmed it was.

'Good, get it booked in, assign all the computers to the technical people, and leave the paperwork until tomorrow. We've been ordered to go and have a roast dinner, apparently.'

'I don't know about you, but I could murder a good Yorkshire pudding,' Jenny said. 'Do you think your Super will have any spare?'

They laughed.

'Before we go,' Fiona said, 'we've got to work out how we're going to pick up McQueen tomorrow morning.'

'We don't even know what he looks like,' Alaya said, entering the room.

'Don't worry about that,' Cornwell said. 'I took possession of his personnel file before I got here. I'll pull out some photographs. They're a bit old, but I'll get our tech guys to run some computer-generated aging software to help us identify him.'

'Great, reconvene here at 7.30am tomorrow,' Fiona said, 'that'll give us a couple of hours to put together a makeshift surveillance team. Remember, nothing on the computer, we're doing things the old-fashioned way.'

As the team wound up for the day, she turned to Jenny and Jane.

'We can go and find a roast dinner if you want, but I'm going to have to come back here afterwards to do some preparation work.'

'No worries, I'll give you a hand,' Jenny said.

'Count me in too, I'll make a start on that paperwork from Cutter Associates,' Jane added. 'After all, I've only got the hotel to go back to otherwise, and somebody's got to keep an eye on you two.'

Jenny noted the look of mischief on Jane's face as she said this and decided to let the remark go.

'Don't worry, Jane, we're getting to the end of this case, you'll soon be reunited with your husband.'

Fiona sighed.

'Are you two coming, or are you just going to stand there squabbling for the rest of the day?'

Chapter Twenty

The next morning Jenny was awoken by the insistent buzzing of her phone. Fiona groaned and turned away from the noise.

An abnormally warm night had meant that they were both sleeping naked on top of the covers, a fact that now tempted Jenny to ignore the call altogether and indulge in more carnal activities instead.

She gently stroked Fiona's back, kissed her on the nape of her neck, and then reached for the phone. It was a WhatsApp video call from Dawn.

Quickly, she leapt out of bed and ran into the bathroom, almost tripping on the discarded duvet as she did so and closed the door. It was only five-thirty in the morning, what could her wife want she wondered,

Dawn was sitting up in bed looking as if she'd just woken up. Her swollen lip and bruising were now not so noticeable. She smiled as Jenny came into view, having activated her own camera.

'Hey gorgeous, I hope I didn't wake you up.'

No, no, I was about to take a shower,' Jenny lied. 'Got an early start this morning.'

'I just wanted to say how nice it was to see you the other night, even if it was only for an hour. I'm sorry I was too busy to talk yesterday. It's frantic here, even on a Sunday, but I think we're past the worst of it. I can't wait for you to come home.,

'Me too. I hope your journey was uneventful the other night.'

'Yes, apart from Jack being grumpy because I made him stop off for a drink.'

Jenny laughed.

'He's been quite attentive since the assault, even offered a bodyguard,' Dawn added.

'Just take your mother with you, that'll frighten them off. But seriously, if anybody comes near you, they'll have me to answer to.'

She was conscious that Fiona was starting to stir in the bedroom. She could hear movement and realised that she needed to end the conversation quickly to avoid being found out.

'Listen,' she said, 'I must go. We've got an important briefing in an hour and Jane will be knocking on my door shortly to accompany her to the station. I haven't showered yet and I'm starving. I'll ring you later, I promise.'

Dawn smiled and blew her a kiss before ending the call, just before Fiona came into the bathroom.

'What's going on,' she asked, still half asleep.

Jenny stood and kissed her.

'Good morning, beautiful. Just taking a call from Dawn. Shall we get ready for our big day?'

She was shocked at how effortlessly she'd lapsed into a state of deception and betrayal, how easily she'd been able to lie to Dawn. She told herself again that it was just sex, but she knew that there were greater insecurities at play that she'd not yet come to terms with.

For now, however, there were more important things to get on with. She turned on the shower and started getting ready for what she hoped would be the last day of this investigation.

* * *

A few hours later they were sitting in the squad room examining a series of photographs produced for them by Cornwell's tech team.

'These are all extrapolated from the picture we have on his personnel file,' he said. 'I'm afraid it's an imperfect art so we're going to need to use our instincts in knowing when we have the right man.'

Jenny mused over a photograph showing a middle-aged McQueen with long dark hair, a beard, and glasses.

'Your technicians have really gone to town,' she said. 'There must be two dozen different versions of our target here. Have you anticipated him having one of those rubber masks as on Misson Impossible?'

Cornwell grimaced.

'If you can do better, go for it.'

'No. you're right, I apologise. These will be very helpful.'

'Thank goodness for that,' Fiona said. 'Right, the plan is that Jenny and I are going to be inside the café, while Jane and Pat cover the entrance from the north. Alaya and David, you set up to the south.

'We'll have earpieces so that we can monitor communications and a radio each if we need to call for back-up. Once our man enters the café, you four are to move closer to prevent him escaping but leave the arrest to us.

'We have no idea what time McQueen is going to show up if he comes at all. We just have the two-hour window that Cutter believes our man will make an appearance. Let's hope he's right or we'll be doing this again on Wednesday.

'Right, we all know what we're doing, let's get on with it.'

* * *

An hour later, Jenny was sitting opposite Fiona in a small café a few streets away from Leicester Square. They'd positioned themselves so that between them all ten of the tables and the door were in view. A pot of coffee, a jug of milk and two mugs sat on the table in front of them.

In addition, Jenny had a large pain au chocolat, which she had half-heartedly offered to share. As she plunged a knife into the pastry, she was pleased that Fiona had rebuffed the offer.

All the tables were occupied with a variety of people, tourists, commuters and locals, tucking into cooked breakfasts.

One fastidious looking man in a pin-stripe suit sipped his coffee while slowly eating a croissant, piece by piece, keeping crumbs to a minimum. It was performance art at its best and had Jenny captivated, so much so that Fiona had to warn her against staring.

At another table, a couple were seated with two pre-teen children, demolishing full English breakfasts and a mound of toast. Next to them two women wearing denim romper suits were having an animated discussion over a pot of tea.

Jenny looked at her watch, it was just nine-o-clock, there was still plenty of time. She would have preferred to have spent more time in the office before taking up position, but when making the arrangement with the owner, he'd insisted that they come early, or he couldn't guarantee them a table.

A voice in her ear confirmed that both Alaya and Jane were in position with nothing yet to report. Fiona, who'd also had the same message looked across at her.

'I suppose we just wait now,' she said. 'I do think that we need to talk though, and this seems to be as good a time as any.'

'What do you want to talk about?'

'Us, I suppose. I know Dawn rang you this morning. What are your plans once this is all over?'

Jenny put her hand on Fiona's.

'You know I'll be going back to Cardiff and married life with Dawn. We're on the verge of buying a house together, and I think I need to give that life a chance. We might even consider children.'

'Of course. I just wanted to get things straight in my own mind.'

'We've said all along that this is just sex. getting the wild side out of my system. I hope you didn't think that it was more than that.'

'No, of course not.'

Fiona seemed a bit flustered and was clearly struggling to control her own emotions.

'I'm sorry,' she said. 'You're right of course. We've both been very clear that this was just a fling. It's just that since that moment outside the car park on Saturday night I've become a bit more attached to you. It's going to be hard watching you go back to domestic bliss.'

'Perhaps we'd better cool it down then. I don't want to hurt you,' Jenny said. 'If it's any consolation, I'll miss you terribly. It isn't going to be easy settling back down in Cardiff.'

They lapsed into an awkward silence, still holding hands over cold coffee cups, almost oblivious to the movement around them.

The clientele at the café had now switched completely. The early breakfasters had moved on and were being replaced by people dropping in for more social interaction - the two women enjoying pastries and coffee while discussing the latest goings on in their street, an elderly man with a long-dishevelled beard reading his newspaper, and two cyclists, wearing all the professional gear, grabbing some sustenance before heading on their way.

The detective's reverie was broken by Cornwell's voice coming through their earpieces.

'I think I see him,' he said. 'Heading your way.'

'Are you sure?' Fiona said quietly, activating a microphone fixed to her lapel.

'Yes, almost certainly. His appearance has changed markedly, but Alaya and I are both positive that it's him.'

'Okay, take up your positions nearer the cafe and stand by.'

The door rattled as it opened, and Jenny felt a blast of air hit her face. She glanced in the direction of the street to see a tall, thin man enter.

She already knew from his personnel file that McQueen was in his mid-thirties, but she wasn't ready for the transformation from the photo held by the security services.

He had thick, yellowy hair fashioned into a quiff, which hung loosely over his forehead. His skin was smooth, almost translucent, with sunken cheeks and large eyes.

He was dressed in a black polo neck, black trousers, a black jacket and expensive black leather sandals with yellowing toenails poking out in a way that caused her to gag, He sat down at a table near the door and started to consult his phone.

Jenny pulled her own device out and opened the photographs that Cornwell had given them. There was no doubt about it, this was their mark. She showed her phone to Fiona, who nodded, and the two women stood and approached the man.

McQueen looked up nonchalantly as they approached, unphased by the warrant cards that they were holding out for him to look at.

'Can I assist you, officers?' he said, quietly.

'Yes, you can,' Fiona responded. 'We believe that you are Harold Anthony Lawrence McQueen, and we would like you to come with us to answer questions about a number of crimes we are currently investigating.'

McQueen got slowly to his feet and pulled a wallet out of his pocket.

'I'm afraid that you've mistaken me for somebody else,' he said. 'My name is Edward Teach. I'm a website designer and I know nothing about any crimes. Here is my driving licence.'

He handed Fiona a plastic card containing his photograph and the name Edward Teach. There was also an address on it, in south London.

Jenny laughed.

'You really expect us to believe that?' she said. 'If you're going to masquerade as Blackbeard the least you could do is grow some facial hair. Will you be coming quietly or do I have to arrest you formally and handcuff you.'

Fiona stared at her for a minute, wondering again how she knew all this stuff and then focused on McQueen who was scanning the premises for a way out. He took note of the four other detectives who were now blocking his escape from the café and inspected Fiona's warrant card again.

'Well, naturally, I'm perfectly happy to accompany you Inspector if only so we can clear up this confusion. Please be good enough to lead the way.'

As they left the café, Jenny turned to Jane.

'Would you believe his alias is as one of the pirates of the Caribbean?'

'He doesn't look much like Johnny Depp,' she replied. 'Maybe he has hidden depths.'

Jenny groaned.

* * *

Back at the station, Jenny and Fiona took McQueen to be booked in. The custody sergeant looked on bemused as their prisoner produced not just his driving licence, but his passport as well, to back up his claim to be Edward Teach.

He sighed and shook his head, contemplating the ingenuity and stupidity of the criminal classes as he entered the name in the record book, before escorting McQueen to the cells where he was to be allowed to cool his heels for a few hours while the police searched his home.

When they got back to the squad room, Alaya was waiting for them with a search warrant. Fiona already had the keys from McQueen to his house. The three detectives piled into a car and headed across London to get there.

It was an anonymous semi-detached sitting quietly at the end of a suburban cul-de-sac. The front garden was well-maintained with a manicured lawn and weed-free flower beds, while the more modern-looking UPVC windows and front door looked like they'd only recently been installed.

At Fiona's request, they donned all-in-one forensic suits and PVC gloves so as not to compromise any evidence. Jenny was sceptical but she understood that protecting the chain of evidence was essential.

Alaya was sent around the back in case anybody else was in the property and were seeking to escape and then approached the front door cautiously. There didn't appear to be an alarm though she noticed that the hallway, and presumably all the rooms were monitored by cameras.

Together, the two Inspectors checked the downstairs room by room before opening the back door to allow Alaya inside.

The house, a three-bed semi, was modestly furnished with a single combined living and dining room dominated by a massive television screen. A fully fitted kitchen completed the downstairs arrangement.

Alaya picked up a laptop sitting next to a large sofa and bagged it before the three women moved upstairs. One of the bedrooms had been converted into an office containing a laptop docking station linked to three large screens and a large colour laser printer.

A filing cabinet stood next to the equipment, but it didn't contain anything useful apart from a bottle of Scotch and three glasses, some computer manuals and a tool kit. The expected hoard of compromising documents was absent. Nevertheless, Fiona decided to bag the Scotch for fingerprints and DNA comparisons.

Jenny pulled down the loft ladder and tentatively climbed it with a torch in hand. Pressing a light switch by the entrance revealed that the attic was fully boarded and contained several boxes full of books. They decided to leave these for the forensic team to sift through, then made their way back downstairs into the kitchen.

There was a walk-in pantry near the entrance, leading under the stairs. It was empty apart from a wooden trap door in the floor.

This was unexpected, although it was common in the richer parts of central London for residents to expand downwards, they were not aware that this trend had extended to the suburbs and Fiona said, as far as she knew, she didn't believe that any of the properties in this area had cellars.

The entrance was obviously well-used as it opened easily for Alaya and there was a hook arrangement to keep the door open. They descended wooden stairs into a well-lit passageway that sloped further downwards. At the far end was a large metal door.

Fiona searched the set of keys that had been taken from McQueen until she found one that would fit and opened it. They switched on the light to reveal a large mainframe computer happily buzzing away inside some sort of metal cage.

The room itself was about ten feet square and just high enough to allow an adult male to stand comfortably. The walls had all been whitewashed. There was no other furniture in the room, which meant that they were able to walk around the cage comfortably and examine it from every angle.

Further examination revealed that the mesh that formed the walls of the cage was made of some sort of conductive material.

'It's a Faraday cage,' Alaya said.

'Sorry, what?' Jenny was not familiar with the term.

'A Faraday cage, it's designed to shield the computer from external electromagnetic forces and also acts to stop anybody else finding the machine other than from walking right up to it as we've just done.'

'This is most probably what he's using to hack our computer system,' Fiona said.

Jenny went to open the cage, but the others stopped her.

'Let's leave that to the boffins,' Fiona said. 'We don't want to inadvertently destroy any evidence with our inexpert ways.'

Alaya was studying the set up closely.

'Do you think that the laptop is networked with this? If so, we might be able to access it that way. I'd imagine that there must be some cabling underneath the floor. It's certainly going to need an internet connection of some sort.'

'Well, the odds are that this computer genius has some pretty strong security on all this techie stuff,' Jenny said.

'Let's hope that our people are up to it then,' Fiona said. 'If not, we're going to have to persuade him to let us in.'

Alaya dialled the number for Forensics, but there was no signal, either because of the Faraday cage, or probably because they were in the cellar.'

'I don't have a signal, has anybody else?'

Both Jenny and Fiona checked their devices and confirmed that they were in the same position.

Once they were back in the kitchen, they were able to make the calls they needed to. Alaya offered to stay behind to coordinate the operation while the other two left for the office.

'Right,' said Fiona, 'I think it's time we found out what Mr McQueen has to say for himself, and perhaps get this laptop open. We'll have you back in the arms of your loved one before you know it, Jen.'

She strode purposefully to the car, leaving Jenny looking askance at this last remark. Had their conversation earlier upset her lover more than she realised. She shrugged.

There was nothing she could do about it now, but still, she didn't want to leave on bad terms with Fiona. They needed to have a conversation soon.

Chapter Twenty-One

A couple of hours later, Fiona, Jenny, Jane, and Cornwell gathered in the squad room to discuss their interview strategy. Appleton was there as an observer. Just as they were starting, Pat walked in holding McQueen's laptop. He looked exasperated.

'I've spent an hour with the technicians on this machine,' he said, 'and they tell me that it is the most secure system they've ever come across, some sort of biometric access plus at least two levels of passwords and a remote access verification.

'Our only chance of getting into it is to ask McQueen to open it for us.'

Appleton harrumphed loudly.

'Bloody infernal machines,' he said, 'in my day the villains used brute force and their wits to steal from you, nowadays they can do it from the comfort of their own bedroom.'

Jenny, enraptured by his broad accent, struggled to get visions of Monty Python's Four Yorkshiremen sketch out of her head. Cornwell came to her rescue before she started sniggering openly.

'I've got a boffin in my team that might have a bit more success,' he said. 'I'll get him to come in and give you a hand.'

Fiona indicated her agreement.

'Thanks, I think this machine and the mainframe its linked to are going to be the key to unravelling this case and maybe unravelling some criminal networks involved in people smuggling and drug running as well.

'Where are we on breaking McQueen's false identify?'

'He's been quite thorough,' Jane said. 'I've been in touch with the General Register Office who've confirmed that there is a birth certificate registered there in the name of Edward Teach. It gives the same date and place of birth as McQueen so clearly; he didn't fancy having a second birthday like the King.

'There's no death certificate for that person, so this is not classic ID fraud when somebody assumes the identity of a deceased child…'

'Like *Day of the Jackal*,' Appleton interrupted.

'Yes, like that really old film,' Jane continued, enjoying the putdown. 'It's likely that he hacked their computer to create the record. It looks like he also did the same to get himself a National Insurance number, and then used that documentation to obtain a driver's licence and a passport.'

'So, we're stymied,' Fiona said. 'We can't prove he's not who he says he is, which means that he's got the drop on us from the outset.'

Jane smiled.

'Not necessarily. Fortunately, David here, has got us McQueen's personnel records from when he worked in GCHQ. These are not standard employment files. They also contain his DNA profile and fingerprints.

'While you were searching his home, we were carrying out forensic comparisons and we can confirm absolutely that the man we have in the cells is Harold McQueen.'

'Well, thank God for that,' Appleton said. 'Couldn't you have started with that?'

Jane looked nonplussed, but Jenny intervened on her behalf.

'I think, sir, that Jane was making the point that this man is clever and slippery by giving us a detailed account of the effort he's made to disappear. I thought her explanation was well-worth listening to.'

Appleton harrumphed again.

'Well, you'd better get on with it then,' he said as he left the room muttering to himself about 'bloody cheeky detectives from South Wales'.

'Okay,' Fiona said, 'I'll lead on the interview, with Pat assisting. Jenny and David can observe. Jane, can you please liaise with Alaya on cataloguing any evidence coming back from McQueen's house.

'We'll start by breaking the false ID and then use the documentation we got from Allison Hill to press him on the money laundering and the associated activities such as the human trafficking you unearthed in Swansea, Jenny. And then we'll move on to the murders.

'I think we've got a pretty strong case already with those documents, Cutter's evidence and what we got from Abadi. What we're missing is proof that the order to kill Councillor Tresham, Casey Hill and Gerald Rebane came from McQueen.

'If he doesn't admit it then we'll need to rely on the technicians opening his computers. Frankly, I don't like those odds, so we need to get this interview right.'

Half an hour later, Fiona, Jenny, Cornwell, and Pat were standing in the observation room looking at a closed-circuit TV feed of McQueen and his lawyer conferring in the interview room.

The sound was off, so they couldn't hear what was being said, but it was obvious that McQueen was getting quite animated in instructing his brief.

Jenny noticed that the lawyer was Michael Suderman, the same man who'd represented Cutter. She didn't believe in coincidences. This reinforced the connection between the two men. She watched as Fiona and Pat entered the room and introduced themselves and then turned the sound on.

Fiona started by reading McQueen his rights and then asked him and his lawyer to identify themselves for the recording. McQueen introduced himself as Edward Teach.

'I think it's time we ended this charade, Mr McQueen,' Fiona said.

Suderman started to intervene, but Fiona held up her hand to stop him.

'You may well have a done a good job in carving out a new identity for yourself, but we have DNA and fingerprint evidence from your previous employment at GCHQ. We are one hundred percent certain that you are Harold McQueen.'

Suderman looked shocked as if he hadn't been briefed properly. McQueen was unphased.

'No comment,' he said.

'Okay, now we have that out of the way, shall we start with the money that's being laundered on your behalf. John Cutter has given us a statement that he's been washing cash you've passed to him; money that he tells us has been obtained through you facilitating people trafficking and drug smuggling. Can you confirm if that is the case.'

'No comment.'

Fiona laid out a series of documents in front of McQueen,

'These were obtained for us by the late Casey Hill and have been authenticated by John Cutter. They confirm the details of the money laundering and traces it directly back to you. The evidence is irrefutable.'

'No comment.'

'Are you denying that these documents relate to activity initiated by you?'

'No comment.'

Suderman took the papers and started to glance through them, while Fiona moved on.

'I note that you're not denying any of this, so let me outline some of the consequences of your criminal activity. A safe house in Swansea, which we believe was provided by you and which you managed on behalf of an organised crime group, was raided by the police, and although the occupants had moved on, they left behind the body of a ten-year-old boy, an Albanian national.

'We believe that you hold a personal responsibility for that death.'

McQueen looked unfazed.

'No comment.'

Fiona was about to move on when Suderman intervened.

'Hold on a minute, Inspector. Looking through these documents again, I can see no direct connection to my client other than the disputed testimony of John Cutter. However, as you've introduced that connection, I am going to have to recuse myself from this case.

'Mr Cutter is my client and it's clear that I cannot represent him and er… Mr McQueen given that they have conflicting interests. I must insist therefore that this interview is suspended while Mr McQueen finds new counsel.'

Fiona looked furious. She recovered quickly.

'Okay, but when you pass this on perhaps you'll alert your successor that Mr McQueen is facing charges of money laundering, facilitating drug and people smuggling, hacking secure government computers, including the General Register Office, fraud, dishonestly obtaining a driving licence and a passport and most seriously, two counts of murder and one charge of attempted murder.'

Neither Suderman nor McQueen reacted to this list of crimes, so Fiona picked up her papers and tablet computer and left them to it.

Watching, Jenny suspected that this conflict of interest had been deliberately manufactured to play for time, but of course they wouldn't be able to prove that. On the screen she saw two uniformed officers arrive to escort McQueen back to the cells. It was time to take stock.

'It's funny how it took so long for that solicitor to discover he had a conflict of interest,' Cornwell said.

'Do you think so?' Jenny said. 'These tactics aren't going to help him.'

She walked with Cornwell back to the squad room where Jane was set to brief Fiona and Pat on the latest developments.

'I've just heard back from the Met's IT people,' she said. 'They've been rooting around in our computer system and have managed to identify a very sophisticated trojan that has been communicating directly to McQueen's mainframe computer. Superintendent Appleton is apoplectic.'

'I bet he is,' Fiona said. 'I imagine that there'll be some choice words higher up the food chain as well.'

'Now that we know what to look for, a search is underway to see if there's a comparable virus in the computers operated by Customs and Excise, Inland Revenue and the DSS,' Jane continued.

'This finding has confirmed what we were told by John Cutter, that McQueen has been using the information he obtained with this trojan to sell an early warning system to criminals, and to find holes in our networks through which goods and people can be smuggled.

'If Councillor Tresham hadn't found one of these safe houses and been subsequently murdered, then we may never have found out what he was doing.'

Fiona whistled softly.

'So, we've stumbled onto a massive criminal enterprise,' she said. 'And one that has shown up major vulnerabilities in key computer systems used by law enforcement agencies.

'I know that this guy is a genius, but I think that once this is sorted out, we're going to need reassurance that this can't happen again, otherwise we'll be back to doing everything on paper and card indexes, and we saw how disastrous that system was during the Yorkshire Ripper investigation.'

'We're going to need access to McQueen's computer if we're to find out the full extent of this infiltration,' Jenny said, 'so David, when can you get your boffin here. This is urgent.'

Cornwell jumped to his feet and started to head out of the door.

'I'm on it right now,' he said as he disappeared into the corridor.

'Is there anything else, Jane?' Fiona asked.

'Yes, I've now got access to McQueen's bank accounts.

'The concern is that the amount of money in these accounts is large enough to fund incidental expenditure such as hiring somebody like Abadi and renting safe houses, but it doesn't really reflect the scale of the operation.

'Colleagues in the financial crimes unit have suggested that, other than the cash Cutter washed for him, most of his money is held as bitcoin, which means that it could be anywhere. They say that the bulk of the cash is likely held in what is called a 'non-custodial cold hardware wallet'.

'That's like an offline hard drive that can only be accessed by a private decryption key and can't be hacked. In other words, recovering funds under the Proceeds of Crime Act will be impossible.

'Fortunately, that doesn't affect our case against McQueen. The payments out of his petty cash account pretty much tie him to the murders.'

'Some petty cash,' Jenny said,

'Thanks to Inspector Keaton persuading the Swiss to open up Abadi's numbered bank account to us,' Jane continued, 'I can now link payments directly from McQueen's accounts to hers, and at the appropriate dates.'

'Got him,' Fiona said triumphantly. 'Let's see him 'no comment' this one.'

'Totally,' Jenny said, 'but I also want to know what his motives were.'

'What do you mean?'

'Well, think about it. He's had this operation running for years, under the radar, enabling all sorts of criminal activity because of the information he's been able to take from us without us knowing.

'And then suddenly, he kills two people and incapacitates a third, drawing attention to his operation and to himself. Did he have no choice? It doesn't look like we would be probing into his activities in anything like this depth and determination if those murders hadn't happened.

'He might well have continued to carry on unnoticed, with law enforcement picking up on one or two of his operations, perhaps suspecting we had people on the inside being paid to tip off the gangs, maybe wondering about too many coincidences, but never getting to the nub of the problems... that our so-called secure computer systems were feeding him information like there was no tomorrow.

'So why draw attention to himself by commissioning these hits?'

'All very good questions,' Fiona said. 'I suggest we ask him once he's got himself lawyered up again. In the meantime, I'm starving. Does anybody fancy going out for food?'

The nearest pub was the one they'd frequented on Jenny and Jane's first night in London. That evening seemed an eternity away now. Once more Jenny admired the solid oak bar, polished brass, and the pictures of various celebrities on the walls, again she gasped at the prices.

Shortly after they'd arrived, Jenny, Jane and Fiona were joined by Alaya, straight from supervising the forensic sweep of McQueen's house. She didn't have much to report that they didn't already know.

The search had failed to uncover any paperwork related to McQueen's criminal activities, or anything else. She surmised that he kept everything online, which was to be expected given his expertise and line of work.

They'd been unable to find any fingerprints other than McQueen's and, apart from the hidden mainframe in the cellar, the house could have been any one of thousands in suburban London.

'So, we're back to square one, then,' Fiona said. 'We can connect him to the murders and have a reasonable case on the money laundering, conspiracy and some other minor offences, but if we want to get into the real nitty gritty, we must get into his machines.'

They ate in silence, pondering the enormity of the enterprise they'd uncovered but unsure how they were going to get the information to put the case to bed.

As they finished, Jane stepped outside to take a call from her husband, while Alaya headed back to the office to write up her report for filing on HOLMES 2 once the system had been cleared and declared secure again.

Jenny wondered whether the others had taken the diplomatic route by leaving her alone with Fiona. If so, their efforts were lost on her colleague, who decided that she too must get back to the office.

'Before we go back, have we decided what we're doing tonight?' Jenny asked.

Fiona hesitated as if struggling with a painful dilemma.

'Oh. I don't know, Jen. I don't want to complicate things for you any more than they are at present.'

'You won't be,' Jenny said trying to reassure her. Fiona, however, was having none of it.

'Look, Jen, this isn't easy for me. You know I've developed feelings for you. It's no longer just sex and a bit of fun. You're heading back to domestic bliss very soon, leaving me alone back in London.

'You've already made it clear that this relationship isn't going anywhere. I've got to think about my emotional wellbeing, I can't afford to get even more involved. You've made your choice, now you must let me get on with my life.'

Jenny could see the logic behind those words. She had no right to expect anything else given her commitment to Dawn. Still, she hadn't expected Fiona to fall for her like this.

'So, you're ending it?'

'Really, you're putting this on me. This is on you, Jen. If you want to make a go of this then do so, but don't think you can play me off against your wife. If you want me, then choose me. Otherwise, let's call it a day.'

She stood up as if to leave. Jenny took her hand to delay her.

'Please don't let this end on a sour note,' she said. 'You know I have feelings for you, but I also have a life in Cardiff. I accept your decision. Let's stay as friends if nothing else.'

Fiona blushed a little and then kissed Jenny on the cheek.

'Of course,' she said. 'We're both adults. Let's act like it. Friends it is.'

Jenny couldn't help feeling empty somehow, as if her own anxieties and insecurities had been laid bare for all to see. What was it about her that she couldn't be content with a steady relationship? Why was she so unsettled in her own life?

She knew she had to focus, get this investigation out of the way first and then try and sort herself out. Just twenty-four more hours and then back to domestic bliss in Cardiff when she would have the space to explore her own feelings and try to get back on an even keel.

Despite all the angst, she couldn't wait.

Chapter Twenty-Two

When they got back to the squad room, Alaya was waiting for them. McQueen had a new lawyer; he'd arrived half an hour ago and was being briefed. They would be able to resume the interview shortly.

Furthermore, Cornwell had returned with his ICT expert, and he was starting to look at the laptop. Fiona grinned.

'Let's hope he can break into it,' she said. 'I'd like a chat with him before we go back in. Do you want to join me, Jenny?'

The two of them walked to the small side office where Cornwell was settling his technician in. The two men stood as they entered.

'Ah, Fiona and Jenny, can I introduce you to Jim Walters. If anybody can break into this machine, then he can.'

Jenny was a bit taken aback by Walters' appearance. He was tall and thin, almost emaciated, wearing jeans and a bright red T-shirt. He had a long thin face, straggly blonde hair, and a wispy beard.

She tried to pinpoint who he reminded her of and then it clicked, he was almost a double of Shaggy from the Scooby Doo cartoon. She shook his hand and joined Fiona on the other side of the table, where they could inspect the laptop.

'I must confess, I've never seen anything like this before,' Walters said, 'but I'll give it a go. I've also asked for access to the trojan that infected your mainframe computer, as that might give me some clues as to what we're dealing with. Give me an hour or so and I'll hopefully be able to put together a few ideas as to what this guy has been up to.'

The two Inspectors agreed and walked out with Cornwell back to the squad room, where Fiona laid out the order of business.

'I propose to take Alaya into the interview room, with Jenny and David observing as before. Jane can you and Pat liaise with the IT guy, er…Jim Walters, and ensure he has everything he needs.

'Oh, and keep trawling through McQueen's mobile and internet records to see if anything useful comes up. I believe that the providers have given us access by now. At least that's one thing we don't need a two-hundred-character password to get into.

'If you find anything give me the nod. Both Alaya and I will be wearing earplugs so that messages can be passed to us from the observation room.'

She looked around to see if there were any comments or questions. There weren't.

'Great, let's do this then.'

The new lawyer could well have been a clone of the old one. He was four or five years older than Suderman, with closely cropped hair and designer stubble, but he wore the same uniform of an affluent practitioner, an Armani suit, monogrammed shirt, pocket handkerchief, expensive leather brogues, gold cufflinks and tie pin.

James Erbury worked for the same firm as Suderman, where both were partners. It was a company that specialised in commercial law rather than criminal matters, but Jenny reasoned that they knew enough to make life difficult for the police.

As Fiona and Alaya entered, he stood and introduced himself. Judging by his accent, Fiona reckoned he was a product of one of the more elite public schools.

They settled down and Alaya switched on the recorder, got everybody to introduce themselves and read McQueen his rights once again. Fiona went straight for the jugular.

'In our last session I outlined some of the charges you're facing, Mr McQueen and, just before your previous solicitor pulled the plug, I indicated that we would also be charging you with two murders and an attempted murder.

'We have access to some of your bank accounts and can prove that money was transferred to the offshore account of Rachel Abadi as payment for her to kill Cardiff Councillor Gareth Tresham and Mr Casey Hill, an accountant working for your friend, John Cutter.

'There are also payments to Ms Abadi that coincide with the attempt on the life of Gerald Rebane, a consultant with Mr Cutter's firm and the attempt on my life. Rachel Abadi has confirmed to us that these payments were made for this purpose.

'What do you have to say for yourself?'

McQueen looked shocked, so much so that he couldn't even get his customary 'no comment' out.

Fiona started to outline the circumstances behind Tresham's murder, including details of the safe house the councillor had stumbled on and the death of the ten-year-old boy as the people smugglers fled the house. McQueen stopped her in mid-flow.

'Hold on, Inspector, this is preposterous. I've had nothing to do with these murders. I didn't transfer this… this money and I've never heard of this Rachel Abadi.'

Fiona scoffed.

'You're really doing this; you're just going to deny everything and hope it goes away. Okay, these are the statements that back up what I've been telling you.'

She started to place a series of documents on the table in front of him, one by one. McQueen picked them up and glanced at them, his face growing paler by the second.

In the observation room, Jenny pressed the microphone button.

'I don't know about you, Fiona, but if this guy is acting then he should get an Oscar. He seems genuinely shocked.

Fiona nodded her head to indicate that she'd heard and understood the message. She ploughed on.

'Did you know Casey Hill?'

'No, not really. I knew of him, I think John - that is John Cutter - had mentioned him to me once.'

She placed copies of the documents supplied by Allison Hill on the table.

'Were you aware that he took these documents, which prove you were using Cutter Associates to launder the proceeds of your crimes, to hand them over to us?'

'No, no, of course not. How would I. I've never met the guy, John said nothing to me.'

'So, why did you have Rachel Abadi murder him then?'

'What, are you insane? Of course I didn't do that. I'm not a killer.'

'The evidence says otherwise.'

McQueen put his head in his hands and started to rock back and forth, Erbury turned to look at him and then requested a break.

'I believe my client is unwell,' he said. 'Perhaps you can get a doctor.'

McQueen raised his hand to indicate that he didn't need medical help.

'I'll be okay,' he said. 'I just need a break, some time to think.'

Fiona gathered up the papers and suspended the interview.

'Fine,' she said, 'it's getting late anyway, we'll resume first thing in the morning.'

She walked to the observation room with Alaya while a uniformed officer took McQueen back to the cells. Jenny and Cornwell were still in the observation room. Fiona was furious.

'Can you believe that fuck?' she said, 'he thinks that by denying everything it will all go away.'

'Well, we know that's not going to happen,' Jenny replied.

They went back to the squad room where Walters was waiting for them.

'I hope you've got good news for us,' Fiona said.

Walters shrugged.

'I have news, but I'm not sure you'll like it.'

He led them into the office where he'd been trying to access McQueen's laptop.

'This is a dead loss,' he announced, brandishing the machine. 'The biometrics on this thing are unreal. The only way you're going to get it unlocked is if McQueen does it for you.'

Jenny nodded. She'd had a feeling that would be the conclusion, as had Fiona, but they had to let him try.

'All the information you need will be in the cloud,' Walters continued, 'and the laptop may not be the only way in. If I could have a look at the mainframe computer he keeps in his basement, I may be able to link into it.'

'Great, I'll come with you tomorrow morning,' Jenny volunteered. She'd been feeling like a spare part for some time, and knew that really, she and Jane should head back to South Wales and let Fiona and her team wrap up the case, but she was reluctant to depart before they had a signed confession from McQueen that she could present to Mrs Tresham and her daughter.

'Besides, there was more to say to Fiona. She knew that there was no chance or purpose to reestablishing their relationship, but she also felt that neither of them had secured full closure. If Fiona really had fallen for her, then she thought she had a duty to properly rebuild their friendship before leaving, after all she had feelings for her, too.

As Jenny volunteered for this task, she was conscious that Jane had joined them and was looking aghast at further time away from domestic bliss in Cardiff.

'There's no reason for you to stay, Jane,' she said. 'You should go back to your husband tonight if you can. Take a few days off, you deserve it.'

Jane beamed.

'Are you sure?'

'Yes, absolutely. This case is all but wrapped up. I'll most probably follow on tomorrow once we've had a crack at this computer in McQueen's house.'

Jane took the hint and headed back to the hotel to pack. Meanwhile, Walters had started to brief them on the trojan that had been found in the police computer system.

'I've had a look at the programming behind this bug of McQueen's,' he said, 'and it's very impressive. It's highly sophisticated and suggests that it's constantly learning and updating. Your tech boys had a real job finding it as it can change its appearance, integrate with the other software and basically adapt to whatever they threw at it.

'In the end they had to wipe the whole system and reinstall from back-ups. Even then they're not convinced that they've got it out of there completely.

'My point though, is that having examined some of the work McQueen did when he was with us and knowing what this trojan can do, there is a strong possibility that the mainframe its feeding is an advanced version of that work. It's a highly sophisticated AI, and very possibly heuristic.'

'I'm sorry, you're going to have to put that in English,' Fiona said.

'Of course, the bottom line is that this machine is learning and then updating its own programming. It may even be taking decisions on its own without reference to McQueen, just using the objectives it's been programmed with as a guide.'

'Are you saying that this computer is conscious and acting as an independent entity?' Alaya asked.

'Conscious no, acting independently, quite possibly. Essentially, McQueen told it to get information from our computers and act to protect his paymasters from being exposed. It may well have interpreted that instruction as licence to find other safe houses, pass on warnings, order equipment for them and so on.'

'Bollocks,' Fiona said, dismissively, 'you're making out a case that the computer not McQueen hired Abadi. Not only is that impossible, but you have no evidence to back up your theory. It's pure speculation.'

Walters shrugged.

'I'm just saying that it's possible that McQueen lost control of his invention and didn't realise it.'

Jenny scoffed.

'There's no way he's getting off that easily. The man is a monster and he's going down for it.'

'Oh, I don't doubt it,' Walters said. 'Whether it was him or the computer, he's ultimately responsible for what happened. I'm just saying that if he's busily protesting his innocence in there, he may genuinely not know what really happened.'

Fiona and Jenny left the room in disgust, closely followed by Alaya. Cornwell stayed behind to consult further with Walters.

'Do you believe any of that shit?' Fiona asked.

'Not for one minute, it sounds like pure science fiction to me.'

'And me, but I wouldn't discount it,' Alaya said catching them up. 'There's been massive strides forward in artificial intelligence. If this guy really is a genius, then he may be years ahead of other scientists in developing the sort of machine that can do all of that.'

Fiona looked appalled.

'Not a word of this in front of McQueen or his brief,' she warned. 'I'm not going to give him any sort of get-out clause. He's going down for this, and if he wants to blame his box of tricks then let him convince a jury on his own. He's not getting any help from us.'

Jenny managed to get Fiona on her own just outside the squad room. She seemed reluctant to talk but relented anyway.

'Listen, I'm sorry if things got a bit sticky back in the pub,' Jenny said.

'Don't be daft,' Fiona said. 'Everything's fine.'

'Good, because whatever happens, I want us to stay as friends.'

'And I'm good with that. Look, Jenny I can see that you're struggling. I don't know if it's your PTSD or just that you really are torn between Dawn and me, but you've got to pull yourself together.

'We're on the verge of tying this up, so we'll be able to go our own separate ways, and yes. I'm happy to stay in touch.

'I notice that you've sent Jane home, why don't you go tonight as well? We don't need you to accompany our boffin to McQueen's house. I can send Pat with him if need be. Maybe, you'd be happier getting back to Dawn earlier than you planned.'

Jenny pondered this for a few seconds.

'No, I want to see this investigation out. I need to be able to look the Treshams in the eye when I get back and tell them what happened and why.'

'You don't need to be here for that. I can give you all that once we've wrapped up the interviews and charged him. We've got a custody extension so we might not even be able to conclude things tomorrow. You could be hanging on for another forty-eight hours.'

'I know that, but I'll go back tomorrow, I promise. I've every confidence that you'll have got it all signed and sealed by then.'

'Okay, suit yourself, but for God's sake, chill a bit. We're fine, it was just a brief fling. There's no need to worry and for fuck's sake, get some counselling when you get home. I hate to see you like this.'

Jenny took her hand briefly and then they walked into the squad room.

'Right" Fiona said to Patrick and Alaya, 'we'll call it a day. First thing tomorrow, we'll nail the bastard good and proper. Go and spend some time with your families.'

She turned and smiled at Jenny.

'I'll see you tomorrow, then.'

Jenny took the hint and started to walk back to her hotel. She half-hoped that Fiona would catch her up and propose a last night shag, but it was not to be. She surmised that her one-time lover was at that very moment navigating London traffic on her way home to feed the cat and have a hot bath.

By the time she got to the hotel, Jane had already checked out. Jenny went to her room and put the television on. Should she have a bath and get some sleep? She felt restless.

She picked up her phone to call Dawn and then had second thoughts. She felt lost and alone. If she rang her wife, it would just make her homesick, and that would make her feel worse.

She should have gone home with Jane, perhaps that would have been for the best. Instead, she picked up her coat and left the hotel to find the nearest pub. Good idea or not, she needed a drink.

The place she found was packed with city types unwinding after work with one last drink before heading home to their partners. She sat by the bar and ordered a double whisky, neat, and downed it in one.

She ordered another one. A man started to approach her but had second thoughts when she gave him what she considered her best 'death stare'. She was going to get drunk alone, she decided, and not tolerate any hangers-on wanting to get into her knickers, as if they could.

By the time she'd drunk her sixth double whisky Jenny felt that she'd made her point. She staggered back to her hotel room, puked in the toilet, and fell onto the bed fully clothed. That'll show them, she told herself, as she drifted off into a troubled sleep.

Chapter Twenty-Three

She awoke with a start, shaken from her drunken slumber by the insistent buzzing of the alarm on her mobile phone. Jenny tried to move to switch it off only for her head to fall back on the pillow in agonising pain.

It had been a long time since she'd had a hangover but even so, she couldn't remember it being this bad.

She made a second attempt and this time managed to sit up on the side of the bed, where she tried to take stock. She picked up a water bottle from the bedside table and swallowed half of its contents in one go.

As she stood up, she noted that her blouse and skirt, which she was still wearing. were covered in vomit. She sighed. Fortunately, she still had a clean pair of jeans and a T-shirt she could change into.

Jenny staggered into the bathroom, where she inspected herself in front of a mirror. Her hair was a mess and partially plastered to her face, there were small pieces of undigested food stuck to her mouth and nose and her make-up had run.

She found some pain killers in her bag, washed them down with the remaining contents of the water bottle, stripped off her clothes and climbed into the shower. The hot water was reviving but couldn't completely clear her head, nor could it restore her memory of what exactly she'd done the night before.

There was no doubt about it, she'd been in London too long.

After drying her hair, brushing her teeth, and packing her bag, she went for breakfast. She wasn't sure if she would be able to keep anything down but knew that she had to settle her stomach somehow.

Half-an-hour later she'd checked out of her hotel and was walking to the office, trying not to talk to anybody on the way, while hiding her bloodshot eyes behind a pair of sunglasses.

As she entered the squad room, Fiona looked up and did a double take.

'Bloody hell, what happened to you?'

'I don't want to talk about it,' Jenny responded, plonking her bag on the floor at the side of the desk she'd been assigned for her secondment. 'Shall we just get on with the day, so I can go back to Cardiff.'

'You can go back now, if you wish, I told you last night.'

'Let's not go into that again, please. I'm going to see this through if it kills me.'

Alaya arrived and was swiftly joined by Pat. Both seemed eager to get on with the interrogation of McQueen but were told that they needed to wait for his lawyer. It was just nine-o-clock, Erbury wasn't due for another thirty minutes.

Jenny still had a headache, and she felt a bit woozy but was determined to do what she'd come to do before embarking on the train journey home.

Fiona placed a hand on her upper back.

'Are you sure you're alright?' she said softly. 'You don't look very well.'

'I'm fine,' Jenny said straightening up and looking directly at her. 'Just had one or two too many whiskies last night, that's all.'

'Good, but I suggest you take the sunglasses off before the Super gets in, he likes to see the whites of his officer's eyes when he's dressing them down.'

Jenny smiled and placed the glasses in her bag.

'What time is Jim Walters getting here?' she asked.

'Any minute now, and then you can head out. Don't worry I've got a car for you, but I suggest you let him drive.'

Jenny agreed. Just then Alaya appeared and informed them that McQueen's solicitor had arrived and was briefing his client. Fiona asked Pat to get the locked laptop and McQueen's phone so she could take it in with her and assigned Alaya to be her co-interviewer.

Appleton walked into the room, closely followed by Cornwell and Walters. He took one look at Jenny and smirked.

'Been on the juice, have we?' He asked rhetorically. Jenny ignored him. Even if she'd wanted to answer she didn't feel that she had the wit to come up with a suitable retort.

'Okay,' Appleton continued, addressing the room. 'David and Jim have briefed me on the IT side of things. If what they think is correct, I imagine that we'll have boffins crawling all over this computer once we've managed to access it.

'I believe we've got enough to charge our Mr McQueen with the murders and a whole lot more as well, but it would help if you can persuade him to co-operate and open this damned laptop, Fiona.

'That's our number one priority now and that comes straight from the top. All the brass and their political bosses are anxious to know what damage he's done and, of course, we've got the prospect of closing down quite a few organised crime groups.

'That's assuming that this computer of his hasn't got wind of the fact that he's been arrested and sent out a warning to them.'

'If it has, sir, that won't be because of us,' Fiona said. 'We've kept everything on paper for the time being, nothing on computer, so hopefully Skynet or whatever he's called it doesn't know we have him in custody.'

'Great, good luck,' Appleton said, striding out of the room.

Pat returned with the laptop, and Fiona and Alaya headed down to the interview suite, with Cornwell in tow. Jenny grabbed Walters and they started walking to the carpool area.

* * *

When they got to the interview room, McQueen was still talking to his solicitor. Erbury indicated that the detectives could enter and start the interview. Once Alaya had gone through the rigmarole of introducing those present for the tape and reiterating the caution, Erbury told them that his client wanted to make a statement.

'I've had time to think and reflect since yesterday,' McQueen began, 'and I need to make some things clear.

'Firstly, it's obvious to me that you have evidence of money laundering that may well come back to me and my activities. However, I'm not a killer, I have never been a killer and had nothing to do with the murders you associated me with yesterday.

'I categorically deny ordering the hits you referred to, I am not that stupid. Why would I draw attention to my other activities by assassinating bit players who posed little or no threat to my work.

'This councillor in Cardiff was no threat to me, and while the documents you obtained from Casey Hill would have caused me some inconvenience, I believe that I would have remained free and been able to continue supporting the various groups I am contracted to.

'You would certainly have remained unaware of the trojans I had planted in your computer systems so my core business would have remained unaffected.

'As for the attacks on John Cutter's consultant friend and on one of your colleagues, which I believe I am also accused of, I would have to have been certifiable to have commissioned them. Both attacks were counter-productive and pointless.'

'So, you're continuing to deny any involvement in these attacks, despite the evidence that shows payment to the perpetrator from your bank accounts?' Fiona demanded.

McQueen paused as if he was collecting his thoughts.

'How much do you know about computers. Inspector?' he asked.

'Not as much as you, that's obvious.'

'Yes, well let me put it this way: I constructed a very sophisticated artificial intelligence to facilitate the infiltration of your systems. You may not be familiar with this term, but the objective was to create the world's first heuristic computer, something I was prevented from doing at GCHQ.

'That means that it learns and adapts as it goes along. You will know that I prefer to be called Hal, which is made up of the initials of my Christian names, well if you've ever read *Arthur C Clarke's 2001: A Space Odyssey* then you will know that HAL was also the name of the computer in that book, another heuristic machine.'

'Yes, yes, we know all of this, please get to the point,' Fiona said.

'The point Inspector is that like the original HAL my machine appears to have learnt rather too quickly and learnt all the wrong lessons.'

'So, you're blaming these murders on your computer? Come on Mr McQueen we weren't born yesterday.'

McQueen was unphased, insisting on seeing his story through.

'When I set up my little project, I programmed a series of parameters into HAL and gave it the task of managing the groups who had contracted with me. He was to identify information on the systems I had infiltrated which was pertinent to each group and issue instructions accordingly.'

'Hold on a minute,' Alaya said, 'are you anthropomorphising your computer?'

'Of course, I think of him as my baby. Anyway, if, for example, a group of immigrants were being housed in Swansea, contractors would be hired to install CCTV and the pictures monitored by the machine.

'If something happened that might compromise that operation such as somebody stumbling on it, or a task was entered on the police computer which might lead to a raid, then the contractor would be notified in good time and be able to relocate.

'Equally, if I was asked to facilitate the entry of contraband into the UK, my machine would analyse shift patterns and ongoing operations and identify weak spots.'

'You can get a computer to do all of that?' Alaya asked, impressed despite herself.

'Yes, sergeant, I can.'

'Get on with it,' Fiona said.

'Of course. It has since transpired that my scheme had one fatal flaw, which is the reason I am sitting here with you today.

'Computers have no moral compass, no conscience. This is not the world of Asimov where the robots are programmed with three laws for the safety of humanity, though in retrospect, perhaps that is something I should have done. HAL is not a robot, so it didn't occur to me that such safeguards were necessary.

'Computers do what they're programmed to do, no more and no less, unless that is you allow them the sort of discretion, I built into mine. In this case I set out a path, a set of principles and objectives and let the computer get on with it.

'My HAL did so, following the logic of his programming to the limit, not understanding the value of human life, not being savvy enough to know that certain actions would compromise the whole operation.

'When your councillor stumbled on the Swansea safe house, the computer didn't give instructions to evacuate as he should have done, instead he took steps to eliminate the councillor from the scene and in so doing drew attention to the operation itself.

'I surmise that something similar happened when your HOLMES 2 system revealed that Casey Hill was whistleblowing the money laundering operation. And with each misstep HAL exposed more and more of the business plan until it was too late.'

So, you *are* blaming the computer.' Fiona said, incredulously.

'HAL is my child, my protégé, but unfortunately, he was too innocent for this world, he didn't understand how humans interact, how we reason. He followed his programme to the logical conclusion, which was to hire somebody to kill to achieve his assigned purpose.'

Fiona gave Alaya a look to indicate that she believed McQueen had lost his marbles and then launched into a direct challenge to his narrative.

'Don't give me that bullshit. Everybody knows that computers do what you tell them. If your machine is going around hiring contract killers, and, trust me, I am far from convinced that fairy story holds up, then it's because you told it to.'

McQueen remained unphased by this onslaught, adopting a look of benign superiority as if he were addressing a class of infants.

'It would be very comforting for you if that were the case, wouldn't it, Inspector, but my generation of computers can act independently as I have described, to project manage tasks I have given it. I just didn't foresee that it would take things so far, to their logical conclusion, if you will.

'No, my culpability was my failure to install ethical fail safes, to programme in Asimov's three laws. I wasn't expecting HAL to treat human beings as just another pawn on its chess board and to remove them from the game so heartlessly.

'I deeply regret that. I am mortified, in fact. It was never my intention for people to die.'

This was all too much for Fiona, who momentarily lost her temper.

'You're *mortified*,' she shouted, slamming her hands on the table. McQueen jumped. 'Your victims had lives too; they had children, partners, families, friends. They're not going to be comforted by your mealy-mouthed words.

'You're a monster, and I'm going to make sure we dismantle your Frankenstein-like creation circuit board by circuit board, and then lock you up for life, and just in case, I'm going to have the authorities throw away the key.'

Erbury put his hand on McQueen's to prevent him responding.

'I think we need to take a break at this point, Inspector.'

*   *   *

Jenny and Walters had taken longer than she hoped to reach McQueen's house. Traffic had been awful, and Walters had driven like a learner. He'd told her that he tried to avoid driving in London whenever he could, and she could see why.

By the time they got there Jenny was desperate to offload some of the liquid-poison she poured down herself and had to rush to use the bathroom, leaving Walters to explore the property by himself.

She was confident that he wouldn't find the entrance to the cellar and, sure enough, when she joined him, Walters was wandering around the ground floor like a lost sheep.

She showed him to the cupboard under the stairs, led the way down into the corridor, found the main light switch and walked with Walters to the hidden room.

Jenny opened the metal door, and they stepped inside. Nothing had changed. The computer was still active, complete with flashing lights and the occasional whirring noise, while the white walls dazzled them with reflected light, something that took a minute or two to adjust to.

Walters studied the Faraday cage like a child at a candy store. He was transfixed. Slowly he walked towards the cage and touched it, gingerly, almost as if he were afraid that it would disintegrate in front of him.

Jenny groaned; this was going to be a long visit. She decided to go back upstairs and make herself a cup of tea. That might help to revive her and settle her heaving stomach.

'I'll be back shortly,' she told Walters. 'Do you want some tea or coffee? I'm sure that there's some upstairs though I'm not so confident that there's milk.'

'No, no hot beverages down here, please? It's too risky.'

Jenny shrugged and walked back up to the kitchen. She filled the kettle, found a tea bag and was relieved to see that there was some milk in the fridge and that it hadn't yet gone off.

She sat down at the kitchen table sipping her brew and scrolling through her phone. On the spur of the moment, she decided to facetime Dawn. When she answered, her wife was looking very excited.

'I was just about to ring you,' she said, breathlessly. 'I've just heard from the solicitor, everything has gone through, the house is ours. I'm picking up the keys tomorrow.'

For the first time in a week, Jenny felt homesick and couldn't wait to get back to Cardiff. This was the future she wanted, not some transitory sex on the side with Fiona.

'That's brilliant,' she said, 'as I'm coming home tonight. I've just got to wind up this last thing with the computer technician and I'll be on the train. Shall we get Chinese? I can pick it up on the way from the station.'

Dawn beamed. 'Don't be daft, this calls for more than a takeaway. Let's push the boat out and go to a restaurant. Let me know when you're on the train and I'll book something to fit in with your arrival time.'

Jenny ended the call feeling much more content with her life. She hadn't realised how much she'd missed Dawn until that moment. She vowed to get the current visit out of the way with as soon as possible so she could head back to Cardiff and the welcoming arms of her beloved.

Deciding that she needed to chivvy Walters along, she finished her drink and headed back down into the cellar. She found him inside the Faraday cage inspecting the computer.

'This is going to take some time,' he said.

Jenny sighed.

Chapter Twenty-Four

Fiona and Alaya had reconvened the interview with McQueen and placed the laptop and phone on the table in front of him.

Their prisoner viewed it with disdain. It didn't seem as if he was going to cooperate, but Fiona thought it was worth a try. She just needed to push the right lever to persuade him, but what?

She opened the laptop and booted it up. Erbury watched with interest while McQueen pretended not to notice even when she swung it around so that the screen was facing him.

'I need your help,' she said.

'My life wouldn't be worth living if I let you into that machine,' he replied. 'These people are not playing games. If I give you access to their operations, they'll be after me. I'll be looking over my shoulder for the rest of my life.'

'Perhaps you'll do so to help yourself.'

'How exactly?'

'Well, you've given us a pretty persuasive narrative as to how Rachel Abadi was engaged to carry out a number of attacks,' she lied. 'Surely, it's in your interests to prove that story by opening your electronic records for us to look at.

'I'm sure that once we have access, even our inadequate technicians will be able to trace the instruction back to your AI. It may prove to be an important pillar in your defence.'

McQueen thought for a few minutes, he looked unconvinced, possibly because Fiona was making it up as she went along.

'Technically, it wouldn't be possible to ascertain who gave the instruction,' he said. 'And you've already said that you have access to Abadi's bank accounts and are able to trace the payments back to me, why do you need any more proof?'

'You know full well what I need from this computer,' she responded. 'Even if we put to one side the operational details it may contain, my superiors want reassurance as to the extent of your electronic infiltration into our systems.

'If you work with us on that, I'm authorised to tell you that we will make a recommendation to the judge that you get more lenient treatment, a more congenial prison cell for example. These things can be arranged'.

McQueen laughed.

'Well,' he said, 'this is a huge change of tone from earlier. Weren't you proposing to tie me to a rock or something and have my liver eaten by an eagle every day like Prometheus?'

Fiona grimaced.

'I'm sorry I'm not familiar with that story, however, I do regret my earlier tone. I was responding to an explanation which I thought lacked credibility, but our people tell me that it might be possible after all.'

Fiona hated eating humble pie, but she believed there was no other way to get McQueen to work with them. She thought that he was wavering.

'If we're going to make a deal, I will want it in writing,' he said.

Erbury interrupted.

'I think my client would need something a bit more concrete than what you're offering at present.'

'I understand,' Fiona responded. 'Unfortunately, a recommendation of leniency and a better prison is all I have to offer. People were killed, lives have been wrecked, and at the end of the day, Mr McQueen was responsible for that.

'A rogue computer may well help with mitigation, but he is the one who's going down for this.'

McQueen put his hand on Erbury's shoulder to prevent him continuing the argument.

'I'll unlock the laptop for you,' he said. 'It's not a problem.'

He took the machine from her. Fiona watched as he opened the camera and allowed it to scan his left retina, he then entered a twelve-digit alpha-numeric access code, put a second code into his phone and finally unlocked the computer by scanning his thumb print. He turned the now active machine to face the two detectives.

'I'm not sure how this will help you,' he said, 'but I'll tell you what you will find on here once your tech guys get to work on it. This laptop contains the bank records you already have, several contracts with various nefarious organisations, and numerous internet searches looking for safe houses and transit routes.

'It may not give you what you're looking for.'

For once Fiona was barely listening, instead she was scanning through the lists of documents contained on the machine.

'Thank you for that. I'm going to suspend this interview for half an hour while I get this computer to our tech team and consult with my Superintendent. There's no need for you to go back to the cells, I'll leave you here with a couple of uniforms.

'If you wish they'll get you some refreshments, tea, coffee, water, whatever you need.'

McQueen and Erbury watched in silence as Alaya shut down the recording machine and exited the room with Fiona.

* * *

At the house, Jenny was beginning to lose patience with Walters. She'd been watching him for the best part of twenty minutes as he slowly explored every inch of the machine.

'Are you actually going to try and access this computer,' she asked.

'All in good time. At present, I'm just taking stock, seeing what interfaces are available, trying to assess where its power cable and broadband connections are.

'Do you know, I think they might be buried underneath, in the floor. This is a very impressive set-up, and to think he most probably built this machine from scratch.'

Somehow, Jenny couldn't match Walter's enthusiasm, but there was one thing that was puzzling her.

'If you couldn't get into McQueen's laptop,' she said, 'then what makes you think you can hack into that?'

'Well, this is an entirely different piece of machinery,' he replied, 'but to be honest, I have no idea if I'll be able to open this up. I think I've got to try, and if I fail, well, we'll just have to go back to McQueen.'

He paused as if he had found something, and then carefully pressed a button that was partially concealed on the outside of the computer. A section of the machine folded downwards to form a small shelf, revealing a screen and a number of access ports.

'Aha,' Walters said, 'this is what I've been looking for. We need to plug in a laptop or tablet here to start interrogating it, and presumably to programme it with new instructions.'

He pulled out his laptop, placed it on the shelf and used a cable to connect it. While it was booting up, he took out his phone and tried to make a call.

'Oh, I forgot, there's no signal down here. I'm just popping upstairs to touch base with David, let him know that I might have a way in.'

Jenny started to point out that he didn't yet know if he could access the mainframe, but Walters had already walked away from the room and was halfway up the steps into the kitchen.

Exasperated, she decided to examine the computer in more detail. She stepped inside the Faraday cage. The entire machine was encased in a smooth, white, plastic box, about five-feet tall and approximately four-feet by four-feet square.

The only break in the surface was the shelf that Walters had opened by depressing a small button beneath it. This had concealed a screen, and two USB ports, presumably to attach a keyboard or other device.

There were lights at the top of the structure that occasionally flashed white or red as if the machine were thinking or monitoring their presence. She shivered; the whole set-up gave her the creeps. It was like one of those horror movies where the super-intelligent computer traps somebody and plays with them.

What was that film called, she wondered, the old one with Julie Christie in it. Was it *Demon Seed*? She looked over to check that the door was open. It was, and she could see that Walters was returning to carry out his task.

'I hope you haven't touched anything,' he said.

'No, I'm leaving it to you to break things.'

He laughed nervously.

'Don't worry, I know what I'm doing. David has given me the go ahead to try and get into this machine, so we'll see what's possible.'

Jenny retreated to the far end of the room to give him space to work inside the cage and watched as Walters pressed some buttons on his laptop. An instruction flashed up on the screen to enter a twelve-digit access code.

Walters grumbled a bit and then set some software running on his laptop. It took a few minutes but eventually the machine found the right combination.

A small scanner emerged from above the opened panel and an instruction appeared requesting a retinal scan. At the same time a five-minute countdown appeared on the screen. The metal door slammed shut with a huge bang causing Jenny to jump in shock.

'What have you done?' she demanded as she ran to the door to open it. 'This thing is locked, for fuck's sake get it open.'

Walters looked as shocked as she was. He swore loudly as he tried to shut everything down.

'I'm trying,' he said. 'It won't let me.'

Jenny tried the key, but it was useless. She walked around to look at the screen.

'What's that countdown about? What happens when it reaches zero?'

'I don't know,' Walters confessed. 'I'm doing my best to avoid that scenario.'

* * *

Fiona and Alaya rejoined McQueen and his solicitor an

hour later, having spent time with the technicians examining the contents of the laptop.

They were disappointed that it didn't contain details of McQueen's operations, nor was there any sign on there of the instructions to Abadi… just the payments, which appeared in the online bank accounts, but then they already had that.

'This has been very helpful,' Fiona told him. 'But where will I find the information you've stolen from our computers? And if, as you say, your rogue computer has been running things, including hiring Abadi to knock people off, why is there no evidence of that on this machine?'

McQueen laughed.

'I did tell you that you that logging onto the laptop wouldn't help you with that. That's my personal machine, I use it for day-to-day work and to access HAL. All the stuff you want is on the mainframe.

'HAL stores it, learns from it and uses it to implement his core programming and purpose. If you want access, then you're going to have to take me home and allow me to download it for you.'

Fiona was dubious.

'And what's to stop you deleting it when we get you there?'

'Nothing, I suppose. You're going to have to trust me. But remember, we have a deal. You have me bang-to-rights as some of my more disreputable colleagues would say. Why would I renege on that?'

'Perhaps to prevent you being a wanted man in the prison system when all of these colleagues find out you've sold them down the river.'

McQueen leaned forward and locked eyes with her.

'Inspector, I'm resigned to that already. As soon as they realise you've got me in here and are prosecuting me, they'll be gunning for me. I'm relying on you and your people to keep me safe. You *will* do that, won't you?'

'Of course,' Fiona said, 'trying to calm him down. 'Fortunately, we may not need you to open your big computer. We have an expert there now who is working on that problem for us.'

A look of panic crossed McQueen's face. He stood up, pushing his chair violently backwards against the wall. As a uniformed officer tried to restrain him, he screamed at the top of his voice.

'No, you've got to stop him. It isn't safe.'

The officer managed to get him settled back into his seat, but McQueen was far from calm. He was almost sobbing.

'Please, try and stop him. I don't want another death on my conscience.'

'What do you mean?' Fiona demanded.

'HAL has a failsafe built in, to prevent others trying to steal his secrets. If there is an unauthorised attempt to access him, without the correct biometric data, then all his programmes and data are transmitted to a secure back-up server, and he will self-destruct.'

'What? In what way? Will the machine just burn itself out or will it be more dramatic than that?

Fiona was starting to panic now, she was thinking about Jenny.

'There will be an explosion, it will take out everything in that room. It was designed that way to stop my rivals stealing my proprietary software.'

'But they'll have time to get away?'

'No, HAL locks things down. Anybody who is in there is likely to be killed. Their only hope is if the cage contains enough of the explosion.'

'Is that likely?' Alaya asked.

'I really don't know,' he replied, head in hands, 'I'm a computer programmer not an explosives expert.'

Now it was Fiona's turn to leap to her feet.

'Are you fucking mad', she screamed at McQueen. What sort of demented fuckwit sets up a computer to blow up if it's hacked. If my colleagues are hurt in anyway, I'll throw the fucking book at you.'

Alaya had to drag her away from him, a feat that proved easier once Fiona realised that she must somehow warn Jenny.

She pulled out her phone while running towards the squad room, shouting instructions to her sergeant to formally close the interview down and put McQueen back in a cell.

She dialled Jenny's number, but it went straight to voicemail. Fiona cursed the blackspot in the cellar. Maybe she could get there on time to let them out or to warn them.

She ran to the carpark, got into her car, fixed a blue light to the roof, and drove like a lunatic in the direction of McQueen's house. Would she be in time, she had no idea, but she had to try.

* * *

Walters was desperately trying to shut the mainframe down. He feared the worst but wasn't prepared to tell Jenny what that might be just yet. Nevertheless, she insisted.

'What is that countdown for?' she persisted.

'I think it's some kind of self-destruct mechanism. I'm trying to find a way in to cut off the power and stop it.'

He had unscrewed the panel containing the screen and was delving inside the machine looking for something, anything, that looked like a power cable. The screen itself hung loosely at his side still counting down.

There was now just three minutes to go. Jenny wondered if it was right what people said: that your whole life flashed before your eyes in the last minutes. Was this what her life had come to, dying alongside a geek in a cellar in an obscure suburb of London?

She banged on the door in the hope that somebody would hear and let them out, but she knew that there was no saviour on the other side, nobody in the house or nearby houses who could hear her or know what to do.

She decided that the best hope of survival was to crouch in a corner of the room, making as small a target as she could and hope that the cage would absorb any blast. She told Walters her conclusion and then assumed the position. He promised to follow suit if he failed to stop the countdown. He was still working.

This was punishment for all her wrong-doing, Jenny thought. There was nobody to confess to, and Walters wouldn't want to know, but maybe she should make her peace with God, if he really existed.

She'd taken a man's life in cold blood to protect a woman whom she thought she loved and then had betrayed her with another woman at the first opportunity. And then she'd let Fiona down as well, treated her like a one-night stand, a casual conquest, when the reality was that she loved her as much as she loved Dawn. What a mess she'd made of her life.

She'd told Dawn shortly after the assassination of Morgan Sheckler that there were always consequences, that nobody got off scot-free after committing a major crime, even if it looked like they had.

She'd been right. The horrors of that shooting had come back to haunt her, she'd looked for comfort in casual sex, and now she was going to pay the ultimate price for what she'd done.

Jenny looked across at Walters, he was covered in sweat. The screen now read thirty seconds. He wasn't going to be able to stop whatever it was that was going to happen.

He exited the cage, closed the door, and curled up in a ball in the opposite corner to her. For the first time in her life, she started to pray. The clock counted down to ten seconds.

She closed her eyes hoping against hope that Walters was wrong. Did she really deserve this? She felt that she did.

'It was me, I did it,' she muttered, 'I killed him.'

And then there was a click, a large bang, a blinding light, and everything went black.

* * *

Fiona felt the ground shake as she pulled into the cul-de-sac. She stopped the car and ran to the house. The door had been left unlocked. As she got to the trap door she was overwhelmed by dust and thick black smoke.

The force of the explosion had collapsed the passage.

She staggered out of the choking cloud of dust and into the front garden where she dialled 999, before dropping to the ground, struggling to breath, her face wet with tears. There was nothing she could do now until the emergency services arrived, but surely nobody could have survived that.

It took half an hour for the fire and rescue service to get there and several hours more for them to get the specialist equipment they needed to commence clearing the debris from the tunnel.

By that time, Alaya and Appleton had joined her at the house, and an ambulance was on standby. David Cornwell arrived soon afterwards. Together, all four of them sat anxiously on the front wall of the property as the work to remove rubble from the tunnel got underway.

Fiona had already done her best to describe the layout of the cellar to the Fire Officer in charge, but he was keen to get more.

'Can you recall if there were any vents in there?' he asked. 'We haven't been able to find any outlets on the surface.'

'Yes, the room must be temperature controlled somehow,' Alaya said.

'I don't remember seeing any vents,' Fiona volunteered, struggling to control her emotions. 'I think there was a ceiling fan, but I can't be sure.'

He looked grim at hearing that news.

'Well, if that metal door is sealed then, even if they survived the explosion, there may not be much air in there, combined with the dust and the smoke, I have to warn you that there's only a remote chance that they'll be alive by the time we get to them.'

Fiona gripped Alaya's arm as Cornwell sat impassively. Appleton looked on ashen faced. He'd never lost an officer before. Eventually, he broke the tension.

'That little guttersnipe,' he roared, 'if I have my way, he won't even see the inside of a prison.'

Cornwell placed his hand on the Superintendant's arm to calm him. Words weren't necessary. There was an understanding between the two men.

Alaya drove to a nearby café to get some tea for the four of them. They sat sipping their drinks as the team worked.

By the time the rescuers reached the metal door the sun was setting. The supply of tea and snacks from numerous café-runs was exhausted. Appleton offered to go out and buy something stronger, but nobody could face alcohol. Instead, they sat in silence listening to the cruel buzzing of a drill forcing the lock on the computer room door.

Eventually, the drilling stopped and there was silence broken only by the measured words of the rescuers as they reached their target. A short time afterwards, the police officers and Cornwell watched in shock as two bodies were carried from the wreckage and into the ambulance.

Fiona felt her legs go from underneath her, only to have Appleton catch her. She buried herself in his shoulder and screamed in pain, a primal cry of anguish.

Alaya relieved the Superintendent of his burden, gently pulling the Inspector off him and sitting her on a low front wall of the neighbouring house. She held Fiona tightly as heaving sobs wracked her body, oblivious to the crowds that had gathered on the other side of the police tape.

When the sobs subsided, all that remained was a heavy, painful emptiness inside. Only then did Fiona fish out her phone and find the number.

It was time to ring Dawn.

Acknowledgements

My fond and loving thanks are due to my wife Angela, who has had to put up with my sudden obsession with writing once I lost my Welsh Assembly seat in 2016, and who has always been patient and supportive in all my endeavours, even when it seemed that I had lost the plot completely.

Thanks too are due to my editor, David Lawlor, who once more helped me knock my story into shape, showed infinite patience with my inability to punctuate properly and used his invaluable experience to help me get this story ready for publication.

All the good things in this novel are there because of the assistance of those named above, any mistakes, inaccuracies, curiosities, or inconsistencies are entirely my own.

Previous works by Peter Black

The Assassination of Morgan Sheckler

When Morgan Sheckler becomes Mayor of the Cardiff Capital Region in Wales, he finds himself at odds with his own staff, not just because of his policies but also because of his brash, bullying manner.

Sheckler immediately sets his sights on dismantling plans for a new power plant in the region -- a move that puts him on collision course with some unsavoury American backers who will do anything necessary to have it built.

Caught in the middle is Dawn Highcliffe, Sheckler's director of development, who must do as the mayor orders but yet also, somehow, please the Americans, who have blackmailed her into cooperating with them.

A world of corruption and intimidation is revealed that brings Dawn to breaking point and sees her facing the prospect of a lengthy prison sentence.

But there's hope, because Sheckler's past is coming back to haunt him and a group of those he wronged are circling, and they're looking for blood...

'Loads of sex, murder? If this is what Welsh local government is like, how do they find time to collect the bins?' **Sunday Times 12 April 2020**

Available now on Amazon

The Only Game in Town

The men who run Oldport are corrupt, arrogant, and unchallenged.

What must happen to loosen their grip on the town?

Harry O'Leary has been leader of Oldport Council for nearly twenty years. Together with local nightclub owner and developer John Baker he has the whole town in his pocket, and both have profited handsomely from it.

Frank McColgan is a local institution. He is the transvestite landlord of the Prince Albert, a pub and brothel in the town's harbour area, a meeting place for local movers and shakers and the favoured drinking hole for journalists at the Oldport Observer and their eccentric editor, Jerome Wilson.

When Billy Jones arrives looking for his journalist brother, he finds a berth at the Prince Albert, and together with barmaid Jeanie Carter becomes entangled in some of the town's less-than-scrupulous affairs.

'Vintage local government corruption, fast paced story, read it in two sittings, couldn't put it down but I did have to sleep! The characters felt real and the far from perfect ending very true to life. A bit of romance, a lot of tears and whoever you are you will want to meet the pub landlord.' **Mrs C.E. Hutton on Amazon**

Available now on Amazon

In My Father's Name

Harrison Balham has spent decades building up his property empire, so when he plunges to his death, leaving his brother, Charles in charge of the company, his son, Hywel suspects it might not have been suicide.

With his mother and his uncle living together as a couple, Hywel feels isolated and disillusioned, until he is told about incriminating documents that could bring Charles down and which appear to back up his theory that Harrison didn't take his own life.

As Charles fights desperately for survival, Hywel is in a race to find the documents and discover the truth before he suffers the same fate as his father.

What he unearths will change his life forever

Peter Black's third novel is as much of a page turner as the previous two as we get sucked into the twists and turns of an unusual mystery set in London's corporate business world.

He has created another selection of flawed yet intriguing characters who we soon get to know during a search for the truth which has the potential to blow family, friendships and the board room apart. It is a great read. **JanetMcB on Amazon**

Available now on Amazon

The Morgan Sheckler Legacy

The mayor of the greater Cardiff region, Morgan Sheckler is dead, shot down in front of City Hall just months into his first term, but his ghost hangs over the city and all those who wish to succeed him, or who worked with him.

The battle to preserve or destroy his legacy is underway, and the stakes are huge.

As those who knew him struggle with the consequences of his assassination and try to pick up the shreds of their lives, unscrupulous forces are at work, and they don't care who they trample over to get their own way.

'If you've read "The Assassination of Morgan Sheckler" you'll welcome this sequel. If you haven't read the first book you'll still find this one thoroughly enjoyable, thanks to the snappy recap that reintroduces us to Sheckler's world and the engaging plotting that characterizes Peter Black's work.

It's fast-paced while always giving its characters time to grow and breathe, it's cleverly constructed in a way that entertains the reader and never short-changes us, and every plot development makes us eager to learn what happens next. You'll have to buy this book to learn about Morgan Sheckler's legacy, but Peter Black's legacy as a novelist is already clear; he's a first-rate storyteller who always delivers a great read.
David Jones on Amazon

Available now on Amazon

Printed in Great Britain
by Amazon